THE LAST HONEYMOON

By the same author

A Sisters' Tale

THE LAST HONEYMOON

Shelley Weiner

Constable · London

First published in Great Britain 1992
by Constable and Company Limited
3 The Lanchesters, 162 Fulham Palace Road,
London W6 9ER

ISBN 0 09 471320 0

Set in Linotron Palatino and
printed in Great Britain by
Redwood Press, Melksham, Wiltshire

A CIP catalogue record for this book
is available from the British Library

To Jack

[illegible] animate [illegible] in indirect [illegible] from the [illegible] delightful [illegible] [illegible]

[illegible] the [illegible] [illegible] hair [illegible] [illegible] [illegible] and social [illegible] [illegible] [illegible] [illegible]

[illegible]

SUNDAY

Everything had a mate at All Seasons. The chintz-covered armchairs came in matching pairs, honeymooners entered two by two and even the fire safety precautions displayed in luxurious double rooms were in rhyming couplets. There had been nothing or no one single here at all until Judith Goldman arrived to put an end to her life.

She had come in the middle of Happy Half-Hour, which was ironic for someone bent on suicide. But it could have been worse. It had once been an hour until management decided that having a full sixty minutes of newlywed bliss would encourage false optimism. And so, at half-six sharp, pairs of honeymooners had emerged from bedrooms named after the months of the year and in a sitting-room called Summer they were toasting the future on half-price drinks. All of them except Judith, who had little future left to toast.

Most honeymooners managed a half-hour of harmony. Just. Some tried and failed. Edwin Cockroft (in insurance), for instance, couldn't agree with his new wife, Angela (in teaching, special needs), upon the name of the room in which they were staying.

'It's November, Ange. I know for a fact it's November.'

'Edwin, my sweet, don't be silly. We're staying in October. How could you possibly forget?'

'I can't for the life of me understand why we're arguing. I still think it's November – but if you insist otherwise, have it your way.'

'But Edwin. Darling . . . look at the key. Go on. Tell me what it says.'

'Oh, Ange. This is ridiculous . . .'

'What does it say?'

'Umm – October. And so? What's the difference anyway?'

Judith watched and listened like a solitary dark fly against the pink marbled wall. She saw Edwin, having swallowed his drink moodily, order another and turn towards his wife.

'Ange,' he said in an ingratiating wort of way. 'Ange – why are we disagreeing with one another? It's our honeymoon, remember. Here – drink up. Cheers. To us.'

'To us.'

The young wife sounded sulky. Not entirely enthusiastic. And Judith in her corner had an urge to shake her, to warn her, to protect her from what lay ahead. But she was exhausted. She had reached her end. The most she could manage was to raise an eyebrow and her glass as she drank to Edwin and Angela on the threshold of connubial contentment. 'To you,' she said silently. 'To all of you.'

Arthur, back in London, was miserable. All afternoon he'd kept expecting to hear the grinding of tyres up the gravel path followed by the screech of brakes and the slam of a door and the furious familiar thud-thudding of Judith's returning footsteps. He maintained a constant state of alertness, upper vertebrae poised for a show of moral indignation, abdomen knotted, muscles in various parts of his body flexed. Until, by seven, when his system had been flooded with adrenalin and his entire skeletal structure ached, it dawned on him that perhaps this time she'd meant it. Maybe she was not coming back.

'So be it,' he exhaled as he pulled himself painfully out of his orthopaedically-sound armchair and made for the kitchen with a slow martyred gait. All this tension was bad for his blood pressure. And he was hungry.

There was silence in the four-bedroomed residence. Expensive silence that came as an optional extra with the thick-piled carpeting and double glazing throughout and a wife who had left him. Walked out. And – the spite of her! The sheer malice. She'd taken the television remote control device. Didn't she know full well that the box wouldn't operate without it?

'Bitch,' said Arthur, opening the fridge. The motor convulsed into action, its hum like the roar of a vast turbine engine in the emptiness of the house. Arthur kicked it irritably but not too hard. He took pride in his possessions – unlike she who had defected. Abandoned what many would describe as earth's last remaining patch of paradise. Simply upped and offed to God-knows-where.

'She'll return – eventually,' he muttered to himself as he surveyed the edible options. Not a vast choice when one excluded the pickled cucumbers that lay shrivelled in the bottled contents of a frog-pond and the pasta sauce that had grown a fungus and assorted tail-ends of film-wrapped cheese and salami in various stages of decomposition. Standards of housewifery had definitely slipped of late.

Arthur had gloomily decided that he would have to subject his cholesterol level to the onslaught of a couple of scrambled eggs when he noticed a flat white cardboard box in the top right-hand corner of the cabinet. He lifted the lid carefully. Twenty years of marriage had cautioned his culinary curiosity in the territory he had (rather graciously, he always thought) apportioned as Judith's. She was infuriated beyond reason by signs of disorder and interference and loss of control, and he feared his wife's anger. It made him tired.

'Bugger Judith. She's gone.'

Arthur opened the box defiantly and saw that it contained a strawberry tart and remembered that they'd been invited to the Davises that evening. The tart was to have been their offering. Most Sunday nights (but, alas, it seemed, not this one) the Goldmans were part of the mighty boiling of kettles and buttering of bridge rolls that meant suburban north-west London was inviting or being invited to 'come around for coffee'.

'Just an informal evening,' prospective hostesses would say. 'A few people. Can you make it? Wonderful. That's the 28th – four Sundays from now. We can't wait.'

By 8.30 there'd be rumbling in the roads as family saloons purred and changed blocks and hallways would ring with excited cries of 'Hello' and 'How *are* you?' from people who'd seen one another in the newsagent's only that morning, and wives would accept a small sherry and husbands a splash of whisky ('only one – I'm driving') and they'd dip fresh *crudités* into Marks and Spencer dressings and nibble crisps ('I really shouldn't – I'm dieting'). And by 9.30, having completed Part One of the obligatory quota of consumption and conversation that a successful coffee evening required, they'd be ushered into grand dining-rooms for Part Two. Here, on long white-clothed tables immaculately set for ten, would be displayed an arsenal of high-fat delicatessen that would make even the most efficiently operating arterial system contract with fear. As Arthur would often sagely observe, abnormal clusters of coronary complaints seemed to be reported on Sunday nights.

'But who am I to spoil your fun?' he'd shrug, helping himself to another bagel smothered in salmon and cream cheese and a bridge roll blanketed with chopped herring. He swore to himself that he'd work it off in the gym the following day.

And by 11.15, after most people had consumed at least three cups of tea (hardly anyone ever drank coffee at a coffee evening), a vast sigh would sweep across the neighbourhoods as guests reminded one another of the imminence of Monday morning and the stresses of the week ahead and the lateness of the hour.

'We really ought to be making a move.'

'Yes. Gosh. I ate too much.'

'It was lovely. So good to see you. And *honestly,* you went to so much trouble. You shouldn't have.'

'No no. It was nothing. A pleasure to have you.'

'Thank you – very much. You must come to us. Soon.'

And by midnight there'd be silence as the residents of suburbia, having sorted themselves into pairs (mostly married) and parked their cars and flossed their teeth and put out their cats and unplugged their television sets, would settle into bed.

'Pleasant evening, wasn't it?'

'Mmm.'

'Nice food.'

'Mmm.'

'G'night.'

'Night . . .'

There was little sexual activity on Sunday nights in the suburbs. Coffee evenings rarely provoked strong passion. Most couples tended to sink into the numbness of sleep (mostly medicated), side by side and in peace.

Not Arthur though. Not this Sunday night. Judith had put paid to that. He hesitated over the tart for a minute or two, considering the confection with its blood-red fruity mounds and creamy peaks, thinking of the prospect of two empty spaces at the Davises' repro-Chippendale table that evening, imagining the speculation their absence would arouse:

'What happened to the Goldmans? Couldn't they make it?'

'Haven't you heard?'

'Oh no. Not again? She hasn't done it *again,* has she?'

'Yup. Again.'
'Poor Arthur.'
'Poor man. She *does* give him a hard time. Remember . . . ?'
'Remember! How could I forget? Did you know, by the way, that her father was a family butcher?'
'Really? How funny. How – appropriate – in a sense.'

At the sudden thought of his father-in-law, Arthur stopped hesitating. With a determined squaring of his shoulders (God how they ached), he lifted out the box and shut the fridge and marched to the kitchen table in time to the pulse-beat that drummed in his head (most disconcerting, that drumming – he'd have it investigated). Arthur placed the tart in the centre, dead centre, of the table and took a deep breath. How would a duellist feel when about to face an adversary? Weary? Sore? *As mad as hell*, he decided as he reached for a knife. It was a large and lethal instrument with the sharpness of a cleaver.

Arthur plunged the steel blade through the heart of the plumpest strawberry and triumphantly lifted out a fruity wedge and watched without mercy as the whipped cream wept. He took a mouthful and wiped the red juice that trickled down his chin and chewed and swallowed and shook his head sorrowfully, then helped himself to another slice and wondered whether he ought to telephone and apologize to the Davises, and consoled himself with the thought that at least he'd be at home that evening to watch the box . . . then remembered he couldn't. And viciously stabbed the tart and resolved to eat the lot. He'd indulge himself and blow the consequences. It was Sunday after all. And Arthur Goldman didn't ask much – but he did expect a bit of peace and quiet on an off-duty Sunday. His wife should have seen to that.

She'd been ill-humoured from the start. Snappy and peevish – and clumsy. Knocked over a glass in the sink while filling the kettle, spilt her coffee, cursed in a most unappealing manner. Arthur hated women to swear.

'You're not premenstrual again are you, Jude?' he had enquired (in an understanding sort of way he'd thought). It wasn't as though he was simply asking out of empty curiosity. Professionally speaking, there was a lot that could be done for PMT these days. Evening primrose oil. Vitamin B6. Arthur had written countless prescriptions for various highly regarded preparations

– and been thanked by his patients and told what a kind caring doctor he was. Many times. Not by his wife though. Judith gave him little credit for – anything.

'What do you mean?'

She swung round and faced him viciously. Her black hair, uncombed, clung damply to her frowning face and her fists were clenched. Her eyes, even blacker than her hair, were narrow slits emitting two concentrated beams of fury. He squirmed and retreated, bewildered by the intensity of her reaction.

'Nothing. Nothing at all. I was simply asking . . .'

'No Arthur – I am *not* premenstrual. All those troublesome little female hormones that give caring men such headaches are perfectly under control. Thanks for asking.'

And she'd stormed out, once-white towelling dressing-gown billowing behind her, bare feet thumping dully against the cork-tiled kitchen floor. The dining-room door slammed shut and, with a great discordant crash, Judith launched herself at the piano. The house seemed to shudder with the violence of her music – a dissonant battle between the bile of the bass and the strident temper of the treble. Arthur remembered how he'd once dreamed of being serenaded by his wife with Chopin études. How differently things had turned out.

He waited a while. Sipped his coffee, poured himself a measured portion of high-fibre additive-free muesli, glanced at the front page of the *Sunday Times* and then, slightly at a loss and searching for an activity that would distract him from the distressing noises being produced by Judith, decided to empty the rubbish-bin.

'There,' he said, rather pleased with himself, when the job was done and at last it sounded as though the sharp gunshot notes from the dining-room were diminishing. The malignant roar in the lower octaves had dulled to a less sinister grumble and the high accusing shrieks in top C had faded. Arthur opened the door carefully, hoping – honestly, hoping – to make amends for whatever he was supposed to have done to offend her.

'Jude?'

Gently. Ever so gently. Her head was bowed over the piano, her shoulders sagged, her left hand lay forlornly on her lap and the right one was picking out a sad little tune in the upper reaches of the keyboard. Judith's anger seemed to have been spent.

'Listen – Judith.' He couldn't think what to say that would

make things better. After a moment, her right hand dropped to join the left and she tilted her head in weary response.

'Jude.' Coaxingly. 'Why don't you calm down and come and have breakfast?'

'I'm calm.' Flatly.

'Well then – how about it? Look – I've even cleared the bin for you.'

She turned round slowly until she was facing him and Arthur smiled as he congratulated himself on his tact and restraint. Then he saw she wasn't responding and his lips suddenly turned limp as he sensed the tension in her straightened back, her deep breaths, her black eyes. Judith's eyes were boring through him. Arthur had to look away.

'For *me?'* she demanded in a quiet voice that made him wince. 'You cleared the bin *for me?'*

'Judith . . .'

He tried to explain, but it was no good. Something seemed to have snapped in his wife. Like a large demented animal she raged from room to room, gathering possessions, muttering 'That's it – I've had it' in a crazed sort of way. He stood back, mutely watching, bewildered, cowering and hating himself for his cowardice, until he finally heard the car taking off down the drive.

Several seconds passed before Arthur was able to move. He wondered whether he ought to applaud or to cry. Had this been the final movement of Judith's last sonata? He crossed the room and shut the piano and settled down to await her return.

And now he had quite given up. Sated with strawberry tart and self-pity until he was sure he would expire in a murky pool of saturated fat and salty tears, he decided he'd have to go upstairs in search of his antacid tablets. Indigestion was the last thing one needed on an evening like this.

Slowly he left the kitchen as the fridge hummed a farewell refrain. Lifting heavy limbs up the carpeted stairs, he noticed the worn patches and tried to remember when they'd had the carpet laid.

Judith's towelling dressing-gown had been flung on to the large double bed. Abandoned like an elderly unwanted pet in a frozen wasteland of crumpled white cotton and cream lace. Arthur badly needed to lie down but was afraid that he'd never wake up. He turned from the bed, sighed and burped loudly, and went to the bathroom to find gastric relief. The door of the medicine chest was half open.

Strange, he thought, as his eyes made a quick inventory of the contents. He never would have left the door ajar – and Judith had made it her policy to avoid all medication. Now if Arthur had been leaving home, he'd have made sure of taking . . . but Judith? No – she'd endure the most excruciating pain without analgesic aid. The year before, she had suffered the blackest despair and yet adamantly refused to take the antidepressants prescribed for her.

Where were those antidepressants, by the way? Arthur had noticed the bottle (with its contents intact) only the previous day and resolved to discard it. Now he saw an empty space where the tablets had stood. He stared at the gap, scratching his head as though trying to expunge the thought that had come, unbidden, into it. Surely not. Not Judith. She'd never do anything like that.

He returned to the bedroom, flatulence forgotten, and braved the bed. The duvet was like a giant snowdrift waiting to engulf him, offering oblivion. Arthur wanted to sleep forever. He couldn't bear to think.

Painful thoughts weren't troubling Arthur's stalwart mother, Gertrude. They rarely did. She applied the same stringent set of standards to her moral balance of payments as she did to the family finances. It was thanks to her, she always maintained, that the Goldmans (senior) were never in debt and that Ralph's hardware business had steered a profitable course for forty years and that, owing to her untiring Good Works for the old, the sick, the dead and the influential, they could hold their heads high in the synagogue. If only God handed out prizes for achievement each Day of Atonement, Gertrude was sure she'd be a regular recipient. At least round the bridge table one didn't have to wait for heavenly rewards.

'Well *played*, Gertie,' Marian Willis enthused. The Goldman partnership had just called and made a small slam. Thanks to her.

Gertrude smiled graciously. She did most things graciously and those activities that couldn't be managed with grace were performed strictly behind locked doors. Ralph, for instance, had never in fifty years of marriage witnessed his wife in the act of defecation. She, on the other hand, had nursed him dutifully through recurrent anal fissure repairs and a triple haemorrhoidectomy.

'It was nothing,' she demurred, responding to the praise for her cardplay with a modest shrug. She'd worked on that gesture, had perfected it until it expressed all the weary righteousness and elegant stoicism to which she'd aspired for most of her sixty-nine years. Gertrude was known for her shrug. She was equally renowned for the tasty perfection of the home-baked fare she always provided for her visitors.

'Ralph darling – would you put on the kettle? I think it's almost time for tea.'

He stood up obligingly. Ralph was Gertrude's least inspired bridge partner but as her helpmate (domestically speaking) he'd always been irreproachable. Especially when they had guests. Mind you, after more than two decades of weekly rubber bridge games together, the Willises had almost ceased to be regarded as guests.

'You must come to us next Sunday,' Marian insisted as usual. She'd been saying it for years but there had always seemed to be a reason for the Goldmans to host the game. At first it had been the children. Despite all their arduous efforts (they'd tried thermometers, surgery, hormone supplements, the latest thinking on abstinence – everything possible), Marian and Gordon Willis had, unlike the Goldmans, not been blessed. And so, during the years when Arthur, then Fenella and, finally, Joanne, had needed babysitting it seemed sensible to have the game at Gertrude's. After that, Ralph had been housebound following his operations. And then – well, by then it had become habit. Like buying the Sunday papers.

'Don't know why we waste our money,' Ralph had muttered as he'd paged through the newspaper while they were awaiting their guests. 'Each week it gets heavier and more full of crap. A bit like Gordon Willis . . .'

'Shush!' Gertrude had said sternly. She often suspected that her husband had hidden depths. Not ones she particularly wanted to explore. Now, watching him as he left the table to attend to the kettle, she saw that he'd acquired a stoop and looked frail. Ralph seemed to be getting lighter and lighter. One day he'd float away. Gertrude shuddered. The idea of it frightened her and she hated being frightened.

'How are the children?' Marian was asking with a disapproving eye on Gordon, who was helping himself to another chocolate.

No danger of Gordon floating anywhere. On the contrary – Marian's fear was that he'd sink into an early grave and, although she supposed death at seventy-four wouldn't be classified as juvenile mortality and life with Gordon hadn't been unceasing pleasure (to say the least), she'd been a Willis, half of a couple, for as long as she could remember and to be alone would be terrifying. Also, it would be most inconvenient (in terms of their regular bridge games) to have to keep looking for a fourth. 'How's Arthur?'

'Fine. Very well.'

Gertrude loved being asked about Arthur. Nothing – not her appointment as chairlady of the synagogue guild nor Fenella's acquisition of a house in Bishop's Avenue nor even Joanne's eventual procurement of a merchant banker – had inspired the level of pride she had reached when her son finally qualified as a doctor. She'd been quite set on his medical future almost since his conception and, undeterred by his lack of ambition and mediocre academic prowess, had steered him – forcefully at times, she had to admit – from one hurdle to the next. Until at last they'd done it. Gertrude often felt she deserved to have her name placed alongside Arthur's (in brackets if necessary) in the national register of medical practitioners.

When it came to his marriage, though, she wasn't quite as wholeheartedly proud. Not that there was anything *wrong* with Judith – if one discounted the episode of the previous year. (And Gertrude, who was an expert in the denial of unpleasant occurrences, had drawn a tight veil around that one.) No, Judith had several things in her favour. Everyone said she was talented and intelligent and not bad looking, if she lost a little weight. It was just that – apart from the fact that she hadn't added to Gertrude's sum of grandchildren – she was somehow not quite *malleable*.

Gertrude had always imagined acquiring a daughter-in-law whom she could conduct up the escalators of Brent Cross shopping centre and through the corridors of the Ladies' Guild headquarters and into soup kitchens and out of restaurants that failed to provide decent service and, finally, to the innermost circles of the Burial Society. But Judith refused to be conducted. 'I'm busy,' she'd reply tersely to her mother-in-law's persistent requests for her company. Gertrude sighed at the memory of those rebuffs and then comforted herself with the fact that, despite her misgivings, Judith had turned out to be an admirable wife. Her twenty-year-old marital service record was almost as unblemished as that of the Volvo she drove (too fast). *Almost* . . .

'Yes, Arthur's very well indeed,' she repeated to Marian, whose bright eyes were fixed on her, awaiting elaboration. 'He and Judith – both.'

It was strange, now she thought about it, that she hadn't heard from Arthur during the day. He usually came to see them on a Sunday – or phoned at any rate. Perhaps he wasn't fine at all.

'Ralph,' she asked when her husband reappeared to report that the kettle was satisfactorily on the boil. 'Have you by any chance spoken to Arthur today?'

'No.' He sounded surprised. It had never been his role to maintain contact with his son.

She thought deeply for a moment and succeeded in dispelling the twinges of unease that threatened to disturb her usual equilibrium. She'd felt a similar wave of apprehension that morning for some reason. Silly. It was probably something in the air. Spring had always made Gertrude feel slightly peculiar.

'Oh well,' she shrugged. Beautifully. 'They probably went out together for the day. They often do that, you know.'

The Willises nodded. They couldn't wait to see what edibles Gertrude would provide with the tea.

Don't be ridiculous, Gertrude told herself in the kitchen as she buttered the gingerbread and felt once again that little flurry of alarm. There's nothing to worry about. Nothing in the least. She arranged the slices on a plate alongside the apple strudel and almond fruit torte and filled a sterling silver basket with meringue kisses and cinnamon twists. A nice spread, she thought, standing back to admire the fragrant results of her culinary skill. Not bad at all.

Then it occurred to her that it was a vast quantity of food to have prepared just for the Willises. Enough to feed an army. Enough for a large family at any rate. Quite sufficient to have satisfied the regular Sunday gatherings that no longer took place in the Goldman home. Gertrude felt another disconcerting flutter and this time it was nostalgia as she remembered and longed for the heady days when the house rang with the cries of toddlers being slapped by irate mothers and husbands being snapped at by wives and teenagers brooding in corners and doors slamming and – where on earth was Arthur? He *always* called.

'Need any help Gertrude?'

Marian always offered.

'No thanks.'

Gertrude usually refused.

Like a soldier answering a battle-call, she took up her calorie-charged tray and marched into the living-room.

'My goodness. What a sight. Just as well my diet doesn't start till tomorrow morning. But honestly, Gertrude, you shouldn't have gone to all that trouble just for us . . .'

That was what Marian invariably said. It was part of the chorus of the Sunday night sing-song that rang each week throughout suburbia and called for the mandatory response: 'Oh no. It was nothing. A pleasure to have you.' Gertrude recited it with supreme skill and followed it with another shrug – her most accomplished shrug of all – as she unburdened herself of her laden tray. Just then, the telephone rang.

'Ah,' she said delightedly. 'That must be Arthur now. I knew he'd get in touch. He never fails to on a Sunday, you know. Arthur's the sort of son who would never let one down.'

And was Judith the sort of daughter who would disappoint a parent? Her father, Solomon, wasn't sure. After all the years, he still wasn't sure. Solomon had been expecting three calls since early that morning, none of which had materialized. Apart from no word from Judith (most unusual on a Sunday), the GP locum service seemed to be ignoring his repeated requests to send someone to investigate his intermittent chest pains. And the Meals-on-Wheels organizers, whom he'd contacted to complain about a fly in last night's beef casserole, had failed to respond to four urgent messages he had left on their answering machine. All day, the only sounds that had broken the silent solitude of Solomon's small Willesden flat had been made by Mozart on his ancient gramophone and the regular flushing of a toilet on the floor above. Solomon's upstairs neighbour, Seymour Katz, was having trouble with his waterworks. Again.

'Fine company for an old man,' he muttered bitterly as Mozart and Katz paused between movements. 'A bad recording of a dead composer and an old pisher with plumbing problems banging on my head.'

Emitting a heartfelt groan, he decided to take himself to the kitchen to investigate the package labelled 'Sunday – supper'.

With a little bit of luck it might contain a few glass splinters or a touch of botulism. That would teach Gertrude Goldman and her acolytes for ignoring his complaints. Mind you, it would only give the Burial Society another body to lay out and Solomon had sworn (after its members had taken such perverse pride in what they'd made of his wife's remains) that he would withhold from them that particular pleasure as long as humanly possible.

'Me? Die?' he had always proclaimed with supreme bravado. 'Don't you believe it. I'm planning to stay around for a long time. In fact, you'll never get rid of me.'

This morning, though, he'd had serious doubts about his claim to immortality. That pain in his chest. There was something different about it. Solomon had been frightened and, for a long frightening moment, unable to move.

'Dora,' he'd whispered, instinctively trying to reach for the left-hand side of the bed. But of course it was empty. Had been for more than a year. 'Dora,' he repeated nevertheless. Out of habit. And longing. 'Dora, help me. I don't feel – very well.'

'Solly, take it easy. You'd better stay put,' she would have said if she had stuck to her marriage vows and stayed till the end. *His* end, whenever it was going to be. She'd had no right to go first. If only he could call her back from the dead and hear the clink of the long silver spoon in the tall glass of lemon tea she'd be bringing up to him, with a sugar lump to suck as he sipped. 'There you are, Solinke. Drink this up. You'll feel better right away.' And he would. He always had.

Well – not quite always. Solomon was still not sure whether or not he had been wise to have followed Dora's advice and sold the shop.

'Solly, listen to me, it's time for you to take it easy,' she had insisted at the time. 'We can enjoy life. Get ourselves a small flat. Relax a little.'

'But Dora,' he had protested, 'what will I do? What will I be? A family butcher is what I *am*.'

Her arguments had been convincing though. The turnover had been steadily dropping for years with the northward migration of his Jewish clientele. Judith had long been married and settled. Their responsibilities were now only to themselves. And so on, and so on. Solomon finally agreed after Dr Woolf had been called in for a second opinion.

'Get rid of it,' he'd said without hesitating. Woolf had always been decisive. Had a name, prognosis and course of treatment for every symptom that came his way. The doctor's cure record was not nearly as impressive as his flair for diagnosis but his certainty had tended to make Solomon feel safe.

'No doubt about it, Solly my boy, the sensible thing for you would be to get rid of the shop.'

That had been more or less what he'd told Dora about her womb six months before. Dr Woolf was a great believer in the amputation of offending organs. God knows what advice he'd give Solomon about the pain in the region of his heart . . .

As it turned out, it had been far easier (if more painful) for Dora to divest herself of her women's bits than for Solomon to find a purchaser for *S. Epstein, Kosher Butcher and Poulterer*.

'It's a good corner position. Modern premises. The best marble slabs you'll find anywhere this side of the Acropolis.'

Solomon had tried every means of persuasion. In vain. Who wanted a business that had lost most of its customers? He was finally forced to sell the shop to a nationwide chain of fast food restaurants and (he could hardly bear to think about it) the butchery had been transformed into a branch of Kebab World UK.

In the mean time, Dora was being subjected to the systematic excision of other troublesome parts of her internal machinery.

'Have them out. Out. Out.' Dr Woolf had ordered the scalpel again and again. Until Dora, like the wrinkled shell of a passion fruit out of which every last seed had been scooped, had been returned to the marital bed to await her end.

'Solly,' she had struggled to say, minutes before it was all over. 'Solly – take it easy. Look after yourself – please.'

And he had. He'd tried. Thanks to the Meals-on-Wheels service, he had kept his body more or less intact. And his soul . . . his soul? Solomon didn't like to dwell too deeply on the state of his soul. Instead he concentrated hard on the instructions attached to the plastic pot containing his Sunday night supper.

'Delicious Chunky Cod Hot-Pot', it said. Solomon had learnt that when a dish was labelled 'delicious' it was likely to be particularly foul-tasting. 'Place the container in your microwave oven and set the timer for three minutes. Enjoy your supper.'

Not long afterwards (thanks to modern technology and the rigour of the Meals-on-Wheels portion control system), Solomon was burping a reluctant fishy encore as he returned to his armchair, unsatisfied and feeling more neglected than ever. Wolfgang Mozart and Seymour Katz had resumed their double concerto and Solomon had nothing to do but to wait.

His chest hurt again. Not half as severely as it had that morning but enough to set him off on an unsettling course of thought about death and the doctor and the futile calls to the Meals centre and – Judith. Judith. Perhaps the pain was simply a sore heart because she'd been so – absent of late. And today, for the first Sunday since Dora had passed on, she hadn't bothered to contact him at all. Not even a simple 'Hello, Dad – how are you?' That was all he wanted.

No it wasn't. There were things he wanted to tell his daughter. And Solomon, with his sudden ache of mortality, feared that if he didn't do it soon, it might be too late.

Solomon's fear was well grounded. It was almost too late. But he might have felt a different sort of pain if he had known that it was Judith, not himself, who was about to die. In the All Seasons sitting-room, his daughter was counting her final hours. Happy Half-Hour was drawing to an end. After that there'd be supper. And after that . . .

With some sadness, for her fury seemed to have dissipated, she glanced across the room at Edwin and Angela and saw a newborn couple, melting into an apricot mousse sofa under a peachy ceiling with mouldings and cornices like an ornately iced wedding-cake. They were sitting side by side, facing a real log fire specially designed to forge the marriage vows. But, despite the efforts of the proprietors and staff of All Seasons to provide 'A Perfect Honeymoon Haven in the Heart of the Cotswolds', they were clearly having their first little – er – difference. Not even Chuck Wilmot (former marketing director of North Carolina Dream Parks Inc.) and his highly trained team could prevent that. Nothing could.

'To us,' they chorused rather wryly. As though, only hours after they had sworn lifelong devotion, they had already shed their innocence. Angie, in daring red with a bold black rose at her cleavage, crossed her legs tightly as her husband edged confidently closer. Edwin may have lost the first game, but he seemed quite sure that he would win the set and match.

Judith sighed. She couldn't help it. They turned towards her and she felt middle-aged and conspicuously unattached in this shrine to matrimony. Suddenly uncomfortable, she reached for her key. It was labelled 'April'. Springtime. The month when trees blossomed and new life began. She smiled.

They frowned and looked away. Now *they* were uncomfortable. It was funny though. Funny and sad and somehow appropriate that she should have returned to this place of beginnings to find an ending. She had come back, after twenty years, to the same daffodil-spangled room in the same confection-laced castle in the Cotswolds where Dr and Mrs Arthur Goldman had had seven post-nuptial nights of supposed bliss, to seek – what? Sanctuary? Peace? Finality.

'I'd like to pay for my drink,' she said to the hovering waiter.

'Certainly madam,' with fine-tuned impassivity.

She extracted her purse from her handbag containing (as well as the TV remote control device which she'd brought along in a final fit of spite) a hundred tricyclic antidepressant tablets. Arthur's textbooks had guaranteed that these would make sure that she'd never be married or depressed again.

The room called April hadn't changed in twenty years. While Judith and Arthur Goldman had gained bedrooms and bidets and a neo-Georgian conservatory and moved from minimalism and early Habitat through to art deco and genuine antique, April had remained frozen in an eternal ersatz springtime. It made Judith feel old. Old and tired. She drew the floral curtains and pulled a buttercup-yellow bedspread off the vast four-poster bed and lay down and shut her eyes. Making a marriage had been exhausting but breaking it was almost enough to finish one off. She doubted whether the antidepressants would be necessary after all.

As for her abandoned spouse, she could imagine him bewailing his fate, see him with bowed head and knitted brow, contemplating the inevitability of his ill-fortune. Poor Arthur. But then, he'd always predicted he would come to an unhappy end. After all, how much in the way of optimism could she have expected from the son of a shroudmaker? Arthur, undoubtedly, would retort that he'd been an idiot to have sought fidelity from the daughter of a family butcher.

'And anyway,' he'd persist (Arthur never had been one for letting things pass), 'my mother's Burial Society work is voluntary. Entirely. It's one of many things she does for several charitable causes – which is more than some mothers ever managed.'

'What do you mean? Don't you dare bring my mother into this . . .'

As usual, it was getting nasty. But since when had anyone ever claimed that the rules of marriage included keeping swipes above the belt?

'Oh forget it. It was nothing. It doesn't matter.'

Typical. His retreat, her wrath. Arthur the victim, Judith the bitch. Then Judith drowning in tears of remorse and Arthur, benignly, offering a hand of peace and Judith, unready, unable to take it and Arthur, rebuffed, feeling martyred and rejected. And Judith helpless in the face of his hopelessness and Arthur even more hopeless in the face of her utter helplessness. And so on and for ever after. It was a far cry from the happy endings promised to brides and grooms in every fairy-tale invented. Wasn't it?

'Arthur? *Arthur*, will you answer me? If only you'd stop feeling sorry for yourself we could try and work things out . . .'

It was useless. Their arguments went round and round. Round and round with no ending in sight. That was probably why she'd returned to the beginning, to this sentimentality-encrusted country hotel where couples like Judith and Arthur and Edwin and Angela were launched on their futile and fantastic quest to seek honey on the moon.

She had left London in a fury, driven bullet-like along wet motorways and lurched along country lanes. Then she'd stopped, out of breath and still angry, and stared at the careful tapestry of pastures and hedges and flowering fields and thought of all the hope and effort there'd been in the carving and taming and tilling of those patches of earth. And her anger had dissolved into an enormous sadness as she'd imagined the end. Fields stripped and dying and the hedges overgrown and the lambs that nuzzled so trustingly against their mothers rounded up and sent for slaughter. All for nothing. All the trying and trusting in vain.

Judith had laughed, for the sadness had been too painful to bear. How ridiculous she must have looked – a plumpish, middle-aged woman leaning against her Volvo with her tears making mascara-tracks down her cheeks, crying as her shoulders shook with laughter.

'Judith – calm down. Control yourself.' She imagined her father trying to soothe her. Solomon Epstein, family butcher. 'There's no point being miserable about things – they'll happen anyway. Let me explain . . .'

Oh, Dad, she'd thought tiredly. Always explaining. Next you'll be talking about the great abattoir in the sky.

'Take those baby lambs, for instance,' he'd say in his slow measured way. 'Now someone in my line of work would see them as chops and joints and tender stewing meat. It certainly wouldn't be useful for a butcher to cry over the creatures. It's the same with marriage. Forget the lace and confetti and ideas of romantic love. Marriage, like butchery, is a flesh and blood matter. It's to do with bleeding and breeding and survival of the species. Do you understand?'

He might have put out a hand and stroked her hair, the way she had longed for when she'd been a small child. The way, even now, she longed for.

'Yes,' she'd reply, eager to please him. Still defeated by that enormous need to please him. 'I – think – I understand.'

And she had looked back towards the meadow and tried to see the mutton for the sheep. But when she had tried to think about the meat of a marriage she'd felt tears rising again.

'But Dad, what about when the breeding doesn't happen? What does marriage mean then? And – I thought you loved my mother. I always believed you adored her.'

'Of course I did. But that's nothing to do with being married.'

'Nothing at all.'

She turned round sharply. Another disembodied voice had risen from the countryside. It belonged to Gertrude Goldman, mother-in-law, volunteer shroudmaker and home organizer *extraordinaire*. Judith was glad Gertrude was making her visitation in the spirit. Her mother-in-law's immaculately groomed physical presence always made her feel as though she had egg on her face. She wiped her mouth and surreptitiously checked under her shoes and asked Gertrude what she had meant.

'Economics,' was the reply, as crisp as a new ten-pound note. 'Ralph supplies means and I provide methods and together we keep the marriage afloat. It's all a matter of demand and supply, balancing the books, profit and loss.'

'I see,' Judith said doubtfully. She had always been hopeless with figures. At least she saw why her relationship with her mother-in-law had never added up. One of the reasons anyway.

So. Meat and money made marital stability and for an innumerate vegetarian that had been bad news indeed. But that's what they had told her, and they were veterans in the field. Solomon Epstein, wedded to his Dora for thirty-eight years and parted by her death. And Gertrude Goldman, teamed with her hard-earning Ralph for half a century and still going strong. Apparently.

As for Judith and Arthur – they had somehow stumbled through two decades together, holding grimly on to the couples carousel. Up and down and round and round. Until Judith had stepped off that morning, a spring Sunday morning, her red Volvo grinding down the gravel path. Away, far away, to a field bleating with baby lambs and two disapproving voices.

'Shut up,' she shouted aloud. 'Can't you keep quiet, both of you, and leave me alone. I won't bother you again. I've decided.'

She returned to the car with as much dignity as she could muster and pressed her face against the leather-trimmed steering wheel and thought she'd cry forever and that would be most unpleasant. Even worse than remaining married. Then she remembered the tablets and wondered whether she should end it there and then, and had got as far as fumbling with the cap (bloody hell – it turned out to be child-proof) when she realized she had no water.

That's when she had looked up, tear-stained and red-eyed, foolish and miserable, and suddenly remembered that All Seasons wasn't far away. How ironic that her flight had inadvertently brought her so close to the honeymoon hotel. Judith was filled with a new sense of purpose. There had been something incomplete about the idea of a life extinguished on a random country lane. Untidy. Unsatisfying for all concerned. As a housewife she had always insisted on order and efficiency and as a musician she'd hated to leave chords unresolved. Loose threads and unfinished symphonies irritated her. But a marital coda at All Seasons? A last tragic refrain in the magic castle where the first notes of the first movement had sounded? Most appropriate. Judith thought she heard Apollo chuckling as she set off. Apollo and Hymen. And the ghosts of Darby and Joan, who had probably died of boredom. At least she'd spare herself that. At the very least . . .

There was not a flicker of amusement from behind All Seasons' velvet-padded reception desk, where a perfectly groomed but barely animate being named Barbie looked askance at the unheralded appearance of Judith. Not only was this new arrival unkept and clearly unkempt. She was blatantly unashamed to ask for the prime honeymoon suite.

'Goldman's the name,' she said firmly. 'Judith Goldman.'

'Hang on a minute.' The receptionist sounded doubtful. She unfolded her perfect size eight sheath-moulded form and sashayed, eyeing Judith suspiciously, towards the adjoining Management Office. All Seasons' employees conformed strictly to the physical proportions suggested by the British Mannequin Makers' Guild and management preferred its guests to arrive two by two, looking as though they'd stepped out of department store windows. Judith wore around size fourteen and had damp patches under her arms and mascara smudges under her dark puffy eyes. Barbie needed guidance on this one.

Judith waited, trying unsuccessfully to avert her gaze from the unpleasing reflections in the multi-mirrored walls and remembered how she'd done the same twenty years before. So what had changed?

Nothing, she thought miserably. Absolutely nothing. And how she'd longed for change. Once, long ago, she had believed in the tale about the Ugly Bride transformed into glorious beauty by the noble kiss of her groom. She had dreamed (what a fool she'd been!) that everything would be different after she'd been awakened by her Arthur. That she would graciously bestow on him the sovereignty of her timeless realm. And so? Had it happened? Not bloody likely.

They had signed out of All Seasons, having billed and cooed and bickered and broken bread for seven nights. And as they'd left she had seen reflected in these very mirrors the same plain Judith who'd arrived the week before. The Loathly Damsel, instead of becoming Her Glorious Highness, had turned into a member of the mighty legion of dutifully dowdy matrons occupying the semi-detached houses of Golders Green.

'I – er – need to know how you'd be paying for your accommodation,' hesitated Barbie, who had emerged from Mr Wilmot's office with a false eyelash in slight disarray.

'Oh.' Judith considered a moment. Then she rummaged through her purse. 'Would this do?'

She handed Barbie her Gold Card. Arthur's badge of affluence. Judith's prize for attaining prosperous wifehood. Barbie examined it intently and gave it back.

'Yes, indeed,' she drawled. 'As it happens, there's been a cancellation in "April". Fortunately, we can let you have it, Miss – er . . .'

'*Mrs* Goldman.'

A cancellation? A wedding that wasn't? In the old days Judith would have been overcome with the sort of sentimental melancholy that moved her when she saw newspaper advertisements offering 'Bridal Dress – Never Worn' and desperate pleas by lonely hearts for convivial life-partners. Now she knew better. She suspected that the couple who'd called off 'April' were probably wise.

'Thank you,' she said, accepting the key. Barbie curved her mouth into the statutory well-formed smile, her eyes having shifted their gaze above Judith's shoulder towards the door. A pair of honeymooners had entered, he burdened manfully by a matching set of suitcases, she in white linen with a coy corsage pinned to her chest. Judith moved aside to let them through.

'Cockroft,' he crowed deeply. 'Edwin and Angela – Cockroft.'

'Welcome to All Seasons,' simpered Barbie. 'I've put you in October.'

ALL SEASONS — YOUR HONEYMOON
HOTEL IN THE COTSWOLDS
SUNDAY 31ST MARCH – DINNER MENU

Sizzling Smoked Oysters
(Succulently steamy morsels from faraway ocean beds, caressed by sun-bronzed toast fingers)

★

Turtle Dove Soup
(Gently heated and fragrantly seasoned love-nectar afloat with tender asparagus tips)

★

Sirloin Steak Aphrodite (for two)
(A provocative pound of the leanest flesh imaginable – good enough to eat)

★

Stuffed Peppers
(Rice-filled variation on a theme for vegetable lovers)

★

Salad Sixty-Nine

(A veritable orgy of peeled tomatoes, stripped carrots,
revealing radishes and bare lettuce leaves
in a sultry undressing dreamed up by our head chef
after a visit to the Bahamas
during the steamy summer of '69)

★

Passion Fruit Pavlova

(Whipped cream and other sweet sensations
to make afterplay naughty but ever so nice . . .)

It wasn't easy being a lone vegetarian in an establishment designed for coupling carnivores. Judith tried to shut her ears from the sound of Vivaldi on a synthesizer and caught hold of the tail of her linen serviette which had been cunningly folded into the form of a swan. With a determined flick of her wrist, she made the bird disappear and narrowed her eyes challengingly at its mate across the table (which, of course, had been set for two). A final tragic twist to the story of the Ugly Duckling, she thought, as she spread the starched square across her lap. All that excitement about the emergence of a glorious swan – and it ends up as a receptacle for gravy stains.

'Is – er – madam ready to order?'

A waitress with a cleavage like a fissure between foam-encrusted peaks leaned over Judith with her notepad and pencil. Judith raised her eyes in line with a badge that had been pinned onto the steeper of the twin ascents. HI! I'M MARCY. HAVE A NICE NIGHT! Beyond the uplands of Mount Marcy she noticed that Ed and Ange had been seated at an adjoining table and were engrossed in the menu. Angela was giggling slightly uncomfortably. Edwin was smiling and licking his lips.

'Has madam made up her mind yet?'

Marcy sounded slightly impatient. Her staff training hadn't covered the seduction of the single woman and (compared with the salivation she'd aroused in Edwin) there was little job satisfaction to be gleaned out of Judith. Meanwhile Judith, having perused the menu and recoiled from its coy innuendoes, had concluded that she'd do without her last supper after all. There was no nobility in a corpse sated with Salad Sixty-Nine and even if she'd been a meat-eater, tackling Steak Aphrodite alone would have looked like public masturbation. As for stuffed peppers . . .

No. It would have to be suicide on an empty stomach. She would deliberately disobey the instruction on the medicine label to 'Take after meals'. It would be her final rebellion.

'Actually,' she said, shutting the menu with a decisiveness that made its pink tassel shudder, 'I'm not quite ready to eat yet. Perhaps in a while . . .'

'The kitchen closes at ten,' Marcy said, eagerly pointing her eyes and breasts towards Edwin. Judith rose to her feet with a resigned shrug and started heading towards the door. As she brushed past Angela, she noticed that the newlywed's glance had been modestly averted from Marcy's approaching mountains and the corners of her scarlet lips had dipped.

'Shall we start with the soup, my little turtle dove?' Edwin was saying playfully. 'We want to make sure that we have a nice night. Don't we?' Angie nodded, trying and failing to attain an eager smile.

A few minutes later, as Judith turned the key and entered April, she could still hear Edwin's voice. A nice night indeed. She remembered the way Angela's mascara-rimmed eyes had followed her out of the dining-room. Had they been glinting with unshed tears?

Angela's plight was soon forgotten as Judith set about her suicide. First, the note. Paper and pen had been thoughtfully provided in the pastel pink folder marked 'Billets Doux'.

TO WHOM IT MIGHT CONCERN,

After many minutes of painful indecision about the recipient of this farewell communication, I think it would be easiest all round if I frame it as a general letter of resignation. Thus: I, Judith Goldman, regretfully wish to place it on formal record that as from today, 31st March 1992, I cannot continue as a member of the human race.

This is not something I decided lightly. For months, years, as long as I can remember I have lived with a dragging weight, a pain that has become too much to bear. Until now, I've told myself again and again that I have to endure. Ignore the pain, Judith, I kept saying sternly. If you don't give into it, the despair will go away.

It didn't. It seemed to get worse and worse despite – everything. And then, last year. Even now, I can't bring myself to write about last year. And finally today. I don't quite know what happened today. Something exploded and I find myself here of all places. And – it's time.

Please don't be too

Too what? Judith looked up, frowning, and caught sight of herself in the large oval mirror that backed the dressing-table at which she was seated. The familiar face was staring back with forty-two years' worth of mournful intensity, bringing darkest darkness to the bright buttercup spring-tones of this dreadful room called April. Too – disappointed? Sad? Angry? How dared she (who had chosen not to be) tell them how not to be? What a cheek.

Judith was suddenly filled with scorn for this person, this woman in black who sat there, puffed up with the passion of her passing, so self-consciously dignified in her despair, as she staged her last scene of her last act with the deliberation of the director of a large-scale melodramatic opera. If she'd been doing her job properly, there'd have been ominous rumblings from the kettle drums and the first strains of a sob from the strings as the final minutes ticked by for the despairing and death-bent prima donna. Instead there was muzak and the scent of Spring Flowers room spray and the ridiculous sight of a dowdy middle-aged woman (with a spot on her chin – was that a spot on her chin, of all things? A hideous red and yellow spot?) trying to design an impressive death.

She turned her eyes from the mirror and they rested on a small table tucked at the foot of the enormous bed like a lifeboat alongside a majestic ocean liner. It held a tray with two glasses and a small bottle of port. A card, propped up against one of the glasses, had an inscription in gold: FOR AFTERWARDS – with our compliments.

Afterwards. Judith laughed – well, almost – as she thought about their afterwards, all the afterwards that stretched ahead for the newlyweds of All Seasons – an eternity of post-coital lethargy (alcohol-induced if all else failed).

'How was it for you, darling?'

'Fine. Wonderful. And for you?'

'Absolutely great.'

Was that it? Marriage? Happiness? If so, it left only the ever after of the coupled state to be lived – until at last, at long long last, it was torn asunder by the arrival of the ever afterwards. And

Judith, who'd found the ever after unendurable, tried to imagine the afterwards that a hundred antidepressants would reveal to her. She'd empty the medicine bottle and a genie would transport her to a heaven where people (no wives – please God, no wives) would make love and glorious music and eat vast amounts of fattening food and laugh into large mirrors and see themselves as beautiful and feel – alive. *Alive?*

Isn't this utterly mad? she thought suddenly. I'm killing myself so that I can feel alive.

That was when Judith knew she wouldn't do it. She couldn't. Someone who longed so badly to feel life didn't really want to die. No – she hadn't come here, in the end, to make her final will and testament. Judith's flight to All Seasons had been her biggest and most defiant won't.

So where did that leave her? Now that she'd cornered herself in April, what was she to do? Quite clearly, she was unable to live or to die or be a wife or a mistress or be single or one of a couple or anything at all. Judith Goldman, she told herself, you are stuck.

And as she poured herself a glass, and then another glass, of the port provided for afterwards (why not?), she wondered how it would be if she were never to leave this room called April. How about if she turned it into a permanent parking place for the maritally disabled and flatly refused to budge? There she'd be – entombed, frozen in time, forever forty-two, while April became May and then June and July and so on until it was finally December and the daffodils, having turned to roses, dropped off and disappeared altogether as autumn changed to winter and the polyester drapes drooped and darkness fell . . .

Judith awoke an hour later and thought she was in hell and remembered where she was and thought, taking everything into consideration, she'd almost rather have been in hell.

'Fuck,' she said crossly as she sat up and bumped her head on a stray bedpost and, blinking away the angry–sad tears that sprang up, decided that if fucking was what she wanted she'd certainly come to the right place. Mind you, being mate-less in All Seasons was a bit like being one-legged in a Fun Run. What, for instance, was she to do with the complimentary pack of condoms ('Assorted Colours, Novel Shapes') that she'd pulled out of the folder containing writing paper, hotel information and a 'mini sewing knit for emergency repairs'? Nothing much, apart from filling them with water until they burst or blowing them up to see if they really expanded to four feet as claimed by their makers, or wondering whether and how they'd been electronically tested. After that, she'd have to resort to the thrills offered by the 'Adult-only Video Selection' or the spills afforded by the multi-directional high speed jet-stream in the bathroom or – the pills. In the end there were always the pills.

But meanwhile she was hungry. Extremely hungry. She'd missed the ten o'clock dining-room deadline and it occurred to her that she hadn't eaten all day and even stuffed peppers and stripped carrots now seemed attractive. As for strawberry tart. Judith shut her eyes longingly and had a vision of a flat white box in a corner of a faraway frost-free fridge and suddenly remembered that they were supposed to have been having coffee at the Davises and wondered whether Arthur had gone on his own.

Never, she decided. He would never had disturbed the table plan by creating an odd number. Instead, he had probably swallowed the tart and given himself indigestion and sought medication – and noticed. Of course he'd noticed. Arthur didn't miss a thing when it came to the medicine chest. He maintained a more careful inventory of its contents than Old Mother Hubbard had kept of her culinary provisions – but (unlike Old M.H.'s) Arthur's cupboard was never bare. It contained quick cures for every ill to which the human organism could possibly succumb. Except depression. Tonight Arthur had undoubtedly come upon a sinister gap in the assortment.

Oh well. He had probably taken fright and then found swift oblivion in sleep. As always.

'Arthur!' She wanted to rouse him. To shake him out of his deep snoring slumber and open his eyes, force him to look at her, to speak to her, listen to her. Properly. They'd tried Couples Counselling the previous year but that hadn't done much to provide the 'marriage enrichment' it had offered. Arthur had infuriated her with his benign platitudes and she had answered sharply and he had kept rolling his eyes to the therapist as though to say 'isn't she impossible?', and after each session the bedroom had rocked with recriminations and counter-recriminations and her exhausted tears – and, finally, his snores.

'Arthur – wake up. We have to talk.'

But they'd never managed it. Not there, in the heart of suburbia, where the marriage knot was tied so tight that it strangled.

'Is *any* marriage happy – really happy?' she had asked him despairingly after they'd decided to give up on their bid for enrichment and make the most of what they had. Judith had always felt sympathy for the wartime brides who'd had to make cake out of turnips but, unlike them, she had been unable to rise above her ingredients.

'Of course,' Arthur had replied without a moment's hesitation. 'I can think of two for a start.'

'You mean –?'

'My parents and your parents. Naturally. Surely you don't need better examples than those?'

Gertrude and Ralph. Solomon and Dora. Were Gertrude and Ralph truly content? Had Solomon and Dora achieved lasting marital bliss? Judith had nodded rather doubtfully.

'I suppose not,' she said. Then she'd paused thoughtfully. 'I wonder if they'd agree with you – deep inside? How much do they hide, Arthur? Do we really know?'

He had dismissed her reservations with a scornful 'you're ridiculous'. But still she couldn't help musing on what lay behind those two paragons of connubial contentment. If Arthur's belief was correct, would Gertrude and Ralph and Solomon and the ghost of poor Dora be willing to convince Judith that marriage could work? That the institution was bigger than the sum of the grievances of its partners? That there was no alternative but for her to go back to Arthur and keep trying to make it work?

'I won't,' said Judith fiercely. 'Not on those terms, I won't.' She opened the file marked 'Hotel Information' and began looking through the index. Surely they'd have room service in a place like this? Didn't all the steamy sex make the guests of All Seasons ravenously hungry? If it really took place, that was. Judith suspected that Edwin and Angela, for instance, having imbibed and ingested and argued and sulked, had probably gone to sleep long ago. And Angie, poor little Angie, had discovered that her new husband snored.

It took a falling apple to strike Newton with gravity and an overflowing bathtub for Archimedes to say 'Eureka!' and an entry in the All Seasons directory of services to give Judith Goldman her big idea. Fighting off a Newtonian headache and an Archimedian desire to soak her sore limbs in steamy water, she perused the entry slowly and carefully, stopping only to breathe 'That's it!',

'I've got it!' and other equally enthusiastic exclamations. Who would have said that only an hour or so before, she had been preparing for death? Talk about the resilience of the human spirit . . .

The item that had inspired Judith's excitement was listed between 'Traveller's Cheques' and 'Volleyball' and headed 'Unfinished Business?' It was the question mark that caught Judith's eye.

'Unfinished Business?' it asked.

'Yes,' she answered, nodding slowly. 'Yes indeed.'

For executive bridegrooms: All Seasons makes it possible for you to keep a finger on the pulse of the money-markets and a foot in the corporate door with hardly an interruption to your honeymoon. We offer a wide range of business facilities, including:

★ Facsimile machines in every bedroom. You'll find yours discreetly tucked away in the drawer beneath the right-hand side of the bed.

★ Willing secretarial assistance. Simply dial 100 and ask for Linda. We call all our secretaries Linda to make things easier for you.

★ A regularly updated and fully comprehensive list of all the world's major stock fluctuations on channel 27 of your TV set.

★ A fully equipped meeting-room for the occasions when nothing but an old-fashioned eyeball-to-eyeball confrontation will do. Our specially designed conference chamber (complete with video, fax and computer facilities and satellite link-up if desired) can be hired on a daily basis. Linda (on 100, remember?) will gladly take your booking. She offers a 24-hour service in case of emergencies.

The last facility was the one that set Judith's heart racing. 'Would it work?' she asked herself as she envisaged the conference chamber at All Seasons as the setting for a face-to-face forum on marriage. How fitting. There'd be five participants (not counting the ghost of dead Dora) gathered to examine the institution – in a setting designed as its shrine. Three marriages. The flawed and floundering partnership between Judith and Arthur, and the supposedly heaven-made matches of the senior Goldmans and widower Epstein. At last, thought Judith with mounting excitement, at long last I may have my chance to learn the truth.

She dialed 100. It was 10.30 p.m. – but didn't a life-or-death issue such as this count as an emergency?

'This is the recorded voice of your secretary, Linda. I'm sorry to say that I'm in a meeting at present but if you leave the name of your room and the nature of your – er – business I'll return your call as soon as possible.'

Judith, who was normally rendered inarticulate by the knowledge that a machine was irrevocably recording her inarticulacy, spoke out loud and clear. This call, after all, was far outside the constraints of normality.

'The name of my room is April. I'd like to make a booking for the All Seasons conference room this week. Please let me know urgently if it's available.'

'Arthur?'

'Judith! Where – were you? Where are you? You really had me worried, you know. I had no idea . . .'

'Arthur – listen to me. Listen carefully. It's very important. As you probably noticed . . .'

'Yes – I saw. They were – gone. You're not going to do anything stupid, Jude . . . ? Are you? Judith? Answer me?'

'Arthur, will you *not* interrupt me. I've told you. What I have to say is extremely important.'

'Sorry. I'm – listening.'

'Right. I have the tablets. Enough to kill me – I know because I looked up the fatal dose in one of your books. And I'm quite prepared to swallow them. I mean it and you'd better believe me.'

'Don't, Jude. Please don't . . .'

'It's up to you.'

'What d'you mean? Judith don't be ridiculous.'

'If you listen to me and follow all my instructions, then maybe I . . .'

'Judith, you're mad. Completely off your head. You need to see someone. Tell me where . . .'

'Arthur, I have a hundred tricyclic antidepressants here in my right hand and a glass of water in my left. I'm warning you.'

'Right. OK. What do you want?'

'I want you to prepare for a journey. You and your parents and my father. To come here, the four of you, so that we can sit together and talk.'

'Where? Why? Judith, this is ludicrous. You're threatening me with your life – for *that?* You've sulked about coming to my mother's Friday night suppers for the past – I don't know – as long as I can remember. And now you say you're going to – *die* unless we all get together . . .'

He agreed. He had to. He swore and puffed and spluttered his anxiety and disapproval and baffled despair until Judith, almost drained of the will to resist, held the phone at arm's length till he finally stopped. At last he agreed because he had no choice. As he said to Judith, sadly, before they said goodbye: 'A bad husband – maybe. But a murderer I'm not.'

There was a slight blip in the number of cases of nocturnal unrest in South East England that night. In London, the number of insomniacs (1.873 million on an average spring Sunday) rose by four.

Gertrude Goldman, for instance, normally a rock-steady sleeper and systematic snorer, remained relentlessly awake.

'I knew it,' she kept saying to Ralph, who had taken out his dentures and squeezed his eyes shut but couldn't reach the level of unconsciousness required to obliterate the agitation of his wife.

'I've always suspected that Judith. Never trusted her, you know. Had a feeling she would do something like this – eventually. But honestly, Ralph – this is going too far. Ralph? Are you awake?'

'Mm. Shh – Gertrude, calm down. Please.'

'Really and truly – to hold us all to ransom. All of us. The whole family. I've a good mind to refuse. To stick to my guns. One shouldn't give in to this sort of thing. Hijacking, blackmailing. Where will it all end, is what I keep asking myself . . .'

'Gertrude, she only wants us to come and talk to her. That's all. Isn't that what Arthur told you?'

It had been – more or less. Arthur had meant to assume a tone of bland matter-of-factness when he had informed his mother of Judith's demand. His heart had thudded alarmingly and the back of his pyjama top had been damp with stress. Nevertheless he had been determined not to offer Gertrude confirmation (yet again) that she had been correct about his unfortunate choice of a wife.

'Arthur!' she had exclaimed. 'Arthur – it's so late – where've you been all day? I thought it was you earlier but it was only a wrong number and I said to the Willises – they were here for bridge – I said Arthur always phones on a Sunday, never lets us down – Where *were* you?'

'Mom. Please. There's been a – slight – problem.'

And as he had recounted the events of the day and she had murmured 'poor boy, my poor, *poor* Arthur', he had felt as though he were being cradled in the warmth of a large eiderdown. He had melted, bit by bit, each time she had said it, until he had been reduced to a soft infant. Limp. Weak and limp. 'My poorest darling boy,' she had murmured as, despite his resolve not to confide in her, it had all come pouring out. 'How hard all this is for you.' And Arthur, agreeing miserably, had to keep his thumb a safe distance from his mouth. He was curled like a foetus, cradling the phone to his chest. Then, suddenly self-conscious, he forced himself to sit up.

'Mom – I'll talk to you in the morning,' he managed briskly. 'Jud. . . . she – said she'd ring to give me details about where she was and when we should come.'

Gertrude's first thoughts, as she replaced the receiver, were about all the meetings she would have to cancel that week.

'It's all very well for you, Ralph,' she sighed. 'You don't lead the sort of life I do – although why I rush about so, taking so much on my shoulders, beats me . . .'

Ralph shrugged, not much of a shrug compared with the nonpareil of gestures perfected by his wife. But then he had never tried to rival Gertrude in her particular fields.

'You're a busy woman,' he conceded. It cost him nothing to tell her what she wanted to hear. 'And I'm – well – only a retired hardware merchant with nothing, not even a single appointment, to cancel. Can we go to sleep now?'

She nodded distractedly but continued, at intermittent intervals, to ruminate and speculate and declaim and denounce. 'I always knew it,' she muttered again and again. 'I told Arthur right from the start that he'd made a bad choice.' Ralph despaired of ever getting to sleep.

Solomon Epstein, in the slumbering side-streets of Willesden, had also given up trying to sleep. Arthur's call had shaken him profoundly. It had brought a sharp pain to his chest. A pain quite different from the ache for which he still awaited medical opinion.

'Is she all right?' he'd asked his son-in-law several times. 'Are you absolutely sure she's all right?'

'Of course she is, Pops. It's just that – well – we don't want to take any chances. Do we?'

'No. Of course not. We must go and talk to her if that's what she wants.'

Arthur had sounded confident and reassuring. 'Cautiously optimistic' was the way they'd have described him on the news bulletins to which Solomon was addicted. But just as he prided himself on never being taken in by smooth-talking spokespeople on the radio, he wasn't entirely convinced by Arthur's honeyed tones. Was she really all right, his Judith? And he hated being called Pops. A silly clownish name. Gertrude's idea, naturally, when the children had first married. He had objected from the start, but the Goldmans had stuck to it. 'I'm Solomon – named after the wisest of our kings,' he'd wanted to remind Arthur – again. But what did it matter now? Did anything matter now?

Several hours later, Gertrude and Ralph, having sipped soothing hot chocolate and exhausted every possible nuance of Arthur's revelation, finally went to sleep. They had sat together in the kitchen, a bright formica haven in the darkness, and shared opinions about their errant daughter-in-law and the remainder of the almond fruit torte. And when Gertrude at last said 'Good night, Ralph', she felt warm and safe and married. Ralph, turning over, felt reprieved.

Meanwhile Arthur, who had tussled for hours with a horrifying vision of Judith contorting in the last throes of death by antidepressants, finally succumbed to the lure of the oblivion offered by an emergency dose of a short-acting benzodiazapine which he always kept, just in case. Arthur was careful with soporifics but this, he reasoned, counted as an emergency. Without doubt – an – emergency, he thought dully, as at last his limbs grew heavy and his mind and heartbeat slowed and slowed.

Solomon, however, stayed wakeful. He was frightened that if he went to sleep he would never wake up. And then he'd never see Judith and she'd think he had refused her call and . . . he couldn't think further than that. Solomon remembered the way his daughter had looked at him once, long before. 'I want to die, Daddy,' she had said. 'All I want to do is to die.'

'No, Judith.' He had been dismissive. 'You don't. You can't.' What father could contemplate the wilful self-extinction of the product of his seed? The ultimate negation of his life-force? 'Don't talk like that. You don't mean it.'

But she had meant it. He had known it then and he knew it now, for Solomon Epstein had always been on close terms with despair. His intimacy with Flushing Katz, however, had taken a knock. In a fit of frustration round midnight, Solomon had banged with a broom on the ceiling.

'Shut up, Seymour,' he'd called irritably. 'Go and see a doctor and give me some peace and quiet. It's not a lot for an old man to ask for in his own home.'

There was a satisfying silence after that. But an hour later, Solomon started missing the sounds of life from above and couldn't bear to play Mozart (Judith; it made him think of Judith). He sat in his small dark living-room, feeling utterly alone.

And she? She who had brought about insomnia and fear and confusion in the upper echelons of the Burial Society and incipient benzodiazapine addiction and strife between neighbours? And an ache, such an ache, to the heart of her father? Judith, having commuted her self-imposed death sentence to indefinite imprisonment in All Seasons (with obligatory visiting rights from her nearest and dearest), was light-headed with relief and hunger and too much post-coital port and a sense of – what was that feeling? Could it be *anticipation?* She had forgotten what it felt like to look forward to the dawning of another day.

MONDAY

Between eight and nine each Monday morning, members of the management team of All Seasons gathered for their Communication Hour. It had once been thirty minutes until Chuck Wilmot returned from a training weekend which included transactional analysis and group dynamics. 'We have to give ourselves *space*,' he announced. 'Extra time to *communicate*, to bounce *ideas*, is not a corporate indulgence. It's a *need*.'

His fervour about person-to-person interaction had since veered off towards post-Jungian dream-analysis and then departed in the direction of homeopathic herbalism. But the weekly meetings remained (at least) sixty minutes. And while they may have been long enough to promote fruitful interdepartmental communication, they had done nothing to prevent the current cash flow crisis. All Seasons was in trouble.

'Guys – let me give it to you straight.'

Chuck leaned forward confidentially. There was very little he hadn't been taught about Motivational Management or how to make underlings feel important while kicking them in the teeth. He had even adapted some of the techniques to his female relationships. 'The Old Wilmot One-Two,' he called his most successful ploy. Lead 'em on, throw 'em out, lead 'em on again. Worked brilliantly, as he liked to boast in the bar. Never failed to have them panting for more. But these days Chuck had little to brag about. His tally of sexual conquests had dipped as low as the room occupancy rates and the message from head office had been that unless there was an immediate upturn in the profit-figures, there'd be some merciless rolling of heads.

'There's no point beating about the bush,' he said now, with a raising of the palms which his body-language instructor had told him meant he was being absolutely open. Laying all his cards on the table. Inviting responding candour which he could then use as a weapon to extricate himself from a nasty predicament. Like now.

'We're in the shit.'

Silence greeted this announcement – broken only by regular tapping as Chuck's secretary, Linda (a.k.a. Sherryl Carter of Milton Keynes), fed the minutes into her lap-top computer.

'The meeting opened on a rather low note,' she wrote. Mr Wilmot *loved* her to be creative. He always told her so. 'In fact, it hit rock bottom from the start when the Executive Manager pointed out . . .'

'Linda.' His voice seemed to have shed the velvety timbre acquired at an intensive Verbal Manipulation Workshop. It was hard and flat. 'I think we'd better keep this meeting off the record.'

'Yes, Mr Wilmot,' she said obediently. How boring. 'Would you like me to leave?'

'Yes – no. You may as well stay. At this stage, anyone's contribution would be welcome.' He looked intently at each member of his team, eyes moving from face to face. 'Ideas, folks. Ideas, ideas. Time – is – short.'

After a general round of coughing and shuffling of feet, Steve Maplin (Chuck's deputy) spoke up.

'Rides,' he said with evangelical ardour. 'Chuck, I've said it before and I'll say it again – particularly at this crucial stage in our – er – operation. Rides are the things to attract the punters. It's been proved over and . . .'

'Steve –'

'Listen to me Chuck. What keeps Disneyland ticking over? What put Alton Towers on its feet? There's nothing, absolutely nothing, to beat a couple of good old-fashioned rides.'

'But –'

'Wait. I have a couple of figures. Did you know that an out-of-town shopping centre near Huddersfield increased its mean customer flow by 13.7 per cent in only two months when it installed a Double Dipper in the concourse? And that when Hellfire Hole was built adjacent to a Methodist centre in Connecticut, church attendance rose by 23 per cent almost immediately? Now – please don't interrupt – what I had in mind was a total immersion experience I've provisionally called The Marriage Ride. Beds on an undulating track sort of thing with various adventures along the way and then . . .'

'That's quite enough, Maplin,' said Chuck, using exactly the sort of icy tone he'd practised for weeks in Advanced Assertiveness and rising to his feet commandingly. But suddenly he felt dizzy. The corporate ladder didn't seem safe. 'Don't you understand, Steve?' he said as he felt for his seat. 'There's no money to invest in anything new. There's no money – at – all.'

He remembered how, a year before, his deputy manager had convinced him to have the conference chamber installed. 'It will put us firmly on the map, Chuck,' he'd insisted. 'You take it from me. These days the punters will go anywhere for a fax machine and a couple of willing modems. Even on honeymoon. Did you know that when an airport terminal on the Cayman Islands installed a meeting-room with satellite link-up, the number of double-decker sandwiches sold in the adjacent food court rose by 49 per cent within weeks? And that the rate of elective hernia repairs carried out by a private hospital in Peterborough rose by 17.45 per cent when an executive communication centre was introduced as one of its patient services? Now I had in mind . . .'

Chuck had fallen for it. And that, he thought grimly now, had been the start of All Seasons' current financial embarrassment. It had been a huge investment. They'd installed the latest in business technology – and about the only person to use it had been Linda who faxed a weekly letter to her sister, Charlene, working in the social security offices at Milton Keynes.

'Maplin,' said Chuck rather bitterly, 'when I had to report on how much we'd lost on that meeting-room, I made up my mind that never again would I let you take us for a ride. Ahem. So to speak. Tell us, Linda – when last was it profitably occupied? Was it – five months ago? I have to inform you, guys, there's no answer for it this time . . .'

'Mr Wilmot . . .'

'Please, Linda. Don't interrupt. This is crucial. The bottom line is that weddings are down. And unless . . .'

'Mr Wilmot. There's . . .'

'Linda! Is there by any chance something *useful* you have to contribute? Why the hell d'you keep butting in?'

'Well – uh – the thing is, Mr Wilmot, there was a booking

made for the meeting-room. Last night. A message on my answering machine. From the – er – occupant of April.'

'A confirmed booking? Are you sure?'

'Well, I haven't actually had a chance to confirm it. Yet. But it sounded definite. From the sound of her voice, she seemed quite certain.'

'*She?* Oh my God.'

Chuck suddenly remembered having agreed, out of sheer desperation, to accommodate a distraught-looking fortyish female, knowing she wouldn't fit in, fully aware . . . and now it seemed she was wanting the meeting-room. Where would it end? And how could he possibly refuse the facility to someone with a Gold Card? Fully authenticated, Barbie had sworn. If only the silly cow had remembered to take down the number. To think of all the hours he'd spent training her in Reception Techniques.

Things had certainly declined since those heady days when he'd had visions of All Seasons as a post-nuptial mecca – Britain's ultimate honeymoon theme park. Giving sanctuary to a stray menopausal woman – even a moneyed one – had never been part of his plans. But hadn't he been taught that flexibility was one of the secrets of organizational success? That good managers bent? And bad ones broke? Chuck straightened his back resolutely.

'Well, guys,' he said, flexing his jaw, 'I suppose I'll have to go and have a word with – her. After all, she may buy us some time.'

Judith would probably have agreed to buy the entire hotel in order to avoid having to order the Continental Daybreaker ('Freshly ground coffee and a couple of hot rolls in bed with honey') from the breakfast menu that someone had slid beneath her door. But the alternative (an invitation to 'Get together in the Dining-Room and Tuck into a Goode Olde English Fry-up') was far worse, and she was hungry. Dizzy with hunger and a headache and wondering whether her muddled memories of fury and flight and an aborted farewell and a phone-call in the night were part of a dream. And knowing – as surely as the poly-cotton daffodils were nodding on the curtains and the snowdrops danced on the drip-dry duvet cover and the spring sunshine beamed with blinding cheer into this room called April – that they weren't. She shut her eyes, frowning.

'What have I done?' Judith asked herself wearily. 'What on earth have I done?'

That was exactly what she'd wanted to know twenty years before when she had woken in this very room with the last dying chords of the final wedding waltz in her head and a man beside her still deeply asleep with outflung arms and regular sighing breaths and a beatific smile on his face. My husband, she had thought with wonder. Could it really be that this male person sharing her bed, this unfamiliar creature with a nodule above his right earlobe and four – no, five – unexplained pockmarks on his forehead and strands of grey in hair already thinning and polyps in his nostrils and bridgework in his mouth, was to share her – everything?

She had always hated sharing.

'Judith – please – let Penny have a turn on your tricycle. It's not nice to keep things all to yourself.'

'Give your friends some of your sweets, Judy darling. We don't want them to think you're selfish.'

Reluctantly, she would let Penny pedal for a few measured minutes and bestow upon Joan and Martha a couple of her least-favoured liquorice allsorts. But it wasn't because she cared the slightest about seeming nice or unselfish. Not to her friends. Nor even to her mother who would watch over her, with arms folded and two worried vertical lines between her eyes, saying how difficult it was for Judith being an only child, and what a difference it would have made if she'd had a brother or a sister. It was entirely for *him* that Judith would grudgingly offer her playmate a toy or a sweet – and later, much later, when they were having supper together, the three of them, she'd make sure of his approval by reminding her mother of her generosity.

'Tell Daddy how good I was – how I let Jennifer play with my walkie-talkie doll. Tell him, Mummy – go on.'

And she would watch his face carefully as he heard about his daughter's virtue. She would be searching, searching for the start of the smile that began in the corners of his mouth and leapt up to his eyes and across the table until it landed in a warm place deep inside her. Judith cared, how she cared, about the approving smile of her father Solomon. For him to be proud of her she'd have shared – anything. And she was secretly glad, glad, glad that she didn't have a brother or sister because it would have meant having to share Daddy. And that sort of sharing would have been unbearable.

The other sort became more manageable when Judith, aged seven, invented an imaginary friend called Cathy. She was an all-purpose maintenance-free companion, who demanded neither toys nor turns and told no tales. Cathy would listen tirelessly to Judith's inventions and confessions and sadnesses and triumphs.

'Once, long ago,' she would tell her silent friend, 'there lived a princess who swallowed one of her wobbly milk teeth and it grew inside her into a huge greedy Smile Monster. Hungry, ever-hungry for smiles. Not any old smile though. This monster wanted to eat the smiles given to the princess by her father the king. And the more the monster grew, the more smiles he needed until . . .'

Cathy was the inexhaustible recipient of Judith's endless stories. Until, one day, she was replaced by a large wooden object that came out of a van and was squeezed through the front door and set down with a discordant crash on the living-room carpet. The piano.

'It's for you, Judith,' Solomon announced. 'You're a lucky girl. I never had a chance to learn to play the piano.'

After that, he began to sit with her each evening. Dora stayed discreetly in the kitchen, while Solomon, with tireless patience, listened to his daughter's progress at the instrument. Judith soon forgot about Cathy. She didn't need her any more. She had the regular attention of her father, and that was far more satisfying than even the most perfect imaginary friend. Judith lived for each evening. To please Solomon, she was prepared to practise all day.

'I'm proud of you, darling – very proud indeed,' he told her when she passed Grade Seven with distinction. 'One of the most promising young pianists I have yet encountered,' the examiner had written.

Judith, who was ten, believed at the time that the smile her father gave her as he scrutinized the report was big enough to keep the greediest of monsters satisfied forever. But of course it wasn't. Nothing was. Not even the one she received when, at fourteen, she reached the finals of the annual competition to find Britain's Young Musician of the Year.

'Judith, it's wonderful,' he said, kissing her on the forehead. 'You make – everything – worthwhile.'

And she looked up into his eyes and saw their sadness.

'What is – everything?' she dared to ask. Her mother had once said he'd been a real hero, that the Germans had given him a terrible time. 'He'll tell you about it, Judith,' she'd said. 'He'll tell you when he's ready and you're ready.' But he never had.

'Daddy, what do you mean by – everything?'

He hesitated, about to talk. She was sure he was about to talk. Then he shrugged.

'You think it's easy to run a butchery – to work day and night? Cutting and ordering and estimating and keeping the customers happy and – Judith, you have no idea. All I can say is that you're a lucky girl. A lucky girl indeed.'

And he subsided into silence, deep in thought.

'I am lucky – I know,' she agreed quickly. Lucky, she had decided, meant not having to share. It meant making music on the piano to elicit smiles from her father. Really lucky would be never again having to visit or think about the family butchery, the source of all her luck. Judith hated the shop. It smelt of dead animals and she couldn't bear seeing her father, her father with the melting smile, her hero-father, with a cleaver in his hand, slicing and chopping through bones and sinews and soft bloody flesh. Even the thought made her feel sick. Judith had refused to eat meat from as early as she could remember. 'But Dad – with you – isn't there – anything else . . . ?' she tried again.

He didn't answer. Solomon sat, deep in thought with downcast eyes. Then he suddenly looked up and said, 'Judith – your mother and I think you ought to – mix – a little more. We're worried that you spend so many hours – alone.'

'I need to practise. Musicians need to practise.'

'Yes – I know. And I'm – we're – proud of you. But there must be a little - balance. Every so often maybe, you should go out. Be with young people. Share your time a little. You understand?'

Sharing. Again. Judith wanted to tell him how she loathed it, utterly hated it. Instead she nodded and he smiled and he positively beamed when, the following Saturday night, she agreed to go to the cinema with an accountancy student called Martin Fishman.

'You see?' he said delightedly the next day. 'You see how it's possible to manage everything?'

She agreed. Just as she agreed, four years later, when a certain

Dr Arthur Goldman (nephew of one of Solomon's oldest customers) telephoned to invite her to a concert. He'd heard her playing, had always admired her, had tickets for a Mahler symphony at the Albert Hall and would she join him? Please?

'A doctor?' marvelled Solomon. 'He must be very clever to have qualified so young.'

'He's eight years older than me, Daddy. Twenty-six. Not particularly clever at all. Quite – nice – though. And we like the same music.'

Was that enough? His niceness and his taste in music and the fact that the mere mention of his name evoked the proudest of smiles in her father – and his sheer persistence? Arthur never gave up.

'Judith, will you marry me? We belong together. I know it.'

'Arthur, I can't. I'm young. There's still too much I have to do.'

She cried that night. No, it *wasn't* enough. Yet how much did she really have to do? How much would she do? Wasn't it possible that she had reached her musical peak and that the road ahead would be dotted with diminishing concerts as it narrowed into obscurity? She would have to face the fading of her father's smile. His disappointment. Could she bear it?

Being married to Arthur wasn't enough but perhaps it would have to do.

'Arthur – I don't know. I can't make up my mind.'

'I'll wait.'

That was his talent and it had certainly not reached its peak. He waited. And waited. Until one night, when the weight of the world and the burden of her father's expectations seemed to crush her and Arthur's hands holding hers felt safe and strong, she finally agreed. Tearfully.

'Are you sure?' he asked. 'Absolutely sure?'

'Yes. I – am.'

She thought of the Smile Monster when she told Solomon the news and watched his delight. Would the greedy beast be satisfied with this, the choicest and juiciest morsel he had yet been offered? Perhaps he was, temporarily. Until after the wedding, when she woke up to the yellow hues of a room called April and a headache – and a husband.

'What have I done?' she asked herself in panic. 'What on earth have I done?'

And now, with the same question on parched lips, she'd woken to another afterlife. Feeling like a battle-bruised survivor (after all, she had, apart from anything else, come through a brush with death by depression), Judith wondered dazedly whether she had really blackmailed the family into agreeing to join her in this haven for honeymooners. Had she finally gone mad?

'Oh God,' she groaned. Perhaps she was suffering from a certifiable disorder – in which case, Arthur would be likely to send white-coated men to disarm her of her tablets and lock her away. For her own good of course. They always said that. And in the end, she supposed, they were probably right.

As she lay beneath the scalloped canopy, comparing the prospect of a tranquillized existence in a padded cell to an enforced resumption of life with Arthur and deciding that, on the whole, she would prefer to opt for the mental rather than the marital institution, there was a knock on the door.

'Who is it?' she called. The loony-bin men? So fast? Or, preferably, breakfast? Yes – a couple of hot rolls (preferably *sans* honey) would help her face the future.

'One moment.'

She stood up and started heading for the bathroom (where she'd noticed a pair of matching towelling robes) but the rapping became insistent and Judith, thinking 'the hell with modesty', opened the door. She was barefoot and bare-armed in the sky-blue nylon nighty that had been a fortieth birthday present from Gertrude.

'Excuse me – er - Mrs Goldman?'

It was neither a warden with a straitjacket nor a waiter bearing a tray but a dark-suited male person of indeterminate age with a mid-Atlantic accent and an electrically-tanned body and a bleeper in his hand. A classless corporate being. Judith smiled automatically and disliked him on sight and he exposed a perfect set of teeth. The feeling was clearly mutual.

'Chuck Wilmot,' he said, advancing into the room and offering her the bleeper-free hand. 'Your hotel manager. *Executive* manager. You made a booking for our conference facility, I believe.'

'Yes – I did,' hesitated Judith, stepping back, appalled at her sudden timidity. Why wasn't she icily asking this man what right he had to enter her bedroom and whether, if she had been a male client, he would have telephoned first – and if he would mind waiting outside until she was ready to receive him? Instead, she was nodding compliantly and extending her hand.

'Is that – in order?' she asked, trying to carry herself with as much dignity as her state of undress would allow. 'The meeting-room reservation. Would it be possible, Mr Wilmot?'

'Call me Chuck – please. I think it may just be – but we'll have to talk about terms.'

He spoke caressingly. 487 bedroom encounters (he'd kept a record) had taught him superb modulatory and muscular control. 'Nice firm grip you have, Mrs Goldman,' he added, withdrawing his hand and moving towards the window as he suddenly struggled with a wave of unfamiliar unease. Business terms were not generally what Chuck negotiated with women in bed-chambers and this particular female was unlike any of his 487 conquests – and, anyway, Chuck sensed she'd be unlikely to submit to being number 488 even if he *were* interested in someone so large and dark and aggressive-looking. Attractive shoulders, though. And a majestic sort of bearing. Interesting eyes. Different. A challenge. He turned round, drew himself to his full six-foot-two and sucked in his stomach.

'Mrs Goldman,' he asked, 'what did you have in mind?'

Judith had recovered her composure and faced him squarely. She felt disgust for this executive clone who was so transparently assessing her bedworthiness instead of her bank balance. Vain bastard. As though she'd consider for a single minute . . . not even for a second. And yet, despite herself, she was exhilarated. She realized that for the first time in twenty years, she didn't feel like someone's wife.

'Mr Wilmot,' she said firmly, pointing to the table at which, only twelve hours before, she'd been writing her letter of farewell to the world, 'let's sit down and see if we can come to an agreement.'

Half an hour later, Judith had reserved the meeting-room and three bedrooms for the rest of the week.

'It's for an – encounter workshop,' she had announced with a sudden flash of brilliance. 'An intensive exploration of – er – marital dynamics.'

'Ah.'

This was the kind of language Chuck understood. Hadn't he suggested more than once to upper management that therapeutic encounters could be an ideal sideline for All Seasons in the event of a falling-off of the carnal kind? Perhaps, if this were successful, it could be the start of something big. If honeymoons became obsolete (and the statistics weren't encouraging), All

Seasons could be transformed into a theme park of the mind. There could be a Gestalt Grotto, a Relationships Roller-Coaster, Assertiveness Training after supper-meetings featuring Freud, eggs and chips. The possibilities were dizzying . . .

'I'll pay the going rate, of course,' she was saying.

'Of course,' agreed Chuck quickly. A short while later, when he left the room called April with a signed booking form and cash deposit, there was a spring in his step. New life was stirring in the finances of All Seasons and aggressive Mrs Goldman had agreed to join him for supper to 'finalize arrangements' and then – who knew?

Judith, too, felt a rush of excitement as she watched Wilmot leave. She reached for the phone.

'Arthur?'

He had picked it up immediately – must have been waiting for her call. Judith decided that power induced a far more heady sense of drunkenness than post-coital port. This could be addictive.

'Judith – what's happening? Can you tell me where you are?'

'Listen carefully', she said, 'and I'll give you full instructions.'

'Yes,' said Arthur mildly.

'Yes – I understand.'

'All right, Judith. If that's what you want . . .'

Anyone overhearing the conversation would have wondered at the man's docility and thought him to be a weakling, a wimp – someone who deserved all he got. An eavesdropper might well have poured scorn on Arthur Goldman for submitting to his wife's blackmail so limply. But that was a mistake people often made about him – believing he had given in when, in truth, he was only beginning to gather his strength for a fight. When Arthur wanted something badly, really badly, he dug in his heels and there was nothing that anybody (not even his mother) could do to deter him. And he wanted Judith. Despite all opposition, he always had. Arthur wanted her with the same sort of intensity as, at the age of seven, he had hankered after one of the tortoise-shell kittens that were born to his friend Joey's Mathilda.

Gertrude had refused. Adamantly.

'Arthur, darling, you may as well stop pestering me. I will not have a cat in this house and that's that.'

'But Mom . . .'

'No. Forget about it. I've always maintained that I'd never allow a child of mine to have a pet. Think of the germs. And hair all over our nice new lounge-suite. And Fenella's still a baby – who knows what the creature could do to her? No, Arthur. I'm sorry but you must tell Joey that your mother has refused to let you take one of his kittens. Now go upstairs like a good boy and let Mummy make supper.'

'OK,' he'd said and tramped up obediently, one step at a time. And while Gertrude in the kitchen congratulated herself on producing a boy who took no for an answer ('How did you manage it, Gert?' her friends often asked her. 'How on earth did you create such an obedient child?'), Arthur in his bedroom was gritting his teeth. He was sitting on his blue candlewick bedspread and frowning fiercely at his neatly displayed collection of construction kits and chemistry sets and illustrated Discovery Books and longing for a kitten. I'll have one too, he decided. I don't care what she says.

And he did – for a glorious two days. The following Saturday, while Gertrude was occupied with Fenella (she operated according to a strict schedule, so Arthur knew exactly when feeding time would be), he smuggled the animal into his room.

'Keep very quiet now, Sam,' he whispered sternly. 'If you're really quiet and good, you'll be able to stay with me forever.'

Arthur addressed his kitten in a bossy voice quite similar to the one his mother used on him – and almost like the one he would use on Judith in years to come. But Sam's tenure turned out to be far shorter than that of Arthur's wife. When he returned from school on Monday, the kitten had disappeared.

'Sam – I'm home,' he said softly, extracting from beneath his bed the box in which he'd thought his pet was safely and comfortably incarcerated. It was a good box. Most kittens would have appreciated such fine accommodation (as Arthur had pointed out to Sam when installing him). But Sam, it turned out, lacked gratitude. When his master lifted the lid, he saw that the box was quite empty.

'Oh Sam,' said Arthur in a small reproachful voice. 'You shouldn't have left me.'

He shut the box quickly and pushed it out of sight as he heard Gertrude's footsteps approaching. When she opened the door, he was sitting on the bed with *The Child's Guide to the Human Body* open on his lap. She looked at him silently. He raised his eyes, struggling to keep them dry, wanting to ask her, to tell her, but afraid.

'Arthur, I've fried some fish for supper. Come downstairs and eat. It will do you good.'

She said nothing about the cat. Ever. Arthur never found out whether Sam had left of his own volition or under Gertrude's guard. He didn't dare ask. Instead, he vowed solemnly that the next time he acquired something he had wanted very badly he would hold on to it – tightly.

That wasn't to be for many years, for Arthur wasn't a demanding sort of boy. 'He's an angel,' his mother said to her friends. 'An absolute angel. If only my Fenella and Joanne would be half as good.' It pleased him to please her and after a while he thought he had forgotten what it felt like to please himself. She wanted an angel, so he became an angel. She demanded a doctor and Arthur obliged. But when Gertrude decided that her son should marry Felicity Green, daughter of the best-known local urologist, he set his jaw and refused. Arthur had met Judith and he wanted her. He had never wanted anything so much since Sam the cat.

And he got her in the end.

Gertrude had objected: 'She's not right for you, Arthur. Your father and I both agree that you could do a lot better. Musicians are a funny lot you know – unstable usually. And her father. Well. A butcher, isn't he? A family butcher? Hmm. Arthur, I'm telling you, you'll be making a mistake. There are other girls, you know. Take Felicity Green, for instance . . .'

Judith had resisted: 'I can't do it, Arthur – I'm not ready to settle down.'

But he stubbornly persisted in his quest until at last he succeeded. And this time Arthur fought hard against the impulse to put his prize into a large cardboard box with an order to be very quiet and good and stay with him forever. He had learnt that this was no way to keep her – and he was determined that Judith would not slip away.

His caution didn't help. He lost her anyway. Despite her comfortable life in fine accommodation (which most wives would have appreciated, as Arthur generally managed to refrain from pointing out), Judith, being somewhat deficient in gratitude, had gone. And Arthur, having bemoaned his fate and feared for her life and soaked his anxieties in drug-induced sleep and settled his stomach with bran flakes and tea, had made up his mind to get her back. Alive. He was determined to fight for her – on her ground, if necessary. This time he'd not let his kitten (who, regrettably, seemed to have grown into a sharp-clawed cat) escape.

That was why his mild 'Fine, Judith – OK – see you tomorrow' was not to be dismissed as the last dying squeak of a cornered mouse. But it sounded so much like it that even his mother was deceived. Gertrude couldn't contain her contempt.

'Arthur darling, I simply cannot understand how you're allowing yourself – all of us – to be forced into something like this. I thought I'd brought you up to have more backbone. Believe me, if you'd had the stomach to ignore that wife of yours, she'd have been crawling back home in no time – if that's what you want. Instead, thanks to you, here we are . . .'

'Mom, it's a nice hotel. The height of luxury. Don't you remember me telling you about it – the place where Judith and I spent our – um – honeymoon? Listen, why don't you – all of us – look on it as a break in the country? It's all on me, remember. My treat. Won't cost you a penny. I'll collect you and Dad tomorrow morning at eight. That gives you all of today to get ready. OK?'

'Well, all right,' she'd said reluctantly. Had she ever been able to refuse her Arthur anything?

'Ralph, this isn't like our son,' she said a few minutes later, shaking her head as she watched a pat of butter melting into an oily yellow pond in the centre of her husband's bowl of porridge. When Ralph was in favour, his spouse cooked him oats – and Gertrude had woken with fond wifely feelings in response to her daughter-in-law's transgression. Other people's marriage problems tended to do that to her.

'Here – take a little sugar. Eat up. It's good for you,' she said encouragingly. Ralph needed feeding. They both needed strength. God knows what they'd find in that place Arthur was taking them to.

'Do you want to know something, Ralph?' Gertrude asked, watching him mixing porridge, butter and sugar into a lumpy grey paste which he swallowed in great spoonfuls. Where did all that food go to? How could a person eat so much and never gain an ounce?

'What?'

Ralph was rarely concerned with improving on his knowledge. Nothing had much interested him since his retirement from the hardware world and the frequent forays into the provinces that his working life had demanded. But Gertrude's attentiveness was not unpleasant and neither was the way the porridge was slipping down his throat. He looked up with as much curiosity as he could manage and Gertrude smiled as she caught his eye. Things between them had never seemed better.

'Between you and me,' she said, leaning towards him confidentially, 'Arthur's indulgence won't help them one bit. That marriage is doomed. I don't know how he has put up with her for so long. I told him from the start he'd picked the wrong girl. It's hopeless, this talking idea. A waste of time. So Ralph – d'you know what? Let's make the most of it. Look on it as a break, Arthur said. And he's right. How long is it since we've had a break together? I'm going to tell everyone that you're taking me away. That I've been overdoing things, exhausting myself, and so my two boys, my Ralph and my Arthur, have decided between themselves to organize for me a little holiday. How does that sound?'

'Fine.' Ralph nodded. What did he care?

She stood up energetically and started clearing the plates.

'Wait – let me finish,' said Ralph.

'Come along,' said his wife. 'There's a lot we have to do. I'd better start cancelling some of my meetings for a start. Let me see . . .'

As Gertrude paused to consider whether Rosa Meyerson of the Burial Society or Esther Bliss of the Women's League should be the first to be told about her imminent departure, the telephone rang. It was Solomon Epstein.

Solomon never enjoyed talking to Gertrude Goldman. She infuriated him. The fact that he had telephoned her was a measure of his desperation for news of Judith. Arthur had told Solomon little more than 'We'll call for you in the morning, Pops – be ready at around eight-thirty with enough clothing for a week'.

'But Arthur – tell me . . .' Solomon had tried.

'Pops, sorry. I can't talk. Have to get to the surgery and try and switch round appointments. Tomorrow. Tomorrow in the car we'll have plenty of time.'

Solomon had replaced the receiver and tried to convince himself there was no need for concern. After all, hadn't things improved since the night before? His chest, for instance. He inhaled deeply, testing the tender spot and decided that the pain had almost lifted. He resolved to tell the doctor, when he finally came, that it had been nothing. A false alarm. The Meals-on-Wheels person he wouldn't let off so lightly . . . but what did it matter, a fly in the food? These things happened. One survived. One usually survived. Solomon shook his head slowly and raised his eyes beseechingly – high beyond the flaking ceiling and the Katz residence and the leaking gutters and the cloudy sky.

'My Lord,' he said, 'I know you have plenty on your mind at the moment and, in all honesty, I don't know how you keep going. If I had even the tiniest part of the trouble you have from your children, I'd be hiding in a dark corner of the universe, tired to death. As it is, even one child gives me almost more pain than I can bear. But I can't hide here in my flat any longer keeping – the thing – to myself. You know. Our secret. Mine and yours. No, my Lord. She wants me there, with her, wherever she is. She wants us all to talk.

'Talk. Ha! As though it helps. Everywhere people are talking till they are hoarse – to you and their doctors and their analysts and their rabbis and their priests and around conference tables and in Houses of Parliament and high up, near heaven, in the United Nations headquarters. The noise! It gives me a splitting headache so I can't imagine what it does to you. And does it make things better? Honestly now. What good does it really do? Are people killing each other less and loving one another any more with all the talking? Are they happier? You don't have to answer. I've got enough on my head.

'My Lord, I don't want you to think that I've forgotten you. I know I haven't been in touch recently, but I've been a little distracted and you've been busy – you know how these things happen. When I had the butchery, there was always something I had to consult you about. We had a working relationship – and a good one too, if you don't mind my saying so. Never any problems. No lost orders or late payments. You provided stock and gave me trading instructions and seven days' credit and I kept strictly to all the rules and each Sabbath I settled my account. On the nail. And a few times a year we met at various food festivals and the rest of the time, all being well, things went smoothly. And so the years passed – until I retired from business and Dora resigned from life. And after that – well – we didn't seem to have as much in common any more, you and me.

'But now we're talking again I thought I'd ask you to keep an eye on her. You know, Judith. My daughter. And maybe lend me strength to see her. I'll pay it back, with interest. You know Solomon Epstein, Lord. With me, a deal's a deal. Just enough strength to tell her . . . my Lord, she won't be too disappointed in me, will she? I haven't been *such* a bad father. Not completely bad . . .?'

Solomon sighed. It wasn't easy, this coming clean. Confessing. Facing the truth. Could he really expect God to help? Maybe, instead, he should ask for a sign to say that Judith would eventually live happily and in peace. Wasn't that the important thing? A small heavenly sign. Nothing flashy – did he need a fire in the flat on top of everything else? Even the smallest clap of thunder would do.

But God would be too busy to attend to the troubles of an old man who had almost forgotten how to pray. After all, compared with troubles like warfare and global warming and football hooliganism and famine, of what importance was a single small sad voice? Solomon reckoned that, like most public utilities these days, heavenly services had become big business – and the most he could expect from prayer was a personalized acknowledgement note. Maybe something like the cheery letter he kept getting from the computers of the *Readers' Digest*.

'Dear Mr Epstein,' it might say. 'We note in our records that you wish to renew your subscription for Divine Intervention and are happy to forward your application to the Authority concerned. We shall inform you in due course whether your request is successful. In the meantime, if you wish to take part in our Giant Lucky Draw, please attach the Yes sticker to the reply card and hope for the best. And remember, Mr Epstein – there are big prizes waiting to be won.'

Not by me, thought Solomon. He remembered how, in the old days, Dora would laugh at the way he compulsively entered jackpot competitions and carefully filled in football-pool forms.

'You're an idiot,' she'd say indulgently. 'As if people like us ever win such things. Why do you bother, Solomon? Tell me – why waste your time?'

'Why not?' he would shrug. 'It costs little enough to try – hardly more than the cost of the stamp. And someone has to win. Imagine, Dora – imagine if . . .'

Those were the days when he'd still had big hopes. He had imagined that fortune or fame (preferably both) would make everything almost perfect for the rest of his life. If only . . . if only he were lucky and his number were drawn or his pools permutation came up. Or his daughter won a piano prize. Eventually, when he had begun to despair of ever winning anything, Judith had nearly made it as Young Musician of the Year.

'You see!' he had said to Dora triumphantly. 'It's just as well I didn't listen to you and stop her from entering. Isn't this wonderful, Dora? Doesn't it make up for – everything?'

She'd nodded rather wearily. He had always known that Dora didn't share his enthusiasm for Judith's piano-playing. Once he had accused her of being jealous of the bond it had created between him and Judith. She had denied it, insisting how worried she was about Judith's excessive absorption in the instrument. 'It's not healthy, Solly. She needs other things. Friends, interests, fun . . .'

He had brushed her doubts aside. Sour grapes. What did a simple person like Dora know about the dedication of an artist? And when the competition result had been announced, he had been so excited, so overwhelmed with a sense of infinite possibilities for Judith (and for himself) that he had chosen to ignore his wife's lukewarm response.

'Judith,' he had said later, enfolding his fourteen-year-old daughter in his arms. 'Judith, you make everything worthwhile.'

She had stepped back sharply and wanted to know what he had meant by everything, and had looked at him – disbelievingly he thought – when he had told her about the hardships of being a butcher and the trials of earning a decent living. But what else could he have said? That her success compensated for years of suffering and lies and compromises and longing? He couldn't even begin to admit those things to himself.

And anyway, he'd been wrong about the link between good luck and happiness. Even claiming top prize in the pools brought its miseries, he knew now. And in the end, Judith, who had won concerto competitions and the hand of a doctor, had finally given way to despair.

'Why?' Solomon demanded of the faded photograph that faced him on the mantelpiece. It had been taken at Judith's wedding. The bride and groom, smiling stiffly, were flanked by their proud parents. Dora stood slightly behind her husband, as though allowing him to take full credit for the success of his daughter. Solomon looked smug. Ralph, on the other hand, seemed worried. His hat almost covered his eyebrows. Had Gertrude, who glowered at Ralph's side like an aggressive warrior queen, crushed it in a fit of rage? For some reason, she had been angry all day.

'What went wrong?' Solomon asked the assembled family. 'Please, someone, tell me why it had to end like this?'

And since God seemed to be otherwise engaged and Arthur was busy and Judith preoccupied and Dora dead and Ralph never said anything of importance, Solomon decided that Gertrude – much as he disliked her – was the only person to whom he could try and communicate his terrible anxiety.

'Good morning, Solomon,' she said briskly when he had announced himself in his most mournful voice. 'How are you?'

'How should I be?'

The woman's insensitivity was unbelievable. Next she'd be asking him if he'd had a pleasant weekend.

'Did you have a pleasant weekend?'

Solomon drew breath and replied with melancholy irony. 'Gertrude, tell me,' he said, 'if your daughter was at death's door, calling out in distress, what sort of weekend would you have? A pleasant one?'

'Quite frankly, Solomon, I wouldn't know. With my daughters, thank God, I've never had such troubles. And Arthur – well, you know Arthur . . .'

'A good boy. I always thought he was a good boy.'

'Exactly.'

There was a meaningful pause. Had that been sarcasm he'd detected in her voice? Was Gertrude Goldman by any chance implying that his Judith was *less* than good? How dare she? She didn't have a clue!

'Now listen,' Solomon began severely. And then stopped. Of what use would it be to quarrel and apportion blame, when they should be supporting one another? Surely Gertrude, even Gertrude, wanted to do all she could to help – if not for Judith's sake, for that of her faultless son? For the family?

'Gertrude – listen.' His voice had lifted and acquired a faint pleading note. 'Can't you understand how upset I am – how hard it is for a father to see his – child – upset? I just phoned to – talk about it.'

Was he, too, about to add his voice to the great cosmic babble that was making God deaf? Perhaps this urge to talk was contagious.

'The reason I called', he corrected himself quickly, 'was to hear what you thought about the matter and whether Arthur had told you any more about where he was taking us. And anything else you can tell me about – Judith.'

Prolonged silence.

'Gertrude? Are you there?'

She was there. Waiting, like a vulture, to pounce and tear into the heart of his grief and pick the bones of his uncertainty. No wonder Gertrude offered her unpaid services to the dead.

'Solomon,' she said icily, 'perhaps I shouldn't tell you this but . . .'

She told him anyway. About the incovenience Judith's 'selfishness' was causing her. Did Solomon know, had he any idea, how many people depended on Gertrude's presence? How many organizations rested on her shoulders? As for Arthur giving in to his daughter's blackmail – all Gertrude could say was that it showed what a wonderful nature her son had. 'I personally', she added, 'would refuse absolutely to bow to terrorist demands.' In the end, though, she (and Ralph too) had accepted their fate. For Arthur.

'He wants us to come along to this – place – so we're going. And, as it happens, we've decided we may as well make the most of it. I can't remember when last we had a break and everyone tells me I need a holiday. I do tend to overdo things, put too much strain on myself. So. We'll see you in the morning, I believe? Arthur says we're collecting you.'

And that, thought Solomon, as he finally said a subdued goodbye, was even less satisfactory as a conversation than the earlier one with Arthur or even the one-sided communication with God. But he'd asked for it. Been foolish to have hoped for anything else from Gertrude. Perhaps he should venture upstairs and commiserate with his neighbour. From Seymour at least he could expect a little sympathy. Or could he? Solomon groaned as he lifted himself out of his chair and saw an ancient tired face smudged with grey shadows reflected in the mirror on the wall. He needed a shave, a haircut maybe. He'd make himself look respectable. Iron a shirt or two. Polish his shoes. Brush his suit.

'Judith,' he muttered fiercely, 'I won't disgrace you. Whatever happens, I won't let you down. Not this time.'

*

'The poor man is beside himself,' said Gertrude loftily as she put down the phone and started searching in her black book for Rosa Meyerson's number. 'One would have thought he'd never had a moment's anxiety from his daughter before. After last year's episode, nothing surprises me. Ralph? Ralph – where are you?'

Her husband was upstairs, deep into his daily evacuation. Oats porridge for breakfast had speeded things up – and, anyway, Ralph was tired of hearing about Arthur's marriage and eager to retreat to the only place where he knew he'd find seclusion and an old copy of the *National Geographic* to fuel his dreams of escape. He looked at a glossy picture of gulls and palms and a sapphire sea and thought with some panic about the prospect of being trapped in a hotel in the heart of England. To talk. Ralph loathed talking.

'Coming,' he called. 'In a few minutes.'

And Gertrude, having tried to telephone Rosa and then Esther and found both their lines engaged, decided to apply herself to the kitchen floor. No matter how much one was prepared to pay one's cleaning staff, she reminded herself, they never managed the sort of shine she achieved after she'd scrubbed it herself. That's what she had always maintained to Judith, whose floor was sometimes dull and rather sticky. Poor, poor Arthur. 'Ralph,' Gertrude called suddenly, pausing with the mop, 'don't you think it would be a good idea to invite Arthur to join us for supper tonight? All this must be so difficult for him. Ralph? What do you say? Shall I ask him?'

'Why not?' came his obliging muffled voice after a delay of several seconds, during which time he had returned with a bump from his South Sea island to a bleached and limescale-free lavatory in Golders Green. At least, he consoled himself as he pulled the chain, at least the presence of Arthur would inspire his mother to produce a lavish meal.

Gertrude, meanwhile, was already applying her thoughts to the menu. 'It's the very least I can do for Arthur, under the circumstances,' she was saying to herself. She'd make chopped liver, follow it with veal schnitzel and then, perhaps, give him a small helping of apple pie and cream. His favourites. To cheer him up.

'Supper? Mom, I don't know if –'

'Come Arthur. It will do you good. A little liver, perhaps, and maybe afterwards some –'

'Honestly Mom, there's so much I have to do. You have no idea what a flu epidemic brings out in people – *and* I'll be away for the rest of the week. Sorry –'

'– some schnitzel with a few roast potatoes – I know how you like them – and then –'

'All right, all right. You talked me into it. I'll be there at seven.'

Arthur returned to his patient. 'Sorry about the interruption, Mrs Martin. Let's have another look at your throat just to make sure,' he said, trying to suppress a feeling that he'd succumbed to bribery. Again. But then, didn't he badly need a good meal on the eve of his departure? Since Judith had left, he had subsisted on biscuits and bran flakes. Hardly a balanced diet.

'Mrs Martin – relax – open your mouth and say AAAAH.'

'AAAAH,' said Mrs Martin obediently. Arthur aimed his torch at her tonsils while surreptitiously adding another item to his lengthening list headed 'Things To Be Packed'. Multi-vitamin pills. Who knew what sort of food they'd dish up at All Seasons? – particularly since he'd heard the place had been taken over by Americans. Averting widowerhood and divorce was one thing – inviting degenerative digestive disorder was quite another.

'Mrs Martin,' he said gravely, 'I can't see anything organically wrong with your throat. Slightly pinkish perhaps – but hardly enough to cause the pain you describe. Tell me – is there anything worrying you? You're not depressed by any chance?'

Mrs Martin's mouth closed. Her lips trembled. Her eyes welled with tears, and she began to tell Arthur how miserable, how utterly miserable she was. 'I know I shouldn't feel so bad – after all I have everything – everything I could possibly want – it's just that my life seems so pointless – and the children – and my husband – no one considers my needs – nobody at all.'

Arthur tilted his head ever so slightly to the left in its sympathetic listener mode, while adding 'Valium – small quantity' to his going-away list. During a pause in Mrs Martin's lament, he enquired, as gently as he possibly could, whether or not she was premenstrual. And when she finally departed, damp and depleted, with sodden tissues, swollen eyes and a prescription, saying 'Thank you, Doctor Goldman – you're most understanding', Arthur couldn't help comparing Mrs Martin's gratitude with the abuse he'd been subjected to by his wife. He was filled once again with self-pity.

'Mom, I don't understand,' he said that evening, as he scraped the last morsel of chopped liver off his plate and transferred it carefully from his fork to his mouth. 'It's not as though I've been a bad husband to Judith. After all, I don't drink or smoke or sleep around or – slap her. What does she want? You know –' He paused to pass his plate to his mother, who loaded it with another liberal helping. '– I've a feeling things would have been quite different if we'd had children. If only . . .'

'Arthur, stop torturing yourself over this. It's not good for you, darling. We'll see Judith tomorrow and you and she can have a long heart-to-heart talk. It's what she wants, isn't it?'

He nodded doubtfully and looked across at his father who seemed totally absorbed in the steady ingestion of his food. Ralph raised his eyes and Arthur caught his gaze and for a moment he thought he saw something warm, alive and amused in the fleeting glance they exchanged. Then it was gone.

'Eat up, Arthur,' his mother was urging him. 'You deserve a good meal.'

Solomon Epstein was receiving no such encouragement. In fact, he was telling himself that he deserved better, a whole lot better, as he tried to find a trace of flavour in the thin yellow fluid that the Meals-on-Wheels woman had tried to pass off as pure golden chicken soup.

It had been a long day.

'Solly, I think we should have this ticker of yours investigated,' Dr Woolf had said worriedly when he had finally arrived and applied his icy stethoscope to Solomon's chest. 'I'm not saying it's serious – necessarily. But if I were you, I'd take myself off to the Royal Free and have a good going over.'

'I can't,' he had replied in panic. 'Not at the moment. I'm – busy. And anyway, it's much better than it was when I called. In fact, to tell you the truth, I believe the pain has gone away.'

Dr Woolf hadn't believed him. 'You're not afraid, are you?' he'd asked. 'You don't have to be, you know. The tests won't hurt – not necessarily.'

'No, no. I'm not frightened, Dr Woolf. It's not that,' he had responded quickly – but been unable to explain to the doctor exactly what it was without telling him about Judith. And that, he felt, was a private matter. One of those things that ought to be kept strictly in the family. 'For various reasons I can't go to the hospital at the moment – and that's that,' he had said firmly. 'I'll give you another call if my chest starts hurting again.'

Dr Woolf had eventually accepted his decision with reluctance.

'I'm not happy about this, Solly,' he had said, shaking his head with foreboding as he opened the door. 'I can't force you to do anything about it, but I'd like it to be placed on record that I'm very far from happy.'

After he had gone, Solomon sat very still, concentrating hard on the organ that was apparently in such urgent need of investigation. He listened for its beats and willed it to keep pumping. Don't let me down, he pleaded. Allow me this week, just this one week with my daughter and I'll give you an examination the likes of which you'd never have believed possible. Name anything you want – X-rays, ECGs. You can have the lot.

He was still engaged in negotiations with his heart when the Meals-on-Wheels representative arrived.

'Mr Epstein, I'm Valerie Markus,' she said briskly, holding out a capable hand. If she'd dared, she would have worn a gold badge saying 'I do good works' on her well-supported bosom. Instead, she sported a permanently understanding smile (outlined with ecologically-sound lipstick) and a track-suit (to express her indefatigable energy) and a voice that vibrated with studied steely sympathy.

'I believe that you have some – comments to make about the service we offer? Why don't we sit down and have a good talk about it?'

From the immediacy with which it sank, Solomon suspected that his heart was not in such poor order as Dr Woolf had indicated. Not necessarily.

'How d'you do, Mrs – er – Markus,' he said as politely as he could. 'Yes, you're quite right. I did have some complaints. Serious ones as it happens. But I've decided on balance not to pursue them. Instead, there are important – personal matters – which need my attention.'

'Are you sure?' she asked earnestly, clearly disappointed that her challenge had not been met. Surely her diploma in Counselling Skills for the Elderly was not going to be wasted – again? 'Maybe you'd like to *chat* about those – matters? It usually helps, you know.'

'No. Thank you.'

'Well then, Mr Epstein, since you've been so co-operative and understanding about your – er – matter for complaint, we – the organization, that is – would like you to accept this as a mark of appreciation. A little gesture of compensation since your meal was not – quite as you'd have liked it.'

And, with a flourish, she produced a box labelled 'Celebration Meal for One' containing, among other things, the chicken soup that tried to claim it had poultry in its ancestry. Other things included a pair of matzo-balls (with microwave instructions), two slices of turkey breast (cholesterol-free), a square-inch of cheesecake (non-dairy) and several generations of coliform bacteria.

'Thanks. Thanks a lot,' said Solomon, urging his benefactress gently towards the door.

'Are you *sure* there's nothing you'd like to tell me about?' she asked as she left – her voice slightly shrill with desperation. Solomon was sorry for her, in a way. But he was far sorrier for himself when he tasted the soup and shuddered with disgust and bitterly regretted that he had let Valerie Markus off so lightly.

Judith was far too well mannered to shudder openly – either at the plate of food set before her on the table or the leer of Chuck Wilmot on the opposite side of it. The smell of his after-shave (guaranteed to contain the secretions of several potent male musk-deers) was overpowering.

'As you see, Mrs Goldman,' he was saying expansively, 'we do offer a vegetarian alternative. Naturally. Here at All Seasons we cater for every taste, all – um – predilections. All you had to do was to ask.'

'Of course. Thank you.' Politeness forced her to attempt eating this amorphous concoction which had been described in the 'special diets' menu as 'Topped 'n' Tailed Beans and Various Gay Greens'.

'What's the matter?' Chuck asked, noticing her lack of enthusiasm. 'Is there anything wrong, Mrs Goldman?'

'Mr Wilmot – I'm sorry. I'm suddenly not hungry. It's been a difficult couple of days and – I suppose I'm very tired.'

'Ah,' he said understandingly and sent a giant tidal wave of concentrated sympathy and musk-scent across the table. Judith sneezed.

'And I think', she added with relief, 'that I may be developing a cold – so I'd better make it an early night.'

'Oh.' The tide lapped back dejectedly. But Chuck Wilmot was far from defeated. Not him. He was conserving his resources for another onslaught, while Judith glanced around at her fellow diners. There seemed fewer, she thought, than the previous night. In a far corner she saw Angela, who was eating alone.

'What happened to her husband?' she couldn't resist asking.

'In bed. Flat on his back. Slipped a disc,' Chuck replied. Judith looked at him quizzically and he, delighted to have captured her interest at last, topped up their wine glasses and leaned forward confidentially as he warmed to his subject.

'You've no idea how many of our honeymooners attempt – things – that are far beyond their physical capabilities, Mrs Goldman. Cheers.'

'Cheers.'

'They refuse to get into training beforehand, despite the advice leaflet we send with our booking confirmation form. We don't take any responsibility for these little mishaps, as you probably noticed in the disclaimer beneath the fire safety precautions. Still – it spoils the fun for everybody when things like this happen. Had management running round in circles all day. And the sweet little wife is beside herself. Inconsolable. Look at her.'

Judith looked – and decided that Angie, eating daintily, appeared far from disconsolate. In fact, she seemed rather more serene and self-possessed than she had the night before. Perhaps she was relieved to have had her marriage role defined so early. A slipped disc called for a caretaker wife. The demands of a healthy husband were far more complicated.

'Poor Angela,' said Judith, aware that she wasn't very sorry for Angela, whose needs seemed so simple and whose choices so clear. No – it wasn't for Angela that Judith's tears were rising. She tried desperately to blink them away, but they filled her eyes unstoppably and fell in great salty splashes into the heart of her orgy of greens. In a way, she supposed her tears were for Angela. For herself and Angela. And Edwin. And Arthur? Oh, everything was sad. Too sad for words. And here she was, still hoping to heal things with words. How, after everything, did she have the energy to hope at all?

'Would you excuse me, Mr Wilmot. Please.'

She pushed her chair back and rose to her feet and felt

Angela's inquisitive eyes on her as she left the dining-room. Chuck followed close on her heels. Long years of experience had taught him that emotionally charged women were highly susceptible. 'Labile means nubile' was one of the bye-laws of the 'Wilmot One-Two'.

'Mrs Goldman,' he said, coming up behind her as she opened the oak door marked April and tenderly stroking the erogenous zone between her upper vertebrae and the base of her skull. As a preliminary technique, it rarely failed. 'Mrs Goldman, you fascinate me. Your tears make me want to gather you in my arms and comfort you. May I? You can tell me everything, anything, Mrs Goldman. I'll make you feel better.'

And Judith, feeling her knees buckling, wondered how on earth this stranger had known that she weakened so alarmingly when touched in that particular spot. Arthur hadn't discovered it after twenty years. Then she saw that Chuck Wilmot had dodged deftly past her into the centre of her room and was waiting with open arms and the sort of anticipatory smile little boys wore when they had planted a banana skin in teacher's path. He was quite certain she would fall.

Judith decided she wouldn't. Not here. Not now, after everything.

'Mr Wilmot, I'm fine thank you. Good-night,' she said firmly, holding open the door.

'Good-night, Mrs Goldman,' responded Chuck without hesitating for a moment. Experience had taught him to recognize when a woman really meant it. Anyway, repeat bids were best left for a separate occasion. Mrs Goldman had clearly been tempted and next time, he predicted, she would submit. 'Sleep well,' he said as he shut the door.

'Sleep well,' she repeated dolefully. Her eyes were now dry and instead of feeling despair or that delicious sense of power, Judith was embarrassed. Something in Chuck Wilmot's knowing smile had woken her sharply to the absurdity of her plight. She had deluded herself into believing she was a tragic heroine making a final dramatic demand to be rescued before her descent into a dignified death when, in reality, she was a laughing stock. A silly frustrated female who had almost (how could she have?) succumbed to a plastic puppet-person because he'd touched her. She hadn't known quite how much she longed to be touched.

'Idiot,' she said aloud and felt herself blushing as she noticed that the port ('For Afterwards') had been replenished and a vase of daffodils had been placed on the dressing-table. They seemed pale compared with the images that bloomed on the curtains and the walls. Pale and insignificant and rather silly. A bit like me, thought Judith, as she crossed the room to check if the flowers weren't plastic after all and decided they were real and wouldn't last long. And as she pondered on mortality and remembered she still had the tablets, she still had a choice, and wondered whether people actually died of embarrassment and just labelled it despair, someone knocked on the door. If it was that dreadful Chuck Wilmot, she'd tell him in no uncertain terms . . .

'Who is it?' she called severely.

'It's me. Linda. The – er – Administrative Assistant. I'm sorry to disturb you at this hour, but there are certain – details – we need to discuss. About your meeting.'

Linda had been promoted. Mr Wilmot had returned in high spirits from his morning encounter with the occupant of April. 'Linda – we're in business,' he'd announced, standing with proudly folded arms over her word processor and interrupting her daydream about a white wedding with handsome Steve Maplin as her groom. Just when they had almost reached the altar.

'What?'

'The conference. The booking you told me about. And four extra guests. It all seems to be in order.'

He had smiled delightedly, triumphantly, and in a moment of expansive generosity, told her that as a mark of recognition for her unfailing efficiency he had decided to upgrade her job title from Secretary to Administrative Assistant.

'Unfortunately, I can't accompany it with a salary increment – yet. But let's see how things develop, Linda. The organization of this meeting – the Goldman Gathering, as I've decided to call it – will be your first real test.'

'Oh, Mr Wilmot. *Thank* you.'

All day she had bustled importantly from the meeting-room to the kitchen to the reception area and back, stopping only to send a quick fax to Charlene ('I've been spotted for management stardom! A member of the team at only twenty-two! Tell Mum and the family!') and to massage poor Mr Cockroft's back.

'Relax Mr Cockroft. Try and relax,' she had purred, applying sensitive fingers to his spinal column. She'd always had sensitive fingers. Mr Wilmot had noticed them long before her leadership potential. 'They're wasted on a keyboard,' he'd often said. But even hands as skilled as hers were ineffective on the timorous twitching torso that had once been Edwin Cockroft's eagerly upright back.

'What *have* we been trying to do?' she'd asked with a suggestive giggle that was greeted with a soulful groan from Mr Cockroft and a fit of coughing from his wife. That was when she'd decided that a more specialized touch was called for and, anyway, in her new managerial capacity she had far more important things to do than to rub oil into troubled joints. There was a conference to organize, for instance.

But somehow, despite her enthusiastic efforts at mustering planning meetings and master-minding menus and thinking about seating-room and sleeping-space and audio-visual aids, by the end of the day her 'Goldman File' was still almost empty. Linda was at her wit's end. Would her rocket to executive stardom ever be launched? There seemed nothing for it but to approach the client directly.

'I'm sorry to bother you so late in the evening, Mrs Goldman,' she said with as much authority as she could manage, after Judith had reluctantly opened the door. 'Do you think we could have a brief – uh – meeting about your conference requirements? It won't take long.'

THE GOLDMAN GATHERING

Preliminary notes prepared by the new All Seasons Administrative Assistant, Miss Sherryl Carter (a.k.a. Linda).

According to its organizer, Mrs Judith Goldman, the Goldman Gathering will be 'a conference to explore the costs and rewards of the married state in a setting far removed from the constraints of suburbia'. It will be a meeting to uncover the truth. So she says. (Confidentially, Mr Wilmot, *is she all there?)* Anyway . . .

There are to be five participants, accommodated as follows:
April – Mrs Judith Goldman.

February – Mr and Mrs Ralph Goldman.
The August Suite – Mr Solomon Esptein and Mr Arthur Goldman.
Meetings will take place in The Solstice Centre from 10 a.m. to 5.30 p.m. each day. Satellite facilities on request.

Catering arrangements:
Breakfast, lunch and supper in the dining-room at 9 a.m., 1 p.m. and 8 p.m. (respectively). Vegetarian meals on request. Participants to be seated at tables for two according to room allocations. Exception: Mrs Judith Goldman insists on dining alone.

For more information or anything else, please ring your Administrative Assistant, Miss S. Carter (professional name Linda), on ext. 100.

Arthur took two antacids, an antispasmodic and a minor sedative before he went to bed later that night. Ralph was sated with protein and Gertrude was drowsy with self-righteousness. Both went to sleep peacefully. Gertrude snored.

Solomon prepared himself for another vigil with Mozart and Katz, while, in his lower intestines, the coliform bacteria he had ingested with the Celebration Meal engaged in energetic multiplication as they passed the time before a dawn attack.

And Judith, having shaken off Chuck Wilmot and mortal embarrassment and, finally, the lovely Linda with her file, drank port alone for the second consecutive night (where would it end?) and turned out the light. She tried not to think about:

(a) why she, who had foresworn any sort of committee work whatsoever at the cost of alienating her mother in-law, should suddenly be organizing a meeting, and

(b) what perverse sense of the ridiculous had inspired her to pick this plastic pseudo-paradise as her meeting-ground, and

(c) whether Arthur and Solomon and Ralph might share the joke – eventually. Gertrude never would. And

(d), (e) and (f) what Chuck Wilmot would have been like in bed.

That didn't leave much material for thought, so she went to sleep.

TUESDAY

An extraordinary management meeting (convened by Chuck Wilmot to 'mull over matters pertaining to the current cash-flow crisis') began badly at 8.30 a.m. in the sitting-room called Summer. Linda, who had developed a new sense of self-importance to match her enhanced company status, refused to take minutes and announced that from now on someone else could serve coffee.

'Linda – be *reasonable,*' said Chuck, struggling to keep his voice low and even. He'd had a long solitary night and woken with a headache and cut himself shaving and wanted to yell out his frustration to this jumped-up little secretary with ideas above her level of seniority. 'We'll manage without minutes just this once, but, well, if *you* don't get the coffee, I might just have to do it myself . . .'

This was a technique his assertiveness training instructor had described as the Martyrdom Manoeuvre. It never failed to effect awe-struck retreat from an aggressive stance. Or so the instructor had claimed.

'Fine,' retorted Linda. 'And, while we're talking, Mr Wilmot, I'd like the team to know that my name isn't Linda. It's *Miz* Carter. Ms Sherryl Carter. D'you think everyone could call me that from now on? Please.'

Shit. If only he'd moved onto Assertiveness III (The Revenge), he might now have some idea how to deal with this sort of insubordination. Hadn't he advised the board about the vital part senior learning could play in inter-personnel relationships?

'OK, OK,' he said mildly, switching to Feint-Submissiveness (a well-established ploy) – then looking helplessly across at his deputy. 'Er – Steve . . . '

'Stay right here, Chuck.' You could count on Steve Maplin.

Generally speaking. 'You get on with the agenda and I'll bring coffee. I don't mind in the least.'

'Good boy.'

By the time the team had settled and coffee been consumed and the Administrative Assistant deflated to manageable proportions, it was almost nine and the first bleary-eyed honeymooner was emerging for breakfast. On his own. Strange things were afoot in All Seasons, thought Chuck uncomfortably. Worrying trends.

'Let's get on with the agenda, guys,' he said in as hearty a tone as he could produce. 'There's no more time to lose.'

He frowned as he riffled through the sheaf of papers on his lap. Things were bad. Even worse than he had thought the day before. A 'Top Secret' communication from head office had informed Chuck that high-ranking executives (himself included) were being invited to agree to a voluntary salary suspension. Temporarily. Until the financial climate improved. As a mark of commitment to the company.

Naturally, he had answered affirmatively – and then remembered that his personal bank balance was even more precarious than that of his company. He was deep in the red, thanks to the previous year's venture into psychoanalysis. And now, not only was he behind with the instalments on his Autogenic Training Kit. Worse – far worse – was the fact that Chuck's annual subscription to the National League of Gifted Young Executives was overdue. Long overdue.

'We regret to inform you that unless we receive the sum of £500 within seven days, we shall have to terminate your membership,' had been the last message he had received. Four days had since elapsed.

Chuck's election as a full voting member of NALGEX had been a peak moment in his career. A boxed advertisement in *Management Weekly* had announced the foundation of the League and warned that only 'the most upwardly mobile' need apply. 'Membership of NALGEX will be your badge of success,' it had declared. Chuck's joy had been unbounded when his application had been accepted. With some trepidation, he'd sent a full curriculum vitae and the special Founder Fee of £200. In return, he had received an enthusiastic welcome letter, one hundred embossed business cards, a personal organizer, a contacts register – and an enormously enhanced sense of status. He was *someone*. A member of a professional body. A person who could (if he so desired) write the letters NALGEX after his name.

Not for long, though – unless his luck suddenly changed. The thought of being expelled from the League was more than Chuck could bear. He'd be nothing. He would sink. He would drown.

He shut his eyes briefly, then grimly called upon his training. Hadn't he been taught that a captain kept in calm eye-contact with his crew in troubled seas? Chuck forced himself to look up – into the eager face of his former secretary.

'Mr Wilmot,' she was saying breathlessly, 'can we begin with my preliminary report on the Goldman Gathering? I've made copies for everybody.'

And before he could reply she was handing out pink Xeroxed sheets and Steve Maplin was breathing 'Wow! Brilliant!' and Ken Mansion, the Catering Executive (a former chef at a topless revue bar in Bognor Regis), was reading dreamily, ' . . . "far removed from the constraints of suburbia" . . . Oh *Linda* . . .'

'Sherryl.'

'Sherryl – how *beautifully* put. You've no idea how *stimulating* that is in terms of sensual gestatory creativity. Vegetables – it's vegetables they want, is it? – for unbounded cross-marital exploration. I can't wait to put my mind to it.'

'Hold it – Maplin, Mansion,' interrupted Chuck tersely. 'Your enthusiasm may be somewhat premature. Granted, Linda . . .'

'Sherryl.'

'Er – Sherryl – has done an efficient job – so far. But we must beware of over-estimating the size of this particular conference. It's only a minor shot in the arm, folks. We need something bigger – far far bigger – if we're to survive.'

'So *make* it bigger.'

Oh no. Not Steve again. With that maniacal look on his face. What was he dreaming up this time?

'How?' asked Chuck warily.

'The popular papers. The tabloids. We'll hook them. Leak luscious little items of rumour – hints that out of this revolutionary gathering in our honeymoon hotel will emerge the last word on marriage. If there's no sex, we can make it up. Tantalizing titbits that the big fish will swallow. And then all the little fish will swim here, thousands and thousands of them. Metaphorically speaking of course . . .'

'Steve –'

'Listen to me Chuck. What keeps the Royal family in business? What keeps *The Times* afloat? Isn't it undeniably true that the gutter-press has vastly enhanced the user-friendliness (and sheer profit) of Real Art and Serious Literature? Just *think* what it could do for the good old-fashioned honeymoon – the kind only we at All Seasons can offer.'

'But –'

'Mr Wilmot, I think Steve is quite right. Absolutely spot-on.'

It was the irrepressible Linda/Sherryl once more. Chuck bitterly rued the rush of blood to his head that had inspired him to raise her status. And he was usually so careful about keeping a safe distance between reason and physical response . . .

'Sherryl. Steve.' He spoke with clearly diminishing patience. 'We – don't – have – time.'

'We'll move fast,' she said with a little gasp, already out of breath from the anticipated effort, her chest moving up and down and up and down. Chuck had to turn away. 'In fact, as it happens, I faxed a copy of the report to my sister in Milton Keynes and she's got a best friend called Denise, who works in the smalls department of the *Evening Echo* and this Denise is having a – you know – a *thing* with the news editor and I'm sure if she were to tell him about . . .'

'Enough!'

Stunned silence. Chuck rubbed the back of his neck. It undulated with tension nodules. He wanted to cry.

'Now guys,' he said quietly, his perfect modulation a triumph of training over emotion. 'Let's go through the agenda, one item at a time. Sensibly. Methodically. With our feet firmly planted on the ground and all eyes on profit. Pure profit. Steve? Ken? Mike? Gavin? Rick? Er - Sherryl? Everyone?'

They nodded, mute testimony to the success of one of A Hundred Ways for the Boss to Talk Himself into Control. There was hardly a single Way that Chuck hadn't employed to cope with one crisis or another.

'Now - first things first. The Goldman Gathering. Let's get down to business.'

While Chuck was urging his mollified team to face reality, Judith was telling herself that it was time to get up.

She had no idea how long she'd been lying, hiding, heavy and half-awake, shielding her eyes from the light and trying to push from her mind the hazy haunting memory of her waking dream. There had been a house – a large house. In the country. A house almost as grand as All Seasons. And Judith, small Judith, thirteen, maybe fourteen, full of sadness, silent tears spilling over her face and almost choking her, was watching as someone slowly retreated. She wanted to call out. 'Daddy,' she wanted to say. 'Dad – don't leave me – please don't go without me. I thought, they told me, you were coming to take me home.' But she couldn't say a word. Not in her dream. In her dream she could only sit helplessly on a hard bed, overflowing with dumb misery as she saw him disappear.

And when she woke with damp eyes and a soaked pillow, she remembered Grove House. She had called out to him then and he had walked away. That had been no dream.

'Judith, I'm so proud of you,' he had said. 'It's a wonderful achievement for you to have been picked. Only three pianists in the whole country and you're one of them. Isn't it amazing, Dora? Don't we have a clever daughter?'

Dora had nodded, looking at Judith intently. Judith had turned away and concentrated on warming herself with her father's smile. 'Are you sure you want to go, Judy?' she had heard Dora ask gently. 'Five weeks is a long time. You don't have to go unless you really want to, you know.'

For a moment she had hesitated. For a split second she had almost turned to her mother and confessed her fear. But Solomon had stopped her.

'Of *course* she wants to go,' he had said firmly. 'Don't give her ideas. Does anyone refuse when they are selected for such an honour? Did the children of Israel say no when they were chosen? – and they suffered plenty, let me tell you. Judith won't suffer. Five weeks? What's five weeks in a lifetime – and in a country mansion with the fifty best musicians in Europe? Such suffering. If she wants to know about suffering, I can tell her a thing or two . . .'

'It's all right, Dad. Of course I'll go.'

And so, on a cold January morning, she had shivered on Platform Ten at Liverpool Street Station, standing on the fringe of a group of the continent's most promising musical progeny, all of them bursting with choral symphonies and string quartets and concertos and sonatas and ambition and guts. Except Judith. She had shivered – sitting alone on the train, in the coach and down the dark corridors of Grove House and in the small bed in the corner of the Blue Room which she had shared with Tricia from Edinburgh (a violinist) and Mirvi from Helsinki (who played the flute) and Maria from Zurich who sang and sang and sang.

'It's funny Judith should be cold all ze time,' Maria had observed lightly between arias.

'Very strange,' Mirvi had frowned as she polished her instrument. She was ever polishing her instrument. 'And she seems such a – robust – person.'

'Wouldn't last where I come from,' Tricia had laughed. 'You think this is cold? It's nothing! Come Judith – let's take a brisk walk. You're playing the Beethoven concerto tonight, aren't you?'

'I c-can't,' Judith had forced out through chattering teeth. 'I can't walk. I can't play. I'm too – cold – to do anything.'

And she had curled into a tight ball beneath the scratchy blankets and they had called her for rehearsals and she had pretended to be asleep and at last it was time for the concerto, her chance to show them what she could do. 'I c-can't,' she had whispered. 'My fingers won't work. They're – too – cold.' And then she had imagined her father looking at her and sadly shaking his head. 'I thought you were strong.' He sounded deeply disappointed. 'I thought my daughter had courage.'

'But I *have*, Dad,' she'd protested. 'Look – I'll show you – I *have*.'

And she had tried, no one could have tried harder. She had emerged, still shivering, from the dampness of her horsehair womb and dressed and confronted the cream of Europe's young talent and failed. 'I'm sorry – I don't feel well,' she'd confessed after the faltering first movement. 'I – can't – carry on.'

Sophia, the ten-year-old Polish prodigy, had taken over and Judith, mortified and still rigid with cold, had returned to her bed. A week later she still lay there, hearing as though from another world the faraway themes of foreign symphonies and snatches of half-familiar tunes and Mirvi enthusiastically polishing her flute and telling Judith she should get up, she really ought to eat.

'I can't understand you,' she was saying distractedly. It was Mirvi's turn to perform a concerto that night and she was determined to shine. 'When a person is cold he must keep moving and eat. In Lapland in the winter . . .'

'Please won't you tell them to phone my parents – I want to go home – I can't bear it here another moment – my father, ask them to tell my father – that I'm – ill.' The words had come out in a desperate rush. Surely if she were – ill – really ill – he'd come and get her? Talk to her? Surely he, even he, would understand?

'Judith, they say you're not well? Can't get up? Won't eat? What's the matter?' His voice on the telephone that night had sounded puzzled and a million miles away.

'I – don't – know. Dad, please won't you come – and fetch me? Please. I – need – to go home. It's so cold here. Please.'

'Don't be silly. You're a big strong girl. Didn't your mother give you plenty of jumpers to keep warm? Judith, this is your chance. A chance in a million. You should be making the most of it. You'll be sorry later on . . .'

'Dad. I can't. I – think – I'm ill. Please? If I have to stay here another three-and-a-half weeks I'll – die. Dad?'

He had come. That Sunday he had arrived by taxi from the station in his best suit and taken her out for lunch and they had sat opposite one another in a café in Colchester and she had told him how lonely and cold she had been, how scared, and he had nodded sadly and she'd been sure, so sure, that he had understood. And they'd eaten together. She had looked into his eyes and put a loaded forkful of egg and chips into her mouth and chewed and swallowed it, still looking at him, and he had smiled. They had both smiled. And for the first time in a fortnight she had stopped shivering.

Then they'd gone back to Grove House and walked upstairs together holding hands and she had managed a laugh as she pointed out the bed where she had spent so much time curled up against the cold. 'It was awful,' she had said, relief flooding through her as she heard herself using the past tense. 'Absolutely awful.' He hadn't responded, but she, bending down to retrieve her suitcase from beneath the bed, had failed to notice.

'Judith.'

She had turned round sharply.

'What?'

'Judith, I must go now or else I'll miss my train. Here – I almost forgot – here's some chocolate and a note from your mother.'

'But – Dad . . .'

'Judith, this isn't easy for me but I know it's for the best – people can't be allowed to give in to themselves like that – where would I be if I'd just given up? Judith – darling – you'll thank me for this one day when you look back. My darling – listen – it hurts me, it kills me, but I can't take you home. It wouldn't be a good lesson. For life.'

'Dad . . .?'

He had kissed her on the forehead and told her to look after herself and keep as warm as she could and try very hard to impress the teachers. It would make him very proud of her if she did well.

'But Dad,' she had said, sitting on the cold hard bed and beginning to shiver again. 'Dad – I thought – they told me – you were coming to fetch me – to take me with you. Don't leave. Please.'

There had been no answer. He had gone.

And now, twenty-eight years later, she had called for him again. Had nothing changed? Would Solomon Epstein tell her once more that she shouldn't give up – that people, his sort of people, had endured much more suffering than she had? And endured? How would she answer him this time? What would she say?

I don't know, thought Judith miserably. I'm more than a quarter of a century older – and still as unsure about everything as ever I was.

She sat up. At least this time she'd force herself out of bed – for she had learnt her father's lessons in fortitude, if nothing else. No one would dispute that Solomon's instruction in stoicism had been superb. Judith crossed the room resolutely and opened the curtain to admit the spring light and decided to order some breakfast. She had a sudden craving for scrambled eggs and chips.

Arthur had eaten nothing for breakfast. He hadn't intended to deny himself sustenance. On the contrary, as the driver he had a responsibility to keep his blood sugar at a reasonable level. But for some reason he seemed to have lost his appetite. He'd also apparently lost three-and-a-half pairs of socks, two casual shirts and his summer pyjamas.

'I don't know . . .' he sighed, surveying his empty suitcase and wondering what one packed for a marriage crisis. Not that he'd had much experience with either packing or picking, since Gertrude had done all of it premaritally and then passed the job on to Judith. His mother and wife had always decided exactly how he should be attired for every occasion and packed his bags each time he went away. Arthur had never questioned it. Dressing him was their duty. Wasn't it? It was *her* duty. So – why wasn't she here doing what she ought to be doing instead of sitting in some fancy hotel and shouting the odds?

'Who bloody cares? I can manage on my own, thank you very much,' he said defiantly, bundling into the suitcase anything wearable that came to hand, slamming it shut and looking challengingly at the chaos in the bedroom as though daring his wife to leap out from a hiding-place and upbraid him for it. She hated his untidiness.

She also said that she hated his pessimism (he called it realism) and his pacifism (she called it cowardice) and his hypochondria and his hard-headedness and the chip on his shoulder and the water on his knee. Not only that. She despised his devotion to his mother (she called it dependence) and his puritanism (he called it strong-mindedness) and his modesty (she called it being a creep) and his incipient hairlessness and his horny heels.

Arthur gloomily concluded that there wasn't a single aspect of his being which he could claim his wife admired or liked or, these days, even tolerated. So why did he imagine that he would persuade her to come home? When it came down to it, why on earth had she agreed to marry him in the first place? At the time, he had thought he understood.

'Are you sure, Judith,' he had asked. 'Absolutely sure?'

'Yes. I – am.'

He had reached tentatively across the automatic gear lever towards the bucket seat (with luxury upholstery and leatherette-trim) in which his newly acquired wife-to-be was seated. She had taken his hand and pressed it against her cheek and he'd been moved by the strength of her grip and the softness of her skin.

'You – trust me, Jude? Don't you?'

She had nodded, the lights of Finchley Road reflected in the tears that filled her eyes.

'I'll take care of you, you'll see. I won't let you down.'

Again she had nodded in silence, moving his hand to her lips and kissing it gently.

'Judith, I – love you.' There. He'd said it. For as long as he could remember he had dreamed about the moment when he would turn with longing passion to the woman of his dreams and say those three words. He had pictured the scene in various settings. On a tropical island, for instance, or in an expensive restaurant, or after a sensuous embrace. But instead of being accompanied by the swish of the sea or the tinkle of a piano or moans of ecstasy, Arthur's avowal had almost been drowned in the roar of traffic. She'd heard it though. She had kissed his hand again, one finger at a time, and then asked if he could take her home as she was tired. Terribly tired.

'But happy?' he had eagerly wanted to know. 'Aren't you happy, Jude?'

'Yes,' she had said softly after the briefest pause imaginable. And he'd expelled the tiny doubt from his mind as he had started the engine and proudly manoeuvred his shiny new Escort into the stream of smart cars and felt huge with success. Who would have thought a Quiz Supper in aid of the Jewish Orphanage Fund could have ended like this?

He had been most surprised when she had agreed to accompany him. 'Um – Judith,' he had hesitated the night before. 'I know this isn't the sort of thing you usually do, but my mother has given me tickets for this charity thing in St John's Wood and – well, I told her I'd go and – the food will be good anyway. And – I'd really appreciate it if you came with me.'

'Fine. I'll come,' she had immediately said. He hadn't dared ask her why or whether she was sure, for fear she would change her mind.

She'd been the only one able to answer the question about the third opera in Wagner's Ring Cycle and he'd been proud of how *different* she'd seemed in her long full skirt and red Liberty shawl and he could almost hear the whispered comments about Arthur Goldman's partner being a famous pianist. Well – not quite yet. But on the way. Definitely on the way. And compared with Felicity Green, the urologist's daughter, who'd been there too, looking so plain and dull and ordinary . . .

'Arthur, drive carefully. You almost knocked over that man.'

'Oh. Sorry, Jude. I'm not concentrating. Judith, I'm – thrilled you said yes. So very, very pleased. And I promise you won't regret it. We'll have a good life, you and me. I'm establishing a good practice and you must carry on with your music. You must. I'll always support you. And after a while – I don't want to wait too long, do you? – we'll have kids – a couple – you do want to have children, don't you? And you must keep up your piano practice in the meantime and when they're older you can go back to it full-time. And there shouldn't be any problem about money. I've been saving. In fact, we can start looking for our first property almost immediately. And we must start thinking about the wedding as soon as we can. Mustn't we, Jude? Don't you agree?'

Such plans. So many dreams. For six months they had met three times a week and he had taken her to films and concerts and ethnic restaurants and coffee bars and told her about his childhood and his mother's hopes for him and how he had longed to have a kitten. Everything. 'I've never been able to speak to anyone the way I can talk to you,' he had said, pulling her towards him and sealing their lips together.

She had told him things too. About how lonely she sometimes was, how she had always hated the butchery and about the time she'd been cold and homesick in a large country house in East Anglia with the continent's most promising young musicians. How she had wanted to leave but her father had decided she should stay.

'He was right,' Arthur had said straight away. He had been determined to seem strong and decisive, for he had believed that would be the way to win her respect. 'It was a good lesson for you – for life.'

'Yes,' she had said softly, and he hadn't been able to understand why she had turned away and was silent for the remainder of the evening. But the next time he had gone to collect her she had seemed herself again and he hadn't thought too much about it and, anyway, the wedding had been creeping closer and there'd been so much to do.

And finally the day had come. Gertrude had grudgingly reconciled herself to the Epstein alliance and armed a cohort of highly trained caterers and a squadron of synagogue wardens and fortified the premises to contain a garrison of Goldman guests. She had sniffed disparagingly at Judith's simple white dress and barely looked at Dora (dumpy in dove grey), and had seethed as she'd sailed down the aisle at Ralph's side. Arthur hadn't understood why his mother had been so angry.

But there'd been no time to find out. Before he knew it he had been married and was gasping to catch his breath in a shower of good wishes, dizzy with champagne and trying to blink away a sudden attack of blinding panic. He had wanted to soothe and be soothed by his mother and tell Judith how beautiful she looked and say to Solomon that he'd take care of his daughter and –

Ralph? What was there to say to Ralph? Everything. Nothing. It hadn't mattered because, before he had managed to utter a memorable word to anyone at all, he had been escorted with his wife (his *wife*) from the synagogue hall and been pointed in the direction of All Seasons. Someone had packed his bags.

And if that someone had been around to pack his bag this morning, thought Arthur crossly, he'd have been ready to leave on time and not had to endure – in addition to everything else – the impatience of his mother.

'Arthur?'

He had guessed it was her when the telephone burst shrilly into his reverie.

'Morning, Mom.'

'We were wondering what had happened to you. Didn't you say you'd be here at eight? Dad and I are ready. Waiting.'

'But Mom – it's only seven minutes past now. I was on my way out. It's not easy managing everything *on my own*, you know.'

'I do know, Arthur darling.' A meaningful pause. 'Can we expect you soon then?'

'Yes. Of course.'

Wearily, he replaced the receiver and lifted his bag and wondered why it seemed so heavy since it contained so little – and worried that perhaps he was exhibiting the first symptoms of an incurable weakening of the skeletal structure. Terminal. That would make Judith sit up and beg his forgiveness for having caused him such anxiety and upheaval during his precious last months, weeks, days . . .

'Ouch!'

That did it. His head. Smack into the half-open door. Arthur swayed and dropped his burden and rubbed his crushed cranium and decided that the possibility of a subdural haemorrhage was far more disturbing than motor-neuron disease. Even worse than that was the chance that he'd inflicted upon himself a base-of-skull fracture which could conceivably cause the leakage of cerebral fluid through his nostrils. Not *very* likely, conceded Arthur. But he blew his nose violently and examined the contents of the tissue just in case. Far better to be careful than sorry afterwards.

That was what he told himself when, having recovered from the prospect of illness and the pain of his injury, he went from room to room on a pre-departure inspection. Doors shut. Windows locked. Burglar alarm operating efficiently. His marriage and health were in jeopardy but his home would be safe. He quickly qualified it: comparatively safe. One didn't want to tempt fate.

When Arthur finally shut the front door and carried his bag to the garage, he saw that it was 8.45 and felt his stomach contract as he contemplated the prospect of his mother's ire and regretted his missed breakfast. Then his eyes rested on the metallic blue bonnet of his BMW, revealed in all its gleaming glory from behind the electronic up-and-over door. He felt instantly better. He stroked the paintwork, in much the same way as he had once patted Sam the cat, and reassured himself with the knowledge that his four-wheeled friend was utterly reliable. No danger of a well-tended car slipping away like a straying pet. Or a wife.

'*You* won't let me down,' he said, making himself comfortable in the driver's seat and turning the key and listening for a responsive purr from the multi-litre engine. There was a moment's hesitation before it came, but Arthur, still distracted by the distress and deprivation incurred by his departure, failed to notice.

Gertrude could not abide unpunctuality. 'Our time on this earth', she said, tapping a freshly manicured nail on the polished oak surface of the dining-room table, 'was not granted to us for the purpose of waiting for latecomers. It is far (*tap*) too (*tap*) precious.'

She looked challengingly at her husband, who was engrossed in the morning paper.

'You're right,' mumbled Ralph, who didn't dare not to respond, but was reluctant to provoke an elaboration of his wife's highly developed views on making the most of one's allotted span. He had often wanted to ask her how she could be so certain (while most people around her seemed to stumble from moment to moment) that there was any purpose at all. But that would invite a lecture on God and charity and the sanctity of life. 'Ralph, I couldn't possibly expect you to understand,' she would conclude in the condescending tone of the insider to the outsider. 'Those of us who lay out the dead have a special sort of – access – into this sort of thing. We know.'

What was there to say to that? As a retired hardware merchant, he could hardly claim insight into anything more spiritual than the workings of a chainsaw or the mixing of paint. If the acquisition of divine knowledge entailed washing dead bodies, then Ralph was happier to remain ignorant. Much happier.

'Are we all packed then?' he asked, hoping to distract her from the anger induced by Arthur's lateness and any possible reference to other late beings. If his days on earth were numbered, Ralph wanted them peaceful. He would tell her so one day.

'Hours ago.' Gertrude had stopped tapping. She breathed in deeply and expelled a large puff of vaporized suffering. 'When someone tells me they're going to be here at a certain time, I move heaven and earth to make sure I'm ready. Haven't you brought the bags downstairs yet, Ralph?'

And Ralph, who needed no special temporal awareness to know that his time had come, folded his newspaper and went slowly up the stairs. A pair of matching suitcases awaited in the doorway of the immaculately tidied main bedroom. 'One thing I insist upon', Gertrude had said, rising with the sun to change the sheets and vacuum the carpets and dust the furniture, 'is to make sure that I always come back to a perfectly clean house. Otherwise my holiday is ruined.'

She seemed to have pushed from her mind the real reason for their journey. Her farewell calls to Fenella and Joanne had been brief and without any reference to Arthur or his errant wife. 'Your father and I are off for a little break in the country,' she had told each daughter in turn. 'Can't chat now – much too busy.' With all the cleaning and packing and telephoning to be done, naturally there'd been no question of preparing oats porridge for Ralph. Not this morning. He had breakfasted without complaint on tea and toast while Gertrude had used the remainder of the loaf to prepare egg-and-onion sandwiches for the journey. 'Arthur will appreciate these,' she'd said, boiling and mashing and slicing and buttering and filling and wrapping without pause. 'Driving always exhausts the poor boy so.'

Merely bringing two suitcases down three flights of stairs exhausted Ralph.

'There,' he said, out of breath, setting them down side by side in the hallway and flexing his shoulders. There was a strange sort of tingle in Ralph's left arm. A curious numb sensation. 'Funny –' he began. He was about to risk Gertrude's scorn by telling her that it felt odd, most unusual, when there was the squeak of tyres in the driveway and she was on her feet and glancing in the mirror and patting her steel-wool hair. She'd had it set especially for the expedition.

'Here's Arthur – at last,' she was saying as she scanned her front teeth for smudges of lipstick and gave a final once-over to the kitchen for traces of crumbs and a last look at her husband. He seemed pale. Perhaps she ought to have made him porridge. On the other hand, she couldn't be expected to see to everything. There were limits. Even for Gertrude Goldman.

'Mom, I'm sorry I'm late. The traffic . . .' Arthur at the door looked flustered. His shirt was crumpled, his tie askew and it seemed as though he had forgotten to comb his hair. His mother melted at the sight of him.

'Come, let's go,' she said, straightening his tie and licking her finger to remove a stain from his lapel. 'Ralph,' she called imperiously over her shoulder, 'will you take the suitcases to the car?' Her fleeting anxiety about her husband had been forgotten.

Before their departure, Gertrude, Ralph and Arthur sank simultaneously into the three-piece suite and (although the men would have preferred to remain seated for a while) almost immediately rose to their feet again. This old family custom guaranteed a safe return from a journey. Gertrude insisted it should be maintained. 'Not that I'm superstitious,' she hastened to point out when she had finally settled herself in the car with the sandwiches, map and travel-sick pills on her lap. 'But there's certainly no harm in sticking to tradition. This one's served the family well, touch wood, for as long as I can remember. So who are we to argue?'

Certainly not Arthur, who was adjusting his position behind the wheel. 'Are we ready then?' he asked. It was 9.45 and he was exhausted. Already. 'We have to travel via Willesden to fetch Solomon.' It looked like it was going to be a long, tiring day.

The morning traffic turned out to be even heavier than usual. It took an hour and a half for Arthur and his passengers to cover the five miles between Golders Green and the outskirts of Willesden. Ralph in the back seat was the only one of the three to remain marginally good humoured. He sat up eagerly.

'Now *this* takes me back,' he said with some excitement. 'Doesn't it take you back, Gert?'

'Yes.'

'Look – isn't that where the delicatessen used to be? And the bakery. Gertrude, didn't there used to be a bakery? Here. There. On that corner.'

'Yes.'

Gertrude, conscious of how elegant she looked alongside her son in his smart BMW that was gliding like visiting royalty through the drab roads of Willesden, had no wish at all to be taken back. She glanced in the rear-view mirror at Ralph, who was peering through the windows and pointing out lost landmarks and thought, with disapproval, that suddenly he seemed more animated than she had seen him in years. How pointless of her to have had that pang of conscience about not providing him with porridge. And how ridiculous her husband looked, all agog here in these dingy streets . . .

'It's funny,' she said off-handedly to Arthur in a voice that sounded as though nothing could be less amusing.

'What?' he asked warily. The crowded roads made him nervous and his mother tended to be critical of his driving. 'What's – um – funny?'

'I don't seem to suffer from – nostalgia. Other people', she indicated over her shoulder, 'tend to be *sentimental* about the past. I'm only too glad, too grateful, that we seem to have risen out of it, thank God.'

And she leaned back against the padded head-rest, sighing and shutting her eyes and managing (almost) to obliterate a sudden nagging feeling that she had left something behind. She concentrated on the contents of the suitcases and mentally ticked off each item. Travel-sick pills. Toothbrushes. Ralph's shaving cream. No – nothing missing. Her packing, as ever, had been meticulous. And yet. And yet. What was it?

'Gert – look – on your left,' Ralph was saying. How she wished he'd be quiet. 'That kebab place. Just over there on the corner. See it? Didn't that used to be old Solomon's butchery? Arthur? Wasn't that where the old man used to trade?'

They nodded. 'Yes,' they said together, she tersely and rather bitterly, and he with a sad shake of his head. They looked at one another for a moment. Then Arthur abruptly shifted his gaze back to the road while his mother, frowning, shut her eyes again and tried and failed to trace the cause of her unease and finally resorted to her favourite time-honoured distraction device. The provision of food. It hardly ever failed.

'Arthur, Ralph,' she announced, sitting up and beginning to

open the Tupperware box on her lap. 'Who wants a sandwich? Egg-and-onion, Arthur. Your favourite.'

'Why not?' Ralph reached across the seat, deciding that it hadn't been such a bad idea to go away after all. That he might – all things being equal – even rather enjoy himself. But Arthur, hands gripped tightly round the steering wheel, was hating every moment. His stomach was knotted, his colon in spasm (a common occurrence when he was especially tense) and there was an itchy spot on his right metatarsus that was steadily driving him mad.

'No thanks,' he said, unable to keep a high-pitched note of irritation out of his voice. Arthur suspected that if he accepted his mother's offering she would give him a brief lecture on weight-watching as she handed him the food. Give and take. One of Gertrude's cardinal rules. With one hand she would offer him sustenance, while with the other, she'd withdraw his appetite. 'I'm not hungry,' he added petulantly. 'Anyway – we're almost there.'

And he swung the car sharply towards the kerb and stopped outside a yellowing three-storey block that had once had 'Willow Court' inscribed in bold blue letters on the ledge above the entrance hall. The W had faded. Only 'illow Court' remained. Solomon Epstein's flat was on the first floor.

'I'll go up and fetch him,' said Arthur. 'Wait here in the car. I'm sure I shan't be long.'

'I should hope not.'

Gertrude pursed her lips as she replaced the Tupperware lid, making sure (as she always did) that she had expelled from the container every last molecule of extraneous air to create a perfect seal. It was one of her particular concerns that the food she had prepared should be properly preserved.

'We're hours later than we said we'd be,' she observed through clenched teeth, waiting for that satisfying snap as the lid attached itself to the base of the box. It came. Her jaw relaxed. 'If the old man isn't ready and waiting, I'll be most annoyed.'

Solomon was far from ready. He was still in bed, his blankets like a collapsed tent about his unmoving form, which encased a gory battlefield. His digestive tract was littered with vanquished lymphocytes and the corpses of several million defeated white cells and a victorious army of E Coli on the rampage, looting and pillaging until not a trace remained of the Celebration Meal For One. Until there was nothing left at all. When the invaders paused momentarily for a strategy meeting and interim celebration, they laughed with raucous glee over how poor Solomon had complained about his tasteless chicken when what he'd been eating was more like Trojan horse.

Solomon, who mostly didn't mind sharing a joke against himself, would not have found this one amusing. He was dying. There was no doubt about it. He had given up. There was nothing to be done except to lie and listen to his churning insides and palpitating heart and wait for the hostilities to end. For peace.

'Lord – oh my God – not now,' he had moaned aloud when dawn had broken over Willesden and the invaders had mounted their attack. He had woken shaking and sweating and heaving with wave after wave of nausea and wondering (between staggered visits to a lavatory that seemed to move further and further from the bed) why he, Solomon Epstein, should deserve such a punishment.

'Tell me,' he demanded weakly, 'my Lord, please would you let me know if there's any – particular – reason. Not that I've been perfect, but who's perfect, tell me? One second – I'll be right back . . .'

And a while later, with even less strength: 'Lord – listen – if you're looking for someone upon whom to inflict your wrath, can I give you some ideas maybe? Not that you really need me to remind you about the murderers and child molesters and embezzlers of synagogue funds – and – adulterers even – who never have a day's illness. Not a care in the world. Naturally, it's no news to you – but just in case you've forgotten and . . . oh – God. Wait. Don't go away.'

By 7 a.m., Solomon's slight form had been wellnigh drained and his voice reduced to a mere whisper.

'Have you no mercy – none at all?' he had groaned. 'Not for me – for her. For Judith. Didn't I tell you that I have to talk to her. That I have something – important – to say? It's not too late is it? Surely it's never too late? Or is that why you're punishing me? For not telling the – truth – all these years? Is that your – reason?'

By 9.15, Solomon had ceased asking for explanations. What was the point when there was nothing left – when all his internal organs and anger and dignity had been flushed away? No – not his dignity. God had spared him that. At least.

'So be it.' His lips had shaped the words as, with his last

remaining ounce of energy, he had arranged himself in an appropriate repose for death and tried not to hear the jubilation of the conquering army as it fanfared its final victory march down his large intestine.

That was how Arthur found him two hours later. A small sad heap beneath the bedclothes waiting quietly for the end.

'Pops!' At first he was sure that his father-in-law was dead. There had been no response to his fourth sharp ring on the doorbell and he had staunchly (his mother was watching him) resisted the temptation to sink to the pavement and hug his knees and howl. Then he had remembered the spare keys Judith had insisted they both kept in the glove compartment of their cars and with an abrupt 'Excuse me, Mom' had fumbled until he had found one. Gertrude, on the point of making a biting remark, had been silenced by her son's set face.

'Pops . . . ?'

The smell. He clenched his fists and tried to will away the nausea and to shut his eyes against the shabbiness of the place. It reeked of decay. From the flat upstairs he heard the sound of a toilet flushing and ponderous footsteps that made the ceiling squeak. In Solomon's flat there was silence. Arthur squinted in the semi-darkness and then, with a shock, suddenly noticed the mound on the bed. Quickly, he crossed the room and reached to feel the artery on his father-in-law's neck. It throbbed reassuringly. Thank heavens.

'Pops – answer me. Please say something.'

He leaned forward, whispering urgently into Solomon's ear, willing him to respond. Arthur had had a feeling about today. A premonition. But he hadn't predicted anything like this. Surely not even a person as difficult as Judith's father would choose a day like today to snuff it? But wait. His lips were moving. Arthur watched intently, hardly breathing. 'What, Pops? What is it?'

'I am *Solomon,*' the old man managed at last. 'Didn't I tell you a hundred times that I want you to call me – Solomon?'

There was a pause before Arthur responded in a soft, almost humble voice. 'Solomon . . .' It sounded like a sigh. Perhaps his father-in-law wasn't about to die after all. Not imminently. Arthur couldn't believe how glad he was.

'Solomon, what's the matter?' he asked. 'Where does it hurt?'

Solomon opened one eye. 'Arthur, my boy,' he replied, shaking his head slowly and mournfully. 'The question you should ask me is – where *doesn't* it hurt?'

He winced and groaned while Arthur probed and considered, wondering whether he ought to call for a second opinion and then remembering that he hadn't yet reached a first. Things weren't going well. At all.

'P—er—Solomon,' he frowned, 'I have to tell you that you're in no fit state to travel – for the mean while. We can't take the chance.'

'Thanks. A lot.' The words came out with difficulty. 'It's – lucky – for me that I should have a son-in-law a – doctor.'

And Arthur, pondering on the nature of the illness and (worse) the call he'd have to make to Judith and (worst) how he'd break the news to Gertrude, failed to notice the sarcasm. He looked down modestly.

'Well. Yes. I suppose it *is* fortunate. Tell you what, Pops . . .' Arthur injected his voice with as much cheer and conviction as possible. Hadn't he always been known for his bedside manner? '. . . I'll go to the car and fetch my bag and then we can have a good old look at you. We'll have you up and about in no time.'

The cheer and conviction may have half-convinced Solomon but they were like embers in the tinder of his mother's impatience.

'For goodness' sake, Arthur!' she spluttered. 'This is the limit. Honestly. Not that I don't feel sorry for the old man. But there's compassion – and compassion. After all, we're not young either. Are we, Ralph? And to expect us to drop everything and run when your wife demands our presence, to drag us exhausted across London and then postpone the whole thing because her father . . .'

'Mom – please . . .'

'I could've told you long ago that he'd pick up something nasty with his flat in the state it's in. Disgusting. Disgraceful the way his daughter, his only child, allows it to . . .'

'Mom, please, there's no point in . . .'

'And now what are we supposed to do? Wait here in the car until he decides to recover? Sit around like *idiots* until we receive our orders? Well, Arthur – I've had it. Everyone seems to assume that I possess endless stores of strength. Even you, Ralph. Ralph!'

'What?'

Ralph, who had been quietly basking in a pleasant haze of time-filtered memories, sat up sharply. His wife's mood was dangerous. He smelt smoke.

'Gert,' he tried soothingly, 'this isn't anyone's fault you know. D'you want us to get a taxi home, Arthur? Then you can see to Solomon and later . . .'

'A taxi! Another expense! Some people seem to think we're made of money.'

'I'll pay,' said Arthur promptly, relieved that pounds and pence had replaced filial neglect and unrequited martyrdom as the objects of his mother's ire. He'd always been more comfortable with cash than conscience. Compound interest was a doddle compared with the complexities of guilt and responsibility. Even the technicalities of a Single European Currency were far simpler than the muddle of the divided allegiance. 'Don't worry about the cost, Mom. It's on me. Tax-deductible anyway.'

'Well,' sniffed Gertrude with haughty resignation, 'I suppose there's nothing to be done. Although, quite frankly Arthur – if you want to hear the truth . . .'

He didn't particularly, but kept silent. It was safer.

'. . . I think it would be only fitting, the right thing to do, for you to tell Judith in no uncertain terms that her duty lies here at the bedside of her sick father. That she must return immediately. And perhaps, since we're all packed and ready to have a little break, the three of us . . .'

Her voice trailed off. Arthur had his stubborn look. There was no future in this particular version of the truth. Even Gertrude could see that.

'Mom, Dad, listen to me,' he was saying in a much firmer voice. 'Come upstairs and I'll call a taxi and we'll see what we can do for the old man and – Mom – perhaps you could tidy the place a little in the mean time? Make it a bit more comfortable for him?'

Gertrude sniffed again, a touch less haughtily. The possibility of accomplishing a few good deeds was not to be sneezed at. Even in her state of debility. *Particularly* in her state of debility.

'Come, Ralph,' she said, opening the door firmly and stepping out into the street with her handbag and her sandwiches and several rounds of grimly determined virtue. It was a fighting force sufficient to smite whole legions of sinners – never mind a mere few million invading bacteria that had grown fat and complacent on Solomon's spoils. 'We may as well get on with it.'

And Ralph, reluctantly following his wife into the fray, remembered the huge relief he had felt when his flat feet had put him in the Pay Corps for the duration of the War. He had never quite managed to find a safe desk job for marital battles and family hostilities.

Arthur, having checked that the car was securely locked and the burglar alarm connected, brought up the rear.

'I'm sorry about this,' he said, out of breath, following his father through the portals of '–illow Court'. Why was he apologizing, always apologizing? He swallowed a sudden wave of anger that made him want to murder his mother and beat his wife and yell at his father and shake Solomon Epstein till he was breathless and blue.

Pull yourself together, he told himself. This was something one couldn't say to hysterical patients these days, with the psychiatric profession and the drug industry competing for their market share. But Arthur had a secret fondness for the old-fashioned slap-on-the-face approach.

'I'll have a proper look at – er – Solomon. Then we'll know exactly where we are.'

He panted up the stairs, aware of a surge in his heart-rate that told him he was out of condition and should plan an intensive session at the gym. Soon.

'And while you tidy up,' he continued doggedly, 'I'll make a few calls. Your taxi. The surgery. Judith.'

He stopped in mid-flight.

'Yes, I'd better get on the phone to Judith and explain our – delay.'

Judith was having a busy morning. The health of her father and the progress of the family's journey had almost receded from her mind. She'd hardly had time to collect her waking thoughts and pull on some clothes before being accosted by someone who had knocked and announced himself as Ken Mansion, head of catering.

'Mrs Goldman,' he had said, *sotto voce* through the door, 'would you be kind enough – I'd be ever so grateful if you could – to spare the time for a fairly brief consultation on the subject of – meals?

For your – um – delegation, if that's what one calls it? I, personally, have had little experience in the area of conference nutrition (a fertile field these days, I believe), but I'm *delighted* to have been given this opportunity to broaden my range.'

His voice sounded as though it had been liquidized. Hardly a consonant remained.

'My – particular specialization, Mrs Goldman –' He had edged sideways into the room as the words oozed out like a rich roux sauce. '– is food for love. Love in all its infinite variations – some of which I was privileged to witness and explore at a centre – I'd almost say a mecca – of eroticism in – *puris naturalibus* – at one of our prime south coast holiday resorts. That was when I was – er – so to speak – headhunted by Chuck Wilmot (you've had the pleasure I believe?) and encouraged to diversify into post-nuptial stimulation. And prose. Ah yes – I was given a free hand with prose. The – ahem – menus are mine, Mrs Goldman.'

'Gosh.' Judith sat down, struck speechless, but wasn't left long to search for words. Mr Mansion's fluency was awesome.

'Yes. And I must confess that I'm terribly fortunate in that I don't have to *work* for my inspiration. The images, the metaphors, the rhythms just – come. And now, with the prospect of this gathering of yours, the possibilities . . . Mrs Goldman, I must confess that last night I hardly slept a wink. The *ideas*. An exploration of marriage. Would you give me licence to express myself freely? Alimentarily speaking, of course. Trust me, Mrs Goldman. I won't let you down.'

'I'm sure, Mr Mansion.' Judith was afraid she might be overcome by his aroma (was it vanilla essence?) and the undressing intensity of his pale blue eyes. And laughter. Hysterical laughter at the sudden thought of Gertrude frowning over unsubtle erotic allusions and Arthur doing an embarrassed double-take over the blatant *double entendres*. And Ralph getting the drift and surreptitiously leering. And Solomon. Solomon? A wave of shame dampened her hysteria.

'The thing is,' she hesitated, 'the – er – participants in my conference are – well – of a rather serious disposition. And . . .'

'Serious? Mrs Goldman, let me assure you that I don't take my work lightly. I understand fully the – weight – of your subject matter, the importance, nay the urgency of it being thoroughly investigated – how was it put? – "outside the constraints of suburbia". Mrs Goldman, I am humble and proud to be honoured with the task of nourishing such a forum and will treat it with all the reverence it deserves.'

'Oh. Well.'

Judith had always considered herself rather adept at maintaining conversational flow but this verbal tide was unstoppable. She searched desperately for a means of diverting it – preferably out of the room and back to the kitchen.

'Mr Mansion,' she said, 'why don't you make a – draft of your ideas and show them to me later? We can talk about – things – then.'

He seemed not to be listening. A rapturous smile had stretched his moustache to a smudge and he was gazing through the window as though at a fantastic faraway feast. Judith was about to repeat her suggestion when he swung round and took hold of her hand with such ferocity that she almost fell off the chair.

'Mrs Goldman,' he said as gravely and sonorously as if he were taking an oath of allegiance, 'I'll repair to my office this very minute and apply heart, body and soul to the matter. And any inspiration I can imbibe from the literary giants I turn to for my source material. Shakespeare, Proust, Honoré de Balzac, Masters and Johnson, et cetera, et cetera. My reference library is superb. And later –'

He paused dramatically, relinquished her crushed fingers and strode to the door. He was leaving. Judith hardly dared breathe for fear that he might change his mind.

'– Later, when I present you with the – er – fruits and other delectations of my labours, you'll agree with every fibre of your being that the feeding of your – think-tank – has been placed in safe and serious hands.'

The rush of euphoria she felt on his departure reminded Judith of the depressive who wore tight shoes all day simply to experience the moment of relief when he finally undid the laces. A regular dose of Ken Mansion would, she supposed, provide the equivalent measure of relative light-heartedness. On the other hand, dread of the next encounter could prove suicidal. Thinking of which . . .

The telephone rang. She wondered why it was that so many of her musings on mortality were interrupted this way and had a couple of brief thoughts about chance, fate and fortune before answering crossly:

'Hello.'

'Mrs Goldman? Is that Mrs Judith Goldman?'

Another male voice. Deeper than Mansion's, but almost as silky and conspiratorial. Who was it this time?

'Yes. Speaking.'

'This is Maplin here. Steve Maplin. Your – second in command.'

'Oh?'

Was this some kind of Wonderland? Had she taken the tablets after all? Judith, suddenly unsteady, clutched the bed-post for support and tried to imagine what Alice would have said. 'In command', she asked dazedly, 'of – what?'

'What?' His composure slipped – for a moment. 'Here. This. The hotel.' He lowered his voice until it was a throaty whisper. 'Your conference.'

The hotel? Her conference? Judith, holding even tighter on to the bed-post, was suddenly afraid of the machinery she had set in motion. Huge creaking turbines and cogs and springs working to turn a revolving stage on which surreal puppets danced and sang silly tunes that no longer seemed funny. She had made a grand gesture, a bid for oblivion, and instead found herself in the plastic paradise of a honeymoon hotel. And then, reaching out for truth, for some kind of real human contact, it seemed she had accidentally turned the starter switch of an absurdly comic carousel. Accidentally? Or was this her way out? After all, wasn't the absurdity of the ridiculous much easier to bear than the pain of the sublime?

'Mrs Goldman,' he was saying, his voice so close to the mouthpiece that she was sure she could feel his breath tickling her ear. She wanted to giggle. Yes. She supposed it was. Far easier. 'Mrs Goldman – I'm sorry to intrude – but if you could spare a few minutes for a meeting, I have a feeling there are things we could discuss that would be to our – uh – mutual advantage. Things that I – for various classified reasons – cannot divulge on the telephone but would be willing to share in a person-to-person situ. . .'

'Mr . . . ?'

'Maplin. Call me Steve.'

'Mr – um – Steve. Listen. I don't think you understand about my meeting . . .'

'Understand? Oh, I understand. Everything. Intuitive understanding is one of my strengths. Mrs Goldman, I can't say anything now – it's too dangerous. Come to the Solstice Centre in exactly thirty-four minutes and we can talk.'

'But . . .'

'Don't let me down. I'll – we'll – be waiting for you.'

The line went dead. And Judith, with a shrug, thought, 'what the hell' and went. After all, there were several hours to fill before the expected arrival of her delegates. Such delegates. She imagined them in Arthur's car. Gertrude regally poised alongside her son, dispensing sandwiches and disapproval and burping her Tupperware with tightly-drawn lips. Arthur worried, nervous and resentful. The driver being driven. Ralph in the rear seat with his maddeningly secret half-smile. And next to him Solomon, his face . . . ?

She tried to picture her father but managed to see only a blur and dismissed a sudden prickle of dread as being the product of her overwrought post-suicidal state. Could it be that this entire venture was an hallucination, a despair-induced dream?

Her suspicions deepened when, at 10.30 sharp, she entered the Solstice Centre and saw chairs and a table and satellite dishes and fax machines, but no sign at all of mysterious Steve Maplin. Then:

'Mrs Goldman.'

A disembodied voice boomed from several stereo speakers set inconspicuously into the pine-panelled walls. The Centre was a small octagonal structure connected by a covered walkway to the main body of the hotel. It reminded Judith of an airport chapel. The design, she decided, was probably governed by the same sub-section of Government Building Regulations covering interdenominational communication outlets. Perhaps market researchers had found that phobic travellers and newlywed businesspeople had similar spiritual needs – the same sort of last-minute desperation to make their peace.

'Mrs Goldman,' repeated the Oz-like voice. Judith almost expected it to expound on her sins. Or announce her flight and its departure time. Instead it chanted: 'We're here. Behind the screen.'

She noticed a shadow – or was it a pair of shadows? – darkening a collapsible projection surface at the far end of the room and, crossing the floor cautiously, discovered a dark-suited replica of Chuck Wilmot together with the curvaceous woman who had accosted her in the bedroom late the night before. Linda? Sharon? Sherryl.

'Sshhh . . . Mrs Goldman, step this way. Quietly. This is highly confidential. I'm – Steve. And this is my Press and Publicity Executive, Ms Carter.'

'Yes. We've met. But I thought you were an administrative ass. . . ?'

'I was, until this morning. Golly, Mrs Goldman, this is all so exciting – I feel quite ill. Nervous tummy. I'm like that, you know.'

Judith wasn't sure whether to express congratulations or sympathy, but didn't have time for either. Steve Maplin was speaking in an urgent non-stop undertone that made Ken Mansion's fluency seem stilted. Something about the promotional possibilities presented by her conference, how his superior, Mr Wilmot, seemed to lack insight, foresight, how he always tended to nip Steve's creative endeavours in the bud. Figuratively, of course.

'But this time – with your help – I'm determined to persevere. This is going to be *big,* Mrs Goldman. It's going to wipe out Wilmot and put me and All Seasons firmly on the map. And – um – Ms Carter, of course. And you, Mrs Goldman. You are going to be launched as the country's leading expert on marriage. How does that sound?'

Horrible, she was about to say. Unbelievably, terrifyingly vile. But Maplin, with a proprietary arm about the shoulder of his side-kick, the radiantly smiling Sherryl, was machine-gunning her with statistics:

'According to the latest available figures, there are 92,874 troubled marriages in South East England alone. A ripe market, Mrs Goldman. A rich crop of discord just waiting to be plucked. Did you know that a single fat person – it was a Mrs Collins from Croydon, if my memory serves me correctly – launched the multi-million pound weight-loss industry? It will take *one troubled wife* – you, Mrs Goldman, this is your big chance – to turn marital disharmony into a prime commodity. But first things first. A press release . . .'

'*No. Stop.* Please.'

Judith shut her eyes and covered her ears. This was no Wonderland. It was a nightmare from which she might never wake. She was frightened and furious.

'I absolutely forbid you to embark on – any kind of publicity campaign,' she said angrily. 'I've a right to privacy – as a citizen, as a guest at your hotel, as a – a person. How dare you! Forget about all of this. Forget about it entirely. Otherwise I'll have to tell Mr Wilmot that the conference is off.' She headed for the door marked Exit, knocking over a chair in her path. 'Blast! Damn!'

'Wait,' called Steve Maplin. 'Mrs Goldman, please wait. Let's talk this through.'

'There's nothing to say. What's the matter with this door? You haven't locked me in, have you?'

'One minute. Give me a chance. Please . . .'

As he pleaded and Judith fumed and Sherryl looked on with the helpless disappointment of a child overhearing her parents cancelling Christmas, the loudspeakers started crackling and someone said 'Ahem'.

'May I have your attention please,' recited a nasal female voice that sounded as though it had been specially cultivated for public announcements. 'I have a telephone call for Mrs Judith Goldman. Would Mrs Goldman please come to the phone.'

'Me? Where?' She looked at Steve.

'Here. There. Everywhere.' He indicated vaguely round the room with its profusion of telecommunications equipment. Cordless. Digital. Cellular. Multi-operational with automatic redial facility and interrupt button. Enough lines to stock a talk-shop. 'Simply pick one up and say hello.'

She obeyed. It was Arthur.

'Jude, I don't know what to say.'

Her anger dissolved. She shook her head sadly. Advance technology had made it possible for the sound of his voice to be carried to outer space and back. But what was the point if he didn't know what to say? Would he ever? Would she?

'Arthur, what's the matter? Is something – terribly – wrong?'

'It's your father. He's – not well. What are you – we – going to do?'

She listened in silence. 'Are you *sure* it's not serious, Arthur?' she wanted to know. 'He's not – a young man.'

'It's gastro, Jude. A moderately severe bout of gastro-enteritis that he picked up from God-knows-where. One of his meals on wheels, I suspect – although my mother swears it's impossible. Anyway, he's responding well to treatment. Amazingly well, all things considered. And he says he wants to come and see you. As planned. He's absolutely determined. So unless . . . ?'

'What? Unless what, Arthur? What are you trying to suggest?'

'Nothing. It's just that – well – with your father ill and my parents dreadfully upset and me – forget about me. It's been very

– difficult for all of us. And I thought that maybe you'd see – you have to admit it, Jude – that all this is rather an over-reaction on your part. We've had worse arguments than the one we had on Sunday. Much worse. But never before have you gone off and threatened . . .'

'Arthur, let's not go through this now. You have no idea about me, us, the way I feel. None at all. And I'm not prepared to talk – to begin to talk – like this on the phone. You know the deal – and I'm sticking to it. I've made up my mind. If, as you say, my father will be in a fit state to travel, then . . .'

'I can't guarantee anything, Jude. Nothing. I'm a doctor, not a plumber. He's old and weak and his heart isn't the strongest. Who can tell? How would you feel if . . . ?'

How indeed? She refused to think about it. After stubbornly insisting to her husband that she was holding firm to her demands, Judith retreated to the sanctuary of her spring chamber. She had given the Maplin – Carter conspiracy a firm warning that press publicity was out of the question.

'Are you sure?' Steve Maplin had asked, somewhat forlornly. 'Can't we even prepare a draft memorandum? Strictly secret, of course.'

'Absolutely not,' she had repeated firmly.

Now in the privacy of April (where the daffodils on the dressing-table already looked as though they'd seen a better day), she heard Arthur's voice joined by the voices of the inquisitive, scandal-hungry world asking 'how would you feel, Judith . . . ? Tell us, Mrs Goldman, how does it feel?'

'I don't know,' she would answer, a look of puzzlement on her face. 'I simply don't know. I haven't felt anything for years.'

After the brief rush of panic on her honeymoon morning, Judith had gone numb. It was as though she had fallen asleep on her wedding night and never properly woken up. Even the Smile Monster had finally been laid to rest. Or so it seemed when the new Mrs Goldman, capable and imperturbable, called on her parents soon after her return to London.

'Judith, how are you? Did you have a good time? Dora, take a look at her. Can you believe that we have a married daughter? So grown up. Such a lady. A – woman. Isn't she, Dora?'

Dora looked at her appraisingly and, slightly doubtfully, agreed. And Judith, turning away in irritation from her mother's familiar caution, fixed her eyes on her father's face and waited for the satisfying inner lurch that meant her Monster was gulping its nourishment and licking its lips after swallowing a smile. She watched Solomon's proud beam – and waited. Until, after a long while, she realized there was nothing to wait for any more. The monster, she believed, was dead.

And for a moment she was furious. She felt cheated and empty. 'How dare you!' she wanted to say – to him and the lost monster and the great big gap, the terrifying void that had appeared. 'Daddy, you created this creature – this hungry beast that I could never satisfy. And now you've killed it. There's nothing left.'

For a moment she wanted to kill him too. Just for an instant.

Then she smiled back. At her father, at Arthur her husband, at her mother who half-acknowledged it and looked away. Goodness – this was easy. Amazingly easy. Why hadn't she thought of it before? With her newfound numbness, she wasn't feeling a thing. Unsurprising really. After all, if anaesthesia could make it possible for patients to withstand heart surgery, why shouldn't it enable Judith Epstein – *Goldman,* she must remember it was Goldman now – to function efficiently as a dutiful wife and daughter?

'We had a lovely time,' she managed with just the right degree of nonchalance. 'Didn't we, Arthur?'

He nodded in a relieved sort of way and moved towards her and took her hand, and his felt warm and soft and for a moment she was almost overcome by sudden vertigo. A desperate longing to fall.

Then she caught herself sharply and extracted her hand and dropped it carelessly on to her husband's shoulder and said they had to make a move, they really had to be off, there was so much to do – and hadn't they promised Gertrude and Ralph that they'd come in and say hello? 'We shouldn't disappoint them, Arthur. We really shouldn't.'

'But Judith – I – we – thought that you – the two of you – were staying for supper. And then I was hoping – well – there's been no sound from the piano for almost two weeks. Such silence. So I thought – a little Mozart maybe . . . ?'

'No. Sorry, Dad. We can't. Arthur's parents are expecting us.'

Whose voice was she hearing – so distant and brittle and controlled? Solomon had probably been right. She must have grown up. Judith remembered a doll she'd been given as a sixth birthday present. A talking doll with a softly padded torso containing a small metal box attached to a string, and a label that exclaimed 'Pull and I'll talk!'. And Judith, ever obliging, had pulled.

'Hello, I'm Mary-Lou . . . I'm very well thank you . . . how do you do?'

Such startling adult noises from the belly of a baby doll. The soundtrack of maturity. Similar, in a way, to the appropriate murmurings that were emanating from grown-up Mrs Goldman.

'Keep well, Dad. Bye, Mum. We'll try and fit in a visit over the weekend.'

She dropped a light kiss on his forehead and slipped her arm through Arthur's and, waving airily, floated down the path. Or thought she had floated until she caught sight of herself in the wing-mirror of the car, as sallow-skinned and graceless as ever. So what. It didn't matter. Nothing mattered now.

'Judith – wait.'

Solomon, out of breath, was calling her urgently. He was hurrying towards her with a large leather-bound book in his hands. 'Here – take this – it's for you. I was going to give it to you later – but . . .'

Mozart's piano sonatas. The complete collection. She held out her arms and they sagged momentarily under the weight of the volume.

'Real calfskin,' he was saying. 'The best. A present – for your wedding. From me.'

She hardly hesitated. 'Dad – how lovely,' she enthused. 'It's just what I've always wanted. One of these days – as soon as I can find the time – we'll sit down together, you and me, and I'll play them.'

'Open it – go on – have a look,' he urged, delighted with her response. 'Feel the quality of the paper. The finest. Look – that one's familiar. Judith, do you remember it? The Sonata in A? It was the first sonata she ever played, Arthur. She played and we cried. Can you believe it? A little girl and she made us all cry.'

There was a pause. Arthur fiddled with a shoelace while Judith looked up the path towards the house and saw Dora's plump form outlined in the open front door, almost luminous against the dark hallway. Yes, she remembered. Her mother had wiped away tears that night. It had been the only time Judith had seen her weep. Solomon's eyes had frequently welled with sentimental tears, but Dora's had always remained dry. Could it have been that her mother had also put herself to sleep? One day, thought Judith, she would ask her about – things. Some day they would talk.

A bus rumbled past. Arthur forced his voice above the noise. 'Jude – come. We really must make a move. It's getting late.'

Her father stood on the kerb to wave them farewell. He had always done that when guests departed. Judith noticed he was wearing the tartan slippers she had bought him for a long-ago birthday. They were worn and torn.

'Wasn't it sweet of my dad to give me the Mozart,' she said as they left. Arthur's clutchwork was smooth and his steering accurate. Judith shut her eyes and thought how easy it would be to drop off with her husband at the wheel and how fortunate she was to have married such a safe driver.

'Funny thing about that sonata,' she said dreamily. 'The A Major. The one he was talking about.'

'What?'

Arthur was concentrating hard on negotiating the traffic. Safe driving demanded a great deal of his attention.

'Don't you remember – the sonata that made everyone cry,' she reminded him patiently. 'For years and years they thought Mozart composed it to express his feelings when his mother died.'

'Really?'

Arthur signalled left. They were almost home.

'Yes – there've been great scholarly essays on the way he used the music to pour out his grief. Then someone discovered that the sonata had been falsely dated. It was composed much later than they'd believed – years after his mother's death. Which shows, I suppose . . .'

Her voice trailed off. What did it show? Why had she begun this irrelevant anecdote in the first place? Arthur wasn't the least bit interested, and why should he be? What did Mozart, dead Mozart, have to do with them, here, now?

'What, Jude?' asked Arthur, turning off the engine and applying the handbrake decisively. They'd arrived.

'Something – about the foolishness of – making assumptions about an artist's heart and mind,' she said vaguely, opening the door and stepping out on to the crazy-paved path. They were extremely lucky to have been able to afford a cottage in the Garden Suburb at such an early stage in their marriage. Everyone had said so. Judith, holding the manuscript to her chest, followed her husband inside.

'What's for supper?' he called over his shoulder. 'I'm starving. I suppose we could ask my mother . . .'

'No. I'll make something. It won't take long.'

A few minutes later, he was looking at her fondly across the breakfast nook, which had been specially designed for informal eating. Arthur applied a piece of wholemeal bread to the last trace of egg yolk on his plate. While he'd already developed a strong sense of roughage, his cholesterol-consciousness hadn't yet been fully raised.

'Jude,' he said, chewing contentedly, 'shall I tell you something? Your father took me aside this afternoon and he said – confidentially of course – that I was a fortunate man. "I can give you any guarantee you like", he told me, "that my Judith will make you an excellent wife." That's what he said. And do you know what?'

He placed his knife and fork together and leaned forward intimately.

'I think he's absolutely right.'

She nodded vaguely and cleared the plates and wiped the surfaces and removed every trace of post-prandial disorder. Yes – she would probably turn out to have a natural aptitude for wifehood. Her father was generally correct about such things.

'He should know,' she said with only the slightest hint of irony. 'After all, wasn't he the one to spot my talent for music? Talking about which, I'd better find somewhere safe to put that sonata book. It's probably quite valuable.'

Arthur was already in the car, hooting impatiently, when Judith finally deposited her calfskin Mozart in its safe place. She had washed the dishes and tidied her hair and plumped up the scatter-cushions on the three-piece suite before finally carrying her wedding gift slowly upstairs. She tried not to think about what she was doing. She tried not to think at all.

'Hurry, Jude,' she heard him calling. 'My mother has a thing about punctuality.'

'Coming. One minute.'

She took a last glance at the Sonata in A before closing the book and tucking it securely away in the depths of her wardrobe. Judith had decided that, in order to be an excellent wife, she was quite prepared to wash clothes and make meals and amends and babies and beds and even bread. But not music. She wouldn't make music. That wasn't part of the deal.

'Funny – I don't seem to hear you playing the piano much any more,' Arthur would say from time to time as the years passed and the instrument they had transported from Willesden (at great cost, as Arthur often pointed out – the insurance premium alone had run into hundreds) became dull from disuse. 'I somehow thought . . .'

'What?' she would answer sharply. 'What did you think? That in addition to all the cooking and cleaning and caring for your clothes and helping to administer your practice and teaching twenty-seven untalented children the difference between crotchets and quavers and the bass and treble clef, I should serenade you with some Chopin each evening? A little Bach before bedtime? A few bars of Schubert after . . .'

'No, no. Of course not. Calm down, Jude – I wasn't criticizing. Honestly. It's just that I'd always believed music was somehow *necessary* to you.'

'Well it isn't.'

'But as for the other stuff – the housework and all – how could I possibly have any complaints? Quite frankly, I often wonder how you manage everything.'

She did manage. Perfectly. No one could have faulted Judith Goldman on the standards of her dinner-party fare or the symmetry of her ironing. The cooker gleamed relentlessly. She saw to it that even her mother-in-law was sometimes stumped for material for criticism.

'Very nice. Very nice indeed,' Gertrude conceded through pinched lips when Judith took her on an inspection tour of the bigger, better house that Arthur had bought to celebrate five years of marriage. Each room was immaculately colour co-ordinated and interior designed. The breakfast nook had expanded to a nosh area (with concealed lighting) and the *en suite* bathroom had gained a bidet. There were 'his' and 'hers' dressing spaces in the master bedroom and a vanity basin in the guest-room.

But the third room, the one papered in sunflower yellow and coyly described by the estate agent as 'an ideal south-facing nursery', was still empty. 'Hmm,' considered Gertrude, pausing at the door. 'This won't be unoccupied for much longer, please God. Eh, Judith?'

'Yes – well - hopefully,' said Judith. 'Wouldn't you like a cup of tea now, Gertrude? Arthur will be back from the surgery soon.'

'First let me give you a piece of advice.' Gertrude wasn't easily distracted once she had focused on a cause. 'I told Fenella and Joanne the same thing and, take it from me, they're glad they listened. You want to have children, I presume?'

'Gertrude . . .'

'Then don't wait too long. I'm telling you, Judith – the longer you wait, the harder it gets.'

Judith nodded. For a moment she thought she heard a tiny cry and felt a small face snuggling at her neck, burrowing into her, waking her up. For a moment she was sure she heard music and she thought her heart would break. But only for a moment.

For she had already discovered that no matter how long she waited, there would never be a baby in that sunflower yellow nursery. And she was also aware that if she stayed sound asleep the waiting wouldn't be hard. Anything would be bearable as long as she remained quite numb.

Arthur didn't notice her numbness. He thought it was maturity. Coping. Not making a fuss. He was particularly impressed with her stoic reaction to the verdict of Dr Benjamin Rogers, widely accepted in the medical fraternity as the nation's top fertility man.

'Jude, it's amazing the way you're handling – things,' he said, frowning over his ratatouille in the Goldmans' new nosh area. 'Some women would have been quite hysterical by now.'

Judith had endured long and often painful investigations to discover why, despite all the effort, the couple remained in an irrevocably childless state. Finally, with formidable calm, she had accompanied her husband to Harley Street to hear Dr Rogers' prognosis.

'Arthur. Judith. I'm sorry. The news isn't good,' he had said gravely. She hadn't flinched.

Rogers had glanced through a file bulging with laboratory reports and X-rays and studies and scans and then put it aside and sorrowfully shaken his silver head.

'Judith, my dear,' he had said with practised sympathy, 'I've already spent some time examining the – er – technical details with your husband. A lot of – *jargon* (you know the way we medical men tend to go on when we get together) – that I'm sure you would find rather – boring and bewildering.'

He had paused and sighed deeply, apparently concentrating on a problematic index finger-nail. Judith had been uncertain whether his expression of hopelessness was about her limited understanding, his torn cuticle or the dire results of the tests. Oh, what was the difference? She had suddenly felt exhausted.

'And so – ' the great man, having concluded his digital inspection, had placed both palms firmly on the vast mahogany desk with its calendar and notepads and pens and executive toys all inscribed with the names of diseases and drugs. 'I'll try to keep it simple and – er – to the point. Far better for us all really. In my opinion, taking everything into account, there is very little possibility of the two of you producing a child. Almost none, I'm afraid. As I said – Arthur, Judith – I'm sorry.'

'But . . . who?' Judith had begun to ask.

'Wait.' The famous Rogers hands, renowned in gynaecological circles for their light touch, were raised as though for a benediction. 'My considerable experience has taught me that it's negative and destructive for couples to become obsessed with questions like "Who?" and "Why?" and so forth. Judith – believe me – there's no question of blame or responsibility in this. It's – well – let's call it fate.'

'I see.'

Judith hadn't seen. But to question further had seemed pointless and she'd had a longing to be in a dark corner somewhere far away, deeply asleep. Arthur, she had noticed, had shifted uncomfortably in his seat and been about to say something and then changed his mind. Rogers had given him no time to change it again.

'Judith.' He had fixed his pale blue eyes on her. 'What I'd like to suggest is that you and Arthur go home and discuss everything quietly and peacefully (get yourselves a nice bottle of wine) and later, when you've had more time to – accept the situation, perhaps we can talk along the lines of – adoption.'

He had lowered his voice and picked up a plastic pyramid puzzle adorned with the name of an oral contraceptive.

'Confidentially speaking, of course,' he'd almost whispered, 'I do have certain connections . . .'

They had thanked him and left silently and that night, over *coq au vin* and several glasses of Yugoslav Riesling, they had chatted about Arthur's troublesome patients and his sporting near-victories and the suspected infidelities of his medical partner and squash opponent, Jonathan Bloom. And the weather.

And the situation in the Middle East and South Africa. And this and that.

'I'm very tired,' Judith had announced at 10.45. 'D'you mind if I . . .'

'Jude – there's something – um – shouldn't we . . .?'

'Arthur, I don't want to talk about it. Not tonight. There's plenty of time.'

'Sure. Absolutely. You're right. We probably both need a good sleep. A rest.' He had sounded relieved.

That night she had dreamt about a dog. A dark and sinister-looking mongrel, who watched her with hungry eyes while she, afraid to show her fear because she'd been taught that dogs attacked those they sensed were frightened, had pretended unconcern. A familiar voice had urged her along. 'Good girl, Judith. You're doing well. You're brave – almost as brave as your father.' But she had known that she wasn't. Not really. That the dog would smell her fear and . . .

With a start she had woken into the darkness and the unease of unresolved terror and the aching weariness of someone who'd been weeping until she could weep no more.

'What's up, Jude? You've been muttering in your sleep. Are you OK?'

'I – yes, I think so. It was a dream. Only a dream.'

And she had lulled herself back into unconsciousness with lists of household chores and the names of people to whom they owed invitations and, at last, on the brink of oblivion, the ingredients she would need for the following night's supper. Ratatouille. That's what she'd try. Wasn't that what everyone was eating?

'D'you like it?' she asked Arthur brightly after he had praised her maturity and the way she was coping. 'It's supposed to be good for you. All those vegetables and olive oil. *Loaded* with fibre and poly-unsaturates.'

'Mmm. Very nice,' he said with rather forced enthusiasm. When it came to his diet, Arthur's tastes were often at odds with his principles. His passion for junk-food caused him moral confusion and he was sometimes troubled by the anger he suppressed when his wife served him the sort of food he recommended to his patients. Like now. Surely after a difficult day she could have come up with something more – *substantial*? He pouted.

Judith noticed and tried not to smile too broadly. Her

husband's internal struggles with the conflicting pressures of greed and guilt and hypochondria tended to provide more entertainment than most other aspects of marriage. 'Good,' she said cheerfully. 'I'm pleased. Listen – Arthur. It occurred to me last night that it's our turn to have the Blooms over for dinner. I know you see Jonathan every day and it'll probably be a *bit* boring but, well, we may as well get it over with. Shall I ask them for Saturday night?'

He stopped eating, surprised. Judith had always expressed disdain for Jonathan ('a self-satisfied philanderer,' she'd once called him) and contempt for Enid who 'allowed herself to be treated like a breeding machine'. Or was she, like himself, desperate for distraction?

'Great. Yes – ask them. Perhaps Jonathan and I can fit in a few sets of squash first.'

With a little more gusto, he returned to his plate.

'Oh – and Jude . . .'

He hesitated, his fork penetrating a plump piece of aubergine and his knife glistening with tomato juice. Judith decided that she wouldn't repeat the ratatouille. There was something slimy and evil about it. On the other hand, maybe she'd prepare it just once more – for that smooth Jonathan Bloom on Saturday night. It would be fitting somehow.

'Mmm?'

'I think that perhaps on Sunday we ought to visit my parents – and yours of course – and tell them about our – er – problem. You know what I mean . . .'

'Yes, of course,' she interrupted quickly. 'We'll do that.'

Perhaps, even in her sleepwalking state, Judith suspected there was something significant about that dinner with the Blooms. She certainly went to inordinate trouble with her appearance for the occasion and Jonathan, she could hardly fail to notice, examined her with new, appraising interest. Judith was aware of his eyes on the curves that were accentuated by her clinging black dress and the way he inhaled her French perfume. Enid was heavily pregnant – was it for the third or fourth time?

'A delicious meal, Judith,' he said, wiping his mouth. The ratatouille had made blood-red stains on the linen serviette. 'Such a talented cook – *and* a musician, Arthur tells me. One of these days you must play for us. I'm a great lover of classical music, you know. Always have been.'

'Yes – well – one day. I'm terribly out of practice, I'm afraid. I seem to be so busy.'

She squirmed uncomfortably – at his smooth platitudes and Arthur's stale anecdotes and Enid's smug fecundity and her involuntary pleasure in response to his hollow flattery. It was as though, despite all her attempts to numb herself, there still remained a part of her that wanted to be woken and wooed. She was almost enjoying herself when she remembered that the following day they were to break to Solomon the news of their sterility. Suddenly Jonathan ceased to be amusing.

'We'd better be going,' said Enid, rising to her feet with great effort. She had noticed Judith's withdrawal and was feeling uncomfortable. 'It's been a lovely evening, but we have to get back. Babysitters, you know . . .'

Judith nodded, averting her gaze from the sight of Enid cradling her huge belly. Her father had so longed for grandchildren. What would he say when he heard?

'Judith, this is terrible for you.' With a clatter, Solomon replaced his teacup on its saucer, spilling beige liquid over the rim. His hands were unsteady as he tipped the contents of the saucer back into the cup. Dora watched anxiously. 'A terrible loss. For both of you. Are you sure you've tried everything possible? Maybe I should have a word with Hymie Woolf? He may not be a genius, but he has a lot of common sense.'

'Honestly, Pops,' said Arthur, 'we've gone all the way to the top. Couples come from every part of the country – in fact, from all over the world – to consult Benjamin Rogers. If he says there's no hope, well then we really ought to . . .'

'Dad, I think we must accept it.'

There was nothing more to say. Dora rose to collect their cups and switched on the standard lamp in the corner of the lounge. It cast a weak yellow light on the room with its flocked wallpaper and four silent occupants as though trying bravely, against all the odds, to brighten the gloom of that late October Sunday afternoon. Judith was trying equally hard.

'So – that's it then,' she said briskly. 'We'd better be off – hadn't we, Arthur? Didn't you say that you'd arranged a game of squash?'

They had already broken the news to Arthur's parents. Gertrude had dabbed at her eyes for the duration of the visit and shaken her head and, from time to time, tried to tousle her son's thinning hair saying, 'Poor Arthur – my poor, poor boy.'

'It's hard for both of you – and for us, of course,' she had said, the folds of flesh under her chin swaying solemnly. 'But, please God –' (she often abbreviated this to PG for convenience, but the gravity of the occasion called for the full appellation) '– we'll all gain strength from our adversity. And, you never know, one of these days there may be a miracle. The fact that I work with the dead doesn't necessarily mean that I'm a pessimist. Does it, Ralph?'

Ralph had nodded. When they were leaving, he had surreptitiously taken hold of Judith's hand and squeezed it – and for a moment she had thought the determined vivacity she'd been pouring into the afternoon had run dry. She had coughed to stop herself from crying and Gertrude had ordered her husband to thump her soundly on the back ('It's the only way!') and Judith, backing off, had finally recovered her composure. 'It was nothing,' she had explained hoarsely. 'Just a tickle in my throat.'

And now, as she tried to take leave of her parents, her throat was threatening to tickle again.

'Come, Arthur,' she said hoarsely. 'We really have to go.' Why was he lingering so? Couldn't he see that she was struggling for air? That this dark house was choking her?

'Judith!' Solomon was summoning her with outstretched arms. She took a deep breath and, holding it in tightly, submitted stiffly to his embrace. He let her go and she released her breath. Then she turned to the door and his bewildered disappointment followed her into the dim hallway. 'I'm sorry,' he was saying. 'Judith – I'm – very sorry.'

'It's OK, Dad,' she said without turning round. 'It's – one of those – things.'

Dora was standing at the entrance, soft and round and concerned. For a moment Judith had an impulse to bury her head in her mother's neck and beg for comfort. Instead, she applied a light kiss to Dora's dry cheek. 'Bye Mum,' she said. 'I'll try and talk to you during the week. Otherwise we'll see you next Sunday. Definitely.'

In the car, Arthur told her again how pleased he was with the way she was managing the – er – situation. She looked at him, puzzled.

'But what about you?' she asked. 'Surely this affects both of us?'

'Of course. But – I always thought – somehow it was worse for a woman. And – I – can't help feeling – responsible.'

'You? Why? What do you mean?'

He shrugged and refused to elaborate. Instead, he launched once again into his hymn of praise to her maturity and understanding, her self-control – and bravery.

Afterwards she wondered whether things would have turned out differently if she had interrupted his mindless sing-song there and then and told him she wasn't brave or particularly mature. 'Arthur,' she might have confessed, 'I'm numb with terror.' She could have tried to explain to him about the lonely little girl who longed to please her father. She might have caught hold of his arm and forced the car to a halt and, above the blare of hooters and the curses of other drivers, insisted that he listen to her truth and tell her his.

But what use would that have been? Arthur, embarrassed, would probably have looked round uncomfortably and made apologetic faces and loosened his tie.

'Jude, try and calm down. Please.' She could hear him. 'I can understand how upset you are at the moment. Rogers warned me that it was only to be expected. But – um – the traffic's rather – heavy and this isn't really the right place for us to talk. Not here. Not now.'

Of course it wasn't. Arthur was, as usual, being sensible. Who, in their right mind, would try and instigate a tête-à-tête in the fast lane to Finchley? Certainly not the efficient and contained Mrs Goldman, who suppressed her sadness and alternated pleasantries with companionable silences and bland observations until they reached home. Then she sprinkled small talk over her husband's eyes and watched him drifting off to sleep.

'G'night Jude,' he said drowsily, smelling of toothpaste and the antiseptic cream he'd applied to a sore patch behind an ear. He sighed, snuggling beneath their new duck-down duvet. 'Shall I tell you something, Jude? I think we'll be all right, you and me. If we can handle – this – well, we should be able to overcome – anything.'

'Of course,' she murmured, stroking his shoulder and suddenly thinking of the smooth, lean shoulder of Jonathan Bloom and then, guiltily, that perhaps she ought to cook something special for Arthur. Perhaps try that recipe Enid had once recommended. Lamb. Shoulder of lamb in orange and wine sauce. Maybe she'd not been fair on Arthur, inflicting her vegetarianism on him. She would provide him with meat. It was the least she could do.

So she soothed him with lamb. And then *bœuf en croûte*. And when she'd perfected that, she moved on to schnitzels in walnut sauce and finally – her culinary triumph – braised veal with lemon and herb stuffing. In time, Judith became known for her veal. 'Oh, goody!' dinner party guests would squeal when it appeared on the table accompanied (as usual) by parsleyed noodles and whole green beans. 'Our favourite dish. Judith, you *are* good.'

'Your cooking's getting better and better,' Jonathan Bloom said appreciatively the next time he and Enid were invited. 'How about the piano? Have you been finding more time to practise? You ought to, you know. I'm still waiting to hear you play.'

Once, when the third (or was it the fourth?) Bloom child was ill, Enid (a conscientious mother, naturally) sacrificed a dinner party at the Goldmans to stay at its cot-side and Arthur (on duty) was called out to a patient between the *crème caramel* and the coffee.

'Well. Here we are then. Just the two of us.' Within minutes, Jonathan had moved to the chair alongside hers and edged so close that she could see the network of small blue veins at the side of his nose. She allowed him to stroke her hands, from the wrists to the finger-tips and back again, and affected disinterest when he told her how lovely they were, how lovely she was, how often he found himself thinking about her.

'Don't be silly.'

She took refuge in the kitchen, making coffee, clearing dishes, dispensing the last of the veal and a dollop of *caramel* and a large nest of leftover noodles into various assorted Tupperware boxes. Carefully, Judith expelled the air, exactly as her mother-in-law had shown her. It had been one of the few lessons she had allowed herself to be taught by Gertrude.

'Judith.' He had followed her and was standing at the door, watching. 'Do you think that some time – we could – get together – just the two of us? I could easily arrange . . .'

'No. I don't think so.' She replied quickly, but with less certainty than she'd intended. She meant it though. At the time. The prospect of a dalliance with Jonathan Bloom was too disturbing even to contemplate. 'I'm – sorry.'

'Are you sure?'

She nodded.

'Oh, well. I tried. How's the coffee doing?'

He seemed to lose interest after that and a few months later Arthur announced that his partner was leaving him to join a practice in Leeds. And Judith, drifting trance-like through the suburbs, dispensing sensible advice and household hints to other people's wives, the rudiments of music to their children, comfort to Arthur and dutiful attention to her parents, hardly noticed. When awake, she was soundly asleep. But sometimes at night, when she was meant to be sleeping, she was uncomfortably awake.

'Jude – you've been tossing and turning and groaning again,' Arthur would complain. 'Is anything the matter?'

'No, it was just another dream,' she would say, sitting up and blinking and rubbing her eyes. 'Only a dream.'

Was this also a dream? Had Arthur really told her that her father, the father whom she loved so dearly, was ill and old and weak with an unpredictable heart and uncertain prognosis? And had she, his darling Judith, instead of rushing to his bedside, actually said (in a cool and decisive voice that she'd had difficulty recognizing as her own) that, whatever happened, she would hold firm to her demands?

'It's up to you,' he had concluded with doom-laden emphasis. And Judith, replacing the receiver with an angry clatter, had loudly denied responsibility for Solomon's ill-health and railed against the ill-fortune that threatened to sabotage her last attempt to talk. She had a strong feeling of finality. That this was it. She would never try again. And she guessed that even Arthur, despite his accusing cynicism, must have detected her seriousness.

And now? What else was there for her to do but get on with the show? She took a deep breath before lifting the receiver again and dialling reception.

'Would you put me through to Mr Wilmot please. I need to speak to him urgently.'

'Certainly. Of course. Is that Mrs Goldman?'

'Yes, it is.' What had given her this new sense of authority? Had it been the power of her death-threat or a self-assurance born out of her solitary state – or just possession of the Gold Card. Who cared? She would enjoy it while it lasted.

'Hold on please, Mrs Goldman. I'll page him for you.'

There was a click and the music-box chimes of 'Here comes the Bride' rang in her ear. Judith winced and wondered if nature's abhorrence of a vacuum was as strong as some people's aversion to telephonic silence. Were the gaps between human babbling too frightening to allow? She had to endure three rounds of the arrival of the bride, one rendition of the 'Wedding March' and, inexplicably, a speeded-up version of 'Land of Hope and Glory' before Chuck Wilmot broke in with a resonant 'Hel*lo-o*'.

'Can I do something for you, Mrs Goldman? Is there anything you need?'

'Yes please, Mr Wilmot. There's been a minor setback with regard to my conference. A slight – postponement. For which I'll foot the bill, naturally.'

'Er – quite.'

'And, incidentally, I'd like you to make sure that the meeting has no publicity whatsoever. It's private. Strictly private.'

'But naturally. Of course. Leave it to me, Mrs Goldman. I know exactly what to do. We'll organize a – a press embargo. I shall give my team explicit – er – instructions. Immediately.'

Chuck replaced the receiver worriedly and began searching in his various manuals for information on how to run a press embargo. It had seemed the appropriate thing to suggest to that domineering Mrs Goldman, but he had no idea what it involved and there was no relevant entry in either the P or E section of his *Advanced Management Handbook*, and he couldn't face admitting his ignorance to Steve Maplin. As it was, he had an unsettling sensation that things were getting out of control. It was an unfamiliar feeling for Wilmot, who had been convinced since successful toddlerhood that he was 'a born leader'. After all, hadn't his membership of NALGEX been confirmation that he was a person endowed with special gifts? That he would one day accomplish great things?

Arthur Goldman never had any such lofty expectations. He had been the boy who was always left to the last when soccer teams were picked and decided then and there that he was a helpless victim of destiny. From an early age he had known that if there were an odd number of players, he would be the one to be excluded from the game. That was life. Arthur had resigned himself to expect misfortune, but that didn't mean he had to be happy with the way things were going. How could he be?

With an intractably depressed, demanding wife and a bitterly disappointed mother and a father-in-law in a most worrying state of health, surely he couldn't be expected to be jumping up and down for joy – even if the weakened cartilage in his right knee allowed such a show of exuberance? So what made his father-in-law think he had the right to ask him to justify his misery?

'Arthur – why such a long face?' Solomon demanded, his own countenance ashen and miserable. 'Things could be worse. A lot worse.'

Could they possibly? Arthur had returned to Solomon's side after successfully depositing Gertrude and Ralph in a Hendon-bound cab and unsuccessfully attempting to reel in his wife. The stabs at her conscience had been futile. Now he was stuck in this dank flat, in the company of a cantankerous old man who had always made him feel uncomfortable. And things could be worse?

'And so – how are we?' he asked, trying, despite himself, to inject a note of encouragement into his voice. He was a doctor after all. 'I've just spoken to your daughter and she sends you her love.'

Solomon, flat on his back, stared fixedly at the ceiling. He did not respond.

'I tried – to persuade her – to change her mind but . . .'

'No. It's what she wants. We must do it for her.'

He resumed his rigid pose. Arthur, following his gaze, saw flaking paint and yellow patches and heard the loud flushing of a toilet in the flat above.

'That's Seymour Katz.' Only Solomon's mouth moved. 'Now *he's* got problems.'

'Pops —'

The eyes slid towards him warningly.

'— uh – sorry – Solomon. I think we seem to have licked this bug of yours. More or less. What you need now is some rest and lots of fluid with – um – the mineral replacement I prescribed and to carry on with the antibiotics, and by tomorrow, I'm sure . . .'

'Did she say what she wants to talk about?'

'Well – not really. I suppose — I suppose what she'll try to do is to make out what a poor husband I've been. How I've failed her. And honestly Pops – I've done my best. When one considers how *some* husbands treat their wives.'

'And she? Judith? Has she been a good wife?'

'Yes. Of course. Everything one could wish for – until last year . . .'

'I heard. But not from her. She didn't say anything. She doesn't – any more. Has she told you how close we were when she was a – little girl? Did she tell you that?'

Arthur nodded and turned away, unable to bear the sight of the pain that was like an open wound on his father-in-law's face. Throughout his career, he had struggled against his squeamishness. Now, fighting back nausea (was Solomon's disorder communicable?), Arthur crossed the room and tried without success to open a window. He longed to be at home.

'Look – Solomon – it's not good for you to upset yourself like this. We have to get you better. Really. Things will seem – different – when you're back to your old self again. You'll see. What I think we need first of all is – some fresh air. The window seems to be stuck – there! Much better. And now – perhaps we ought to get hold of some soup. Light broth. My mother will probably be able to help with that. She'll be glad to. Tell you what – if you're ready to have a sleep, I'll take myself off and . . .'

'No. Stay here, Arthur. Please. Forget the soup. I'm not hungry. I – want you should sit down and – keep me company. I don't know why it is, but I suddenly feel – afraid.'

Solomon was trying to sit up. Arthur saw his frailty and wondered how he could have been in such awe of his father-in-law for so many years. Solomon had seemed a giant. He had cast an enormous shadow that somehow maintained its size long after age had shrunk his body. But now the shadow seemed suddenly to have lifted, revealing an old, sick and frightened man.

'There's nothing to worry about. Honestly, Pops.'

There was no argument in response to the hated nickname. Not this time. Solomon lay back weakly, resigned to the cost of his admission of fear. He'd been in business long enough to know that there was a price to pay for everything. So – he'd manage without dignity. It wasn't the end of the world.

'Arthur, will you stay here? While I have a little sleep? And then – later – we can have a talk, you and me? Please?'

'Well, I do need to get home at some stage and arrange – things with my parents and – er – Judith. Can't we save our chat for tomorrow, Pops? I'm – terribly tired.'

'Please, Arthur. You can rest – there – on the chair while I sleep. Not for long. Arthur – listen to me – I know you think it's stupid – but I'm frightened that I won't manage to get to Judith – in time. And there are certain things I have to say . . .'

'All right then. Go to sleep, Pops. I'll stay.'

What else could a man do? Refuse someone's last wish? As he sank into the armchair that Solomon had indicated, Arthur couldn't help thinking that this was the second time in two days that he'd been subjected to a demand from the dying. He sighed. It didn't seem fair.

Gertrude, too, was feeling wronged.

'It's not as though we were the ones to *ask* to go along to that hotel,' she said bitterly, waiting an extra minute for the tea-bags to take. She had decided that she and Ralph needed a strong brew to help them recover from the stresses of the morning. 'We agreed to support Arthur – and put ourselves to considerable inconvenience in order to do so. Between you and me, Ralph, I'd have thought that with three out of four in our little party ready and willing to make the journey, the fourth member might have been encouraged to stand down.'

'He's sick, Gert. It's not his fault. So, we'll go tomorrow. What's the hurry? Arthur seemed sure Solomon would be well enough by then.'

'That's not the issue.'

She filled Ralph's cup with dark amber liquid, then remembered that there was no milk. She had cancelled it. This was infuriating. Humiliating. By now they should have been sitting back and being served in a luxury hotel as Arthur had promised – not swallowing black tea in the kitchen.

'I've a good mind to . . .'

She looked up. Ralph had resumed reading the morning paper as though he had only been interrupted for a moment to answer the door.

'Ralph! I don't know how you can sit there as if nothing had happened. Here I am, an absolute wreck, having turned my whole world upside down in order to get away, and you don't care . . .'

'But Gert – there's nothing we can do. I'm simply being

realistic. Why don't you sit yourself down and drink your tea and – later, why don't we take ourselves out for a meal? Just the two of us? How does that sound?'

'Well – I suppose so,' she agreed, amazed at how pleased she was by his suggestion. It had been many years since Ralph had summoned enough energy to generate a *plan*. 'I don't mind doing that – as long as we make sure to pick a place where we won't be recognized. It would be *mortifying* to have to explain why we're still in town.'

She tasted her tea, frowning. Its pungency reminded her of the frustrations of the day. 'Really and truly Ralph – this is an enormous amount to expect us to put up with. I hope Arthur appreciates all our effort.'

Arthur wasn't in a position to appreciate anything. The afternoon seemed endless. Here he was, uncomfortably cramped in Solomon's lumpy chair, dozing and dreaming and waking in chilly confusion, while his wife in her fancy hotel was probably taking tea. Nice milky tea. With a scone or two. And a slice of chocolate cake . . .

Judith, meanwhile, would have been grateful even for the dark amber liquid over which Gertrude was shuddering. For more than an hour she had been waiting in vain for the pot of tea she had ordered. The only other occupant of the Summer sitting-room was Angela. On her own. Her husband, apparently, was still out of action.

'Are you waiting too?' Judith asked her.

'Pardon?' Angela had been lost in a mental replay of her wedding. She had reached the magical moment when Edwin had lifted her veil and kissed her and everyone had clapped. After that there'd been married life and so far it wasn't . . .

'Tea? Were you wanting tea?'

'Um – no. No, thanks. I'm allergic. Always have been. But you go ahead. Don't mind me.'

Judith, defeated, decided to give up. She would retire to the yellow shades of April and contemplate her conference. She rose slowly and started for the door.

'Excuse me – Miss – er – Mrs?'

Angela visibly restrained herself from raising a hand for attention. Four years in teaching (special needs) had made their mark.

'Goldman. Judith. Is – there something the matter?'

'No – not really. It's just that it's sort of – quiet – strangely quiet – around here this afternoon and I was wondering if you knew . . . ? You see, I'd thought we, me and Edwin my fia – husband (gosh, I can't get used to that) were coming to this special place for honeymooners. All sorts of – entertainment and stuff – laid on for couples. We'd saved for ages. And – well, I know it's not anyone's fault about Eddie's back and that, but – it's a bit of a disappointment really. Nothing much to do. And now everyone's disappeared and I thought – well, Ed and me both thought – that you might be a sort of *inspectress* and might know what was happening . . .'

'No, I'm not here in any kind of official capacity,' said Judith, smiling at the speed with which Angela had surrendered personal conjecture to the joint stream of the wedded we. She'd be an ideal wife. 'I'm a guest. Like yourselves. But you're right. There does seem to be an odd sort of – lull. It's rather worrying. Especially with several members of my – er – family due to arrive tomorrow. Shall we try and find out what's happening?'

'Yes – let's.' Angela sounded delighted. This partnership promised more excitement than the one that had been sealed before the altar had provided so far. Eagerly, she sprang to her feet, wobbling precariously in her high-heeled shoes. She'd not expected to need sensible footwear on honeymoon. What *had* she expected? 'Why don't we try the reception desk? Let's see if we can wake someone up.'

They didn't need to. Just as they were about to ring the bell for attention, there was a sudden opening and slamming of doors and agitated footsteps and a volley of shrill invective in a man's angry voice.

It was Ken Mansion. He had resigned. Chuck Wilmot, shocked into silence by the furious stream of abuse pouring from the mouth of a member of his team, watched helplessly as clothes and books and assorted haberdashery made of rubber and leather and plastic foam were slung into the boot of Mansion's mauve Mini. 'I've fucking had it,' Ken declared as he squeezed in a final load. 'That's it. I've fucking bloody – had – enough.'

'Ken, don't do this to us,' Chuck spluttered at last. 'You can't. We'll – we'll sue you, you bastard. It's a company car . . .'

But Mansion had made up his mind. In an emphysemic uproar

of coughing and revving, the vehicle took off – carrying the erstwhile catering executive into the Cotswold sunset and leaving the manager bereft. The car disappeared down the road, trailing behind it part of a black satin brassiere which hadn't quite made it into the boot. It was the last thing Chuck saw.

'Oh God, what do I do now?'

He shut his eyes and kneaded his aching head. Chuck, a sworn agnostic, was desperate. Perhaps some heavenly advice would fill the gaps that had suddenly appeared in the reference material recommended by Associated Institute of Management Training Bodies. Until now, Chuck had been sure his manuals were infallible. But nothing he had ever read had prepared him for dealing with the might of the temper and insubordination that Ken Mansion had displayed. Not only that. The books had failed him miserably when he had needed information about a press embargo. He had been forced to swallow his pride and page for his deputy.

'Mr Wilmot, I've tried everywhere. Mr Maplin seems to have disappeared,' Barbie in reception had announced after a long while. Chuck had been standing over her, fidgeting impatiently.

'Keep paging him. Don't give up. And, while you're about it, try and get hold of my – er – secretary, Linda. Sherryl. Whatever.'

'I – um – already have, Mr Wilmot. She also appears to be missing.'

Chuck had shaken his head, mystified. He'd had to stop himself from sitting down with a severe reminder that *The Pecking Order* (an invaluable authority on authority) had advised against the equalization of eye-levels in the workspace of a subordinate.

'And – Mr Wilmot – there's something else.'

She had fiddled uncomfortably with the heart-shaped locket at her throat. Chuck's sense of foreboding had threatened to overwhelm him. He had placed a soothing hand on Barbie's distraught upper arm and stopped himself from pinching her.

'What?' he had asked through clenched teeth.

It had come out in a torrent. Five guests (a couple and a ménage – hadn't Chuck always *known* that threesomes were nothing but trouble?) had checked out and they'd seemed – slightly unhappy with things. And then that Mr Cockcroft-with-the-bad-back in October had summoned her urgently and made a pass at her. And she had a feeling that Mr Maplin and what's-her-name – Sherryl – were busy doing it in the Sundries

Stockroom because she'd heard funny noises coming from there all afternoon and if anyone knew Mr Maplin's – forgive her – mating sounds, she did. And when she had finally gone to Mr Mansion's room to see if he knew what was happening, she'd – oh, goodness, the things she'd seen . . .

'What?' asked Chuck again, succumbing to his need to be seated. The hell with *The Pecking Order*.

She had covered her face with her hands and through the cracks between her fingers had come words like 'whips' and 'life-size inflatable dolls'. 'Pornographic pictures. Underwear. Shiny boots. *Vegetables*.'

'Enough!'

Chuck had reached the point when a man had to do – what a man had to do. In twenty-seven square-shouldered, purposeful strides, he had covered the distance between reception and the tightly shut door of the Sundries Stockroom.

'Maplin! Out!'

There was silence, broken by grunts and gasps and high-pitched squeals of laughter.

'Maplin, you're in there. I know you are. Will you come out – now. I need you urgently. There are some – crises to consider.'

More laughter. Crashing, thudding sounds. What could they have been doing with the Sundries? The *Sundries*? Chuck had stood there, listening, unable to imagine. Oh, well. Steve had never been short of novel ideas.

'Maplin – Steve – please. Linda. Sherryl. Pull yourselves together. At once.'

There had been no response. And Chuck, undermined and half-demented with a generalized feeling of dread, had decided to approach Ken Mansion as the next-in-line senior executive in the team. Chuck would make allowances for Mansion's supposed deviations and try to enlist his support.

'Chuck – come inside – do.'

Mansion had flung open his door and welcomed him into his room and Chuck had successfully concealed any sign of surprise at the lacy black bra and suspenders in which his catering chief was attired. He had looked neither to the left (at the photographs) nor the right (the shackles) but straight ahead (over the heads of the strange blown-up dolls) into Ken's mascara'd eyes.

'Ahem – er – Mansion. There are various problems that have cropped up this afternoon and I need your – well, for a start, do you have any experience in conducting press embar . . .'

'Wait. Chuck. Before we do anything else, I *must* show you the roughs of the menus I've been composing. Honestly, I've been head down, hard at work for *hours* – as you can see. The state of this place! And here – here are the results. Crumbs, Chuck – I'm utterly exhausted.'

He had pushed into his manager's hands several typewritten sheets. But Chuck was intent on other matters. After all, of what practical use were mere menus when the guests had gone and Management was sporting in the stockrooms and Reception seemed to be breaking down? He had put the sheets aside impatiently and continued his speech.

'As I was saying . . .'

'The menus,' Mansion had interrupted. 'Aren't you going to look at my menus, Chuck? I've put my *all* in them, you know.'

Something had snapped in Chuck then. All the years of temper taming and autogenic training and endless series of exercises to control the will-power had been in vain.

'Bugger your menus,' he'd shouted. 'Forget your God-damned menus and listen to me.'

'What?' That had done it. Talk about being blasted! Chuck had always coped moderately well with scorned women, but nothing could possibly have prepared him for the blistering fury unleashed by a slighted artiste. Within minutes, Mansion, enraged beyond reason, had stripped and changed and packed and, spewing malediction, had transported himself from All Seasons.

And Chuck, miserably watching the spot where the company Mini had disappeared into the horizon, wished fervently it were all a bad dream.

Arthur was having a terrible dream. It had begun quite promisingly but, like real life, was turning into a nightmare. He'd been driving a silver Rolls-Royce with a mighty engine and seats as soft as marshmallow and the shiniest fender imaginable. 'A clever boy,' he had heard his mother telling her friends as she had waved him goodbye. 'I've always maintained he was a clever boy.' Then the ground seemed to drop beneath him and he was up in the sky. Higher and higher, until he was floating in the clouds and into an ice-palace where, on glistening thrones, Judith and Solomon were seated. They were smiling superciliously at his shivering awe.

'Look who's arrived. It's Arthur,' Solomon was saying. 'Poor old Arthur.'

Then, all at once, he was springing out of his throne and smashing the window of the car and pulling, pulling at his son-in-law's arm. 'Wake up,' he was shouting. 'It's time you woke up. It's getting late. Late. Late . . . maybe too late.' And he was shaking the car till it rocked on the clouds.

'No,' Arthur was pleading, terrified. 'No, no, no.'

'What's the matter? Arthur – Arthur – wake up.'

Arthur forced himself to consciousness. 'It's – cold. So cold,' he complained.

'Arthur?'

He opened his eyes. Solomon was beside the chair, tapping his shoulder. The flat was in darkness. The stale smell seemed to have intensified and the temperature had dropped.

'Pops – what are you doing out of bed? You're supposed to be resting.'

'Resting? You think a person can rest with the way you snore and moan. Anyway, I'm feeling better. I managed to sleep a little, woke a little, thought a little. And now – well – I . . .'

'I know. You're hungry. You suddenly fancy some soup. Am I right?'

Arthur stretched his arms. His body was sore and stiff. Maybe the old man would forget about his great need to talk and allow him to leave.

'Shall I give my mother a ring and see what she can do?'

Solomon shrugged and turned unsteadily towards his bed and his legs, scrawny and blue-veined beneath his night-shirt, seemed barely able to support even his meagre weight. Arthur averted his gaze. 'So ring her,' Solomon was saying in a resigned voice. 'If you say I need soup, I'll have soup. Who am I to argue with a doctor?'

He spoke with his usual mixture of deference and irony and Arthur, as usual, was thrown into confusion. He nodded and shrugged with embarrassed modesty. Then he stopped and turned to Solomon, suddenly indignant. This was a new reaction.

'Why do you keep doing this to me, Pops? What right do you have? Making me feel – uncomfortable. As though I'm a fraud somehow . . .' Arthur had never confronted his father-in-law before and his daring made his head spin. He forced himself to continue. 'I *am* a doctor. At least I am that.'

*

Yes, thought Solomon, weakly reaching for the sanctuary of his bed, you are a doctor, Arthur. No one could dispute that.

'You're right,' he said aloud, softly.

'After all,' continued Arthur, his confidence clearly boosted by the ease with which Solomon had slipped into submission, 'I worked jolly hard for it – passed every exam – and I don't think anyone would argue about the success of my practice. At any rate, my patients seem to respect my opinion. What I've done may not seem much to you but – well, Pops – we can't all be a hero . . .'

A hero? Solomon lay back, exhausted. Had Arthur any idea how tiring it was – to seem – to be – a hero?

'I'm not.'

The two words hovered forlornly in the silence. They hung in the thick stagnant air and Solomon saw Arthur step forward as though about to try and catch them and toss them back into the void from where they had been expelled.

'Don't be silly, Pops. You're just being modest. Judith has always told me that you're one of the bravest . . .'

'I'm – not – a – hero.'

Arthur smiled disbelievingly.

'Listen to me, Arthur,' he said, looking away from his son-in-law and fixing his gaze on the opposite wall. 'Please. It's important.'

'Pops, this isn't . . .'

'Everything you've heard about me is a lie. I was never imprisoned by the Germans. I didn't save any lives – except my own. Arthur, I was a coward. Will you tell that to Judith if it should happen that – I don't manage . . . ? Tell her that her father was a poor frightened man who ran away.'

'You're not well, Pops. Everything seems worse when a person . . .'

'Arthur, I've had this on my conscience for almost sixty years. Hear me out. Please.'

Arthur sat down. The old armchair creaked under his weight.

'I didn't run away from the soldiers or the guns, Arthur. That, at least, would have been understandable. No, I ran from the family and – myself. And her.'

'Her?'

'A girl. A Polish girl. I loved her, but the family didn't approve.

How could they? Their Solomon with a Polish peasant! A Catholic! They wouldn't have it. And I couldn't choose between them and – her. So I ran. I came to England. To work for my cousin Joe. A butcher . . .'

He paused, shutting his eyes and lying so still that Arthur was frightened.

'Pops,' he said, standing up. 'This is all in the past. It's all over and done with. It doesn't matter any more . . .'

'I worked here as a butcher. And meanwhile – back home – *they* were – butchered. All of them. Even the girl was killed – for trying to help. I left them – to die. In the ovens. The Nazis took them all.'

Another silence. Solomon was breathing hard. Arthur felt helpless. Was the old man about to cry?

'It's not . . .'

'It is important, Arthur. A man can't die with such secrets in his heart. It was Joe – he started telling people what a hero I'd been. It made him feel good, to have a cousin a hero. And I kept quiet. I always meant to speak up with the – truth. But it got harder and harder. And Dora *admired* me so much. Worshipped me. And then, when Judith came I thought this was my chance – to make up. To bring up a child who would be really brave. I taught her . . .'

He stopped. Arthur waited.

'What I taught her was – how to endure – in silence. And now, it seems, she wants to talk.'

'Exactly,' said Arthur, relieved that the confessional had moved to the here and now. This was much more manageable than the old man's agonies about the murky past. 'That's exactly it! Our main aim now should be for you to recover properly so that we can all set out for the hotel tomorrow. To talk. Right? I'm sure Judith will understand how – difficult – things have been for you. And – er Pops? Solomon?'

'Mmm?'

'Look – I didn't mean you to – put yourself down to make me feel better about being – a doctor. That's not what I wanted.'

'It's nothing to do with that, Arthur . . .' Solomon began. Then he stopped. Did he really imagine that Arthur would hear his story from any perspective other than his own? And Judith? How would she hear it? Would it change anything for her? Maybe the truth-telling would only help Solomon himself to feel better. Forgiven. Perhaps, he thought tiredly as he allowed his eyes to shut, perhaps maintaining the myth for this long had been the price he had paid for the years of deception. His lonely act of contrition. Maybe his silence had been a kind of heroism, after all.

Arthur, meanwhile, had picked up the phone and dialled Gertrude's number.

'Hello – Mom? It's good news. The old m . . . Solomon is feeling much better. I'm sure he'd be able to manage a bowl of your soup now. It would be good for him. D'you think that you can organize something?'

Organīz|e, to give orderly structure to, frame and put into working order.

Chuck Wilmot, utterly disillusioned with the collective wisdom of management skills specialists, had turned in despair to the *Concise Oxford Dictionary*. It was his second-last resort. When he reached the New English Bible, he would know that all was lost.

'Orderly structure,' he said longingly, and remembered how that very morning he had still believed in the logical hierarchy of management as firmly as medieval churchmen had trusted the Great Chain of Being. As implicitly as the scientists who saw every particle of matter locked in the embrace of strict mathematical laws of motion. As devoutly as the autocrat who thought he held the key to political stability.

Then along came chaos.

The weak link that broke the Great Chain. The peasants' revolts that shattered autocracies. The flapping of the wings of butterflies in the Amazonian jungles that caused a tornado in Texas. The crumbling of Chuck Wilmot's world. Judith Goldman. Ken Mansion . . .

'Orderly structure,' Chuch repeated helplessly, and recalled how, a million years before, he had counted on his team and kept tallies of his conquests and sworn by the effectiveness of the *ad hoc* committee. And now?

He rested his head on the open pages of the dictionary and shut his ears against sudden peals of laughter that penetrated the office window, despite a sound-proof guarantee from the country's most reputable double-glazing company. Women's laughter. The discomforting kind of female hysteria that Chuck Wilmot feared would push him over the edge. 'Orderly structure.' It was like a last dying prayer.

But Judith and Angela couldn't hear it. They had been caught outside in a burst of spring rain and were deafened by the deluge and their own shrieks of mirth – at their drenched state, the mauve Mini, Chuck Wilmot's face. Everything. While scientists were struggling with chaos and churchmen sought to bring back belief and politicians pleaded for control and the managing executive of All Seasons feared for his sanity, two women had discovered in less than an hour that the world was irretrievably ridiculous. That all one could do was submit to the rain – and laugh.

WEDNESDAY

It had hardly stopped raining all night. Chuck Wilmot, fighting against insomnia and trying to ignore the violence of the intermittent cloudbursts, had attempted to soothe himself with holistic thoughts and meditational mantras and memories of former achievements. Moments of glory. Women rescued from the jaws of respectability and minor sporting successes and major milestones in a career that had been lush with promise. Everyone had said so.

'Wilmot, you're quite clearly a man of the future,' a personnel officer attached to the Department of Agriculture, Fisheries and Food had once remarked. That had been after Chuck had answered an advertisement seeking an ambitious young executive to promote burials at sea. 'Feed the fish and free our farmlands,' had been the theme of the trial poster campaign he had devised. The officer had described it as 'brilliantly innovative, marvellously convincing' and given Chuck the job.

It had been fulfilling – while it lasted. He had developed a successful series of upper deck funeral packages (with coastal cruises as optional extras) and persuaded the country's largest chain of undertakers to open outlets on the piers of several seaside resorts. But then government funds had been diverted to a European joint venture and commercial sub-aquatic interests were attracted by new sources of North Sea oil and there'd been widespread picketing by gravediggers and sympathetic bodies. In the end, a Committee of Inquiry had been set up and decided (after several months of deliberation) that promotional campaigns for burials at sea should be dumped. And Chuck, redundant but unabashed, had moved on to the middle management of theme parks and finally risen to become the most senior executive of All Seasons – where he sometimes longed for the heady, hopeful days with the DAFF. Providing human fare for the creatures of the deep had been far simpler than feeding honeymooning hotel guests. Especially without a catering manager.

Chuck fought back a wave of nausea and tried to squeeze shut his eyes in a futile attempt to fend off the encroaching rain-soaked dawn. The chaos of the day before had deteriorated into an evening of complete confusion. Honeymooners (the few who hadn't checked out) had gathered in Summer for their Happy Half-Hour and grown restive when, after forty-five minutes, no waiter had appeared.

As Chuck knew well from his study of *The Crowd and The Common Enemy*, adversity united the most disparate elements – even married couples.

'Drinks. Drinks. We want our drinks,' they had chorused – and he could have sworn it had been in two-part harmony. Then the Goldman woman (hadn't he smelt trouble the minute she'd walked into reception?) had demanded the bar keys and, with the giggly little Cockroft wife in tow, had dished out double tots of one thing and another. And finally, after a couple of hours and a sing-song, they'd all started demanding food and Chuck (suffering from the double-vision that usually preceded his most acute attacks of migraine) had made his way to the catering quarters and discovered that the chef-less kitchen was minus cooking sherry as well. All eight – or four – or could it have been only two? – remaining members of the food preparation team were in a state of uproarious inebriation.

'Please. Guys – please. What's happened to our spirit of co-operation? Our togetherness . . .'

But his feeble efforts to regain control were like the cries of the last British officer at the Indian Mutiny.

'Take a grip on yourselves,' he'd called. And the only response had been from his migraine, which had finally besieged him with a vengeance. Half-blind with pain and panic, he had made his way to his room and wondered if the scruffy pair (or had it been a foursome?) he'd thought he had seen emerging from the Sundries Storeroom could possibly have included his trusted deputy manager? That must have been when he'd blacked out.

And now, as Wednesday broke wetly on the Cotswold downs, he felt helpless and still headachy in the face of his administrative and financial crisis – not to mention a conference he regretted he had ever agreed to accommodate. The thought of it filled him with dread.

*

Judith awoke and heard the rain and felt inexplicably light-hearted. She reminded herself of her despair and the death threat and the imminent family gathering – and even these weren't enough to dampen her mood. Nor were the after-effects of the alcoholic dissipation of the night before.

With the toxic wastes of a fair share of the hotel's depleted liquor stocks embedded in her liver, she sat up slowly and tasted sourness – and smiled as she thought of the mega-dose of vitamin C Arthur would prescribe for someone in her condition. To flush out the system, he always said.

A great believer in flushing out the system, was Arthur. Clearing the decks. Beginning again. Spring cleaning. Forgetting. That was probably why he had agreed to her summons. He would try and sweet-talk her into submission, into the safety of unconsciousness and insist that they make a fresh start.

That was what he had done the year before. Administered vitamin C (for purification) and valium (for tranquillity) and selective amnesia (for the pain). And she had swallowed the medicine and tried to purge herself calmly and taken no heed of the ache that refused to respond to any drug her husband could prescribe.

'Jude,' he had said solemnly, 'I know this is going to be hard – but I've decided that it would be best – all round – for us – the two of us - to put the whole – thing – behind our backs. Do you agree?'

'Yes.'

What choice had she had? She had wanted to scream at the pompous clumsiness of his speech and to demand what right he had to decide. For the umpteenth time, she had wanted to tell him of her unhappiness. To talk. To talk. But she had been aware that, as a convicted thief and traitor, she could have lost her liberty or her hands or even her life. Instead, she was being offered oblivion. How generous of Arthur. And how ungrateful it would have seemed to refuse.

'Yes,' she had said, trying to sound as convincing as she could. 'Arthur, you're right. Let's make a – new beginning. We must try and forget.'

And she had. She'd tried. That night she had made iced fruit soup followed by pineapple duck with saffron rice and *crème brûlée,* and they had shared a bottle of Chardonnay, and she had heard the brittle tinkling of her voice as she had chattered about food scares and money matters, environmental concerns and the very latest endangered species. And she had thought how the years had crisped their conversation and sharpened their palate for superior dry wines and enhanced their good taste and taught them nothing. And as she had dished out yet another witticism and a little more duck for Arthur, she had felt ill from the effort of swallowing pain and forcing back memories. But he hadn't noticed her nausea. Or if he had, he'd deliberately ignored it. Even Arthur had known that an anti-emetic would have been useless against sickness of the soul.

'Lovely meal, Jude,' he'd said, wiping his mouth and draining the last of his wine. 'You've really done yourself proud.'

She had smiled, graciously accepting his praise for her food and forgiveness for her treachery. But she had known she was guilty of far more than he knew. She had killed. She, Judith Goldman, was a murderess.

It had started innocently enough. What could have been more wholesome than a Traditional Family Friday Night at Gertrude's?

They had reached the time of evening when family news was generally exchanged. Committee procedure had contributed as much to the ritual of Gertrude's gatherings as the dictates of Jewish tradition. Minutes and matters arising therefrom were dealt with as efficiently as the lighting of the candles and the blessing of the wine. Family news had, as usual, been preceded by an item with a spiritual slant. 'To give relevance to our agenda,' as Gertrude liked to put it, piously.

'Guess what?' Arthur, having extracted the last fibre of lamb from a troublesome molar, stretched out his arms and then rubbed his stomach to redistribute the meat and potatoes and barley soup and apple crumble in an arrangement less threatening to his incipient hiatus hernia.

'What?' Fenella, the middle child, could always be depended on to support big brother Arthur.

'What?' echoed Jake, her husband. Jake was a solicitor and generally came into his own in conversations about conveyancing. On other matters he had little to say.

Joanne, the youngest, glanced at her brother with obliging half-interest but Arthur wasn't satisfied with the response of his siblings. He wanted his wife's attention as well.

'Jude. D'you want to know who's coming back?'

'Who?' asked Judith absently. She was still thinking with some discomfort about the contribution that Joanne's husband, Martin the merchant banker, had made to the spiritual part of the meal. He had looked across the table – at her, she'd been sure his glance had been directed at her – and with a wicked gleam in his eye had asked nonchalantly if anyone knew what the sages had decreed to be the duties of a good Jewish husband.

There had been a general mumble of ignorance. A slightly nervous mumble. Martin tended to touch on subjects that no one else dared broach. He flirted with Judith unashamedly.

'Martin,' Gertrude had said warningly. But she hadn't silenced him. As the richer and better-looking of her sons-in-law, he was allowed certain liberties.

And so, in a heavily ironic voice that had seemed to be aimed at Judith, he had proceeded to outline the obligations of a husband: to maintain and clothe his wife, to ransom her if she'd been captured and to provide for her burial.

'And then,' he'd continued meaningfully, 'there is the conjugal duty of intercourse – with a frequency suitable to the husband's station in life.'

'Martin,' Gertrude had repeated. 'The children . . .' But the children (Fenella's twins and Joanne's little Richard) had already left the table and were far out of earshot. 'Ralph . . .' But Ralph was listening intently, with a small secretive smile. Gertrude had looked away.

'Honestly Mom – we're adults,' Arthur had felt obliged to point out. As the oldest, one of his roles was to liaise between parent and children – even now, when most of the children and their spouses were forty or more.

Gertrude had sat back, defeated, while Martin had gleefully elaborated on the required frequency of intercourse for various occupations. Once every six months for sailors, every thirty days for camel drivers, once a week for ass-drivers and scholars, twice a week for labourers and every day for people who didn't need to work for a living.

'How about lawyers?' Fenella had asked mischievously.

'And bankers?' Joanne had wanted to know.

Judith hadn't asked about doctors. Not aloud. She'd had a sudden disturbing vision of millions of her people performing by rote down millions of years – their sexual history laid out like the score of an endless symphony. Meetings and partings at rhythmic intervals. Long rests to mark the voyages of sailors and Sabbath semi-breves for scholars and countless demi-quavers for husbands at home. And doctors? Her doctor? She had looked at Arthur across the snow-white linen cloth that his mother had starched and ironed, and seen the sterility of their couplings. Week by week. Month by month. Nineteen years of intercourse without issue. Little comfort. The withering of hope. And love? Had there ever been love?

'Who is it, Arthur?' she asked now, in weary response to her husband's question. 'Who has come back?'

But even before he had answered, Judith knew. She fixed her eyes on a small gravy-stain she had discovered on Gertrude's cloth and remembered ratatouille and a hard lean shoulder. And a shiver of fear and anticipation spread from the base of her spine to the back of her neck. Martin, she noticed, was watching her curiously. Arthur was intent on his news.

'Jonathan Bloom. An old partner of mine. Went to Leeds – but it didn't work out. He and Enid have separated now and – well – we're taking him back into the practice. Do you remember Jonathan, Jude?'

'Yes,' she said quickly. 'I – believe I do.'

That was the way it started. Innocently enough. In the safe fold of the family, as a news item on Gertrude's Friday Night agenda. A moment when Judith glimpsed the aridity of her years with Arthur and the mere mention of Jonathan's name conjured the promise of other possibilities. Why he? Why then? Judith, who slept fitfully that night, chasing and guiltily evading tantalizing dreams of a man's body, a man's mouth and a lean, muscular shoulder, could only conclude that it was something to do with the hand of fate.

Two weeks later, she discovered that the hand of fate felt rather pleasant. So did its lips, its chest and various other parts of its anatomy. Arthur had gone to Leicester to attend a two-day conference on the common cold and Judith (after a little persuasion) had accepted Jonathan Bloom's invitation to 'come over for a meal and chat'.

'I think – I'm happy,' she said. The brief meal and briefer chat had been followed by a lingering session of lovemaking on Jonathan's folding bed in his small bachelor flat. This was as far away from the family as Judith had ever been and she wondered why she didn't feel even a touch of remorse. His touch had obliterated everything. She sat up and felt him looking at her.

'You're beautiful.'

'Me?'

'Of course you are. Magnificent. Doesn't Arthur tell you how – lovely – you are?'

'Um – no. Not really. No, he hasn't told me anything like that. I didn't think I was.'

He insisted on proving his belief in her loveliness – again. And later, as they shared Chinese take-aways in his cramped kitchen, he told her how his marriage had crumbled in a bleak suburb of Leeds.

'Things hadn't been – good – between us for many years. Enid was my very first girl-friend, you know. And I was the only one for her – still am, I believe. We were too young when we married. Much too young. And now – well, we're giving one another – space. To live. Explore. Grow. I've – er – gone into therapy and suddenly I'm getting in touch with – all sorts of things. With you.'

He leaned forward and reached for her hand and pressed her fingers to his lips. 'Mmm. You taste of – soya sauce. Judith, you're utterly delicious.'

'Jonathan?'

'Hmm?' His tongue was tracing the fine tracks of her fingerprints, the deeper etchings on her palm. Her life-line. She felt it sliding, slithering, slipping away.

'The children – what about your children?' she asked, her voice harsh and loud in the small flat. She tried to dispel a mental picture of Enid, exhausted and ever-pregnant, with shadows beneath her eyes and puffy white skin that seemed to have been squeezed of nourishment and long deprived of the restoration of sleep. 'Surely this must be – very difficult – for them?'

'Yes. It's not easy. For anyone.' He relinquished her hand and took up his chop-sticks and expertly lifted a mound of egg-fried rice and bean sprouts and sweet and sour chicken to his mouth. 'Enid', he said, chewing intently, 'has family in Leeds. They're giving her a lot of support and the children are surrounded by cousins and things. In a way, I'm the one who has to manage on my own.' He swallowed and looked up at her. 'And you, Judith? How about you? How has – marriage – been for you?'

Like a long, long sleep, she wanted to say. A lonely tower on an island in a grey suburban sea. A place where endless silences are broken by pre-recorded conversations and the ringing of preset ovens containing casseroles prepared for two. Numbness. Emptiness. She wanted to tell him how she had sunk into her dreamless slumber when living had become too tiring – when feeding an insatiable Smile Monster had sapped all her strength. And how she was terrified – too scared to wake up.

'All right, I suppose,' she said instead, imagining Arthur in his Leicester hotel room, indulging in the contents of the free hospitality tray and thinking fondly of his wife. He was fast asleep too, she suspected. But his head was filled with pleasant dreams of how a marriage ought to be and the last thing they'd include would be a scene of adultery. Adultery? Was she, Judith Goldman, an *adulteress*? Yes, she had abandoned her body to that of Arthur's partner. But she couldn't bring herself to offer him the contents of her soul.

'It would have been – easier – if we'd been able to have children.' She couldn't keep the wistfulness out of her voice.

'Yes – Arthur told me,' he said, picking out a plump piece of egg from his hillock of rice. 'A pity for you. Both of you. But – children aren't everything.'

Gripping the egg delicately between the wooden sticks, he inserted it into his mouth, frowned briefly, then chewed, swallowed and sipped. He wiped his lips and looked at Judith with an eager smile.

'How about your music? Do you still play? You once said that you'd play for me. I've never forgotten about it, you know. I'm sure you have no idea how many times I've thought of the two of us together. Truly.'

He paused, his face suddenly serious. 'There was something – about you – that I found – irresistible from the time we came for dinner. That first time, years ago. Ratatouille, was it? I'd never tasted it before. Do you remember it, Judith? Feeding me ratatouille and promising you'd play for me some day?'

'Yes,' she said softly. 'I remember.'

'And will you? Will you keep your promise and play? For me?'

She did. Only once. On a hot July day, after she had locked the doors and checked that all the windows were tightly shut, she went upstairs and retrieved from the depths of her wardrobe a leather-bound volume.

'Here we are,' she said lightly to Jonathan, who jumped to his feet when she reappeared with the book. 'Some Mozart. For you. At last. Are you – familiar – with the Sonata in A?'

He shrugged non-committally and nodded towards the piano. 'Very soon I will be,' he said.

And she, nodding back as she approached the instrument, was amazed at her own composure. At how she had descended the stairs without stumbling and was now lifting the piano lid and balancing the music on its ledge and her hands were quite steady. While inside, in a place he couldn't see – or didn't want to – there was a babble of dissent, a wild chorus of anger, furious voices raging to escape while a huge monster rubbed its eyes and turned over . . .

'It starts with a theme, followed by – I think it's six – variations,' she told him. 'A simple, graceful theme. I'm sure you'll recognize it.'

. . . and it stretched and sighed and made ancient toothless smacking sounds and its yawn was wide enough to rip her apart, to tear her in two. Then it rested for a while. Adjusted its position and lay perfectly still. Ah, such relief. But it was temporary relief, followed by a panic-stricken need, stronger than before, to rouse the creature. To shake it, prod it, kick it awake. God – how desperate she was to feel – something. Even fear. At least it would mean she was alive . . .

'D'you know, Jonathan – this is the first piece I ever performed. Apart from playing for my father, that is. For him – well – naturally – I played almost every day. Gosh – it's been such a long time. I do hope I can remember how it goes.'

. . . which was why she'd agreed to see Jonathan again and again. In his flat, in the park, once in the British Museum and this time – the acme of daring – at home. She had bared her body and allowed him to stroke it and heard him tell her she was beautiful. Majestic. And each time there'd been a moment – an instant when she had become a glorious monarch who had reigned supreme with her handsome consort. But before she could catch hold of it, it had slipped away and she was numb again. Even worse than dead. For she had tasted something else . . .

'Yes, *yes*. Of course. I do know that tune. I'm sure my sister or someone used to play it. And you're doing jolly well. See? Didn't I tell you it was like riding a bicycle?'

'Shh. Listen. The variations. Here come the difficult bits.'

. . .and, like an addict in search of the ultimate fix, she had sought it again. With glazed eyes and a head buzzing with devious schemes for another illicit meeting and half-memories of those tauntingly brief glimpses of something she was sure she must have imagined, she had cooked Arthur's meals and made wifely noises and visited her parents and emitted daughterly sounds. And smiled and been agreeable and thought she would surely go mad. Or had she already done so? Was this madness? Or hell? Nightmares haunted her sleep and the daytime hallucinations became so unbearable that she knew she would have to be woken. There was no other way . . .

'It switches to A minor now. An endless legato. Like the sound of an oboe. Smooth. So sad.'

'Hmm? Oh yes. It's lovely, Judith.'

. . .so she'd turned into a kleptomaniac as well. Not the sort who evaded capture while compulsively adding to a secret store of unneeded items, but the kind of thief who called out to be caught. She had stolen minutes with her lover, then hours, then whole days – and each time she had left clues. An open address book. A cigarette lighter. A scrap of paper bearing his name. Catch me, they'd shouted. Catch me. Please catch me. But Arthur had remained blind to the evidence of her infidelity, stone deaf to her cries. And finally, in desperation, in the glare of a July afternoon, she had lured Jonathan home with the offer of her marital bed and – she'd almost choked on the words – a musical interlude. Dangerous bait. But even this, it seemed, was not enough to stir her to life . . .

'Back to the major key. Do you hear the theme – the thread?'

. . . until suddenly, during the brilliant *forte* of the allegro variation, she stole a glance at her audience. And instead of seeing the handsome, politely smiling face of her lover she saw her father in shut-eyed ecstasy. His little Judith was transporting him to paradise. Then his eyes opened and they widened in reproach when he saw it wasn't his innocent child who was playing. He saw – everything. And her lips moved to defend herself and the monster writhed and the pain, oh the pain . . .

'Judith – you're crying. Is something the matter?'

'No, no – not really. This bit – reminded me of something. I think I'd like to stop now, Jonathan. The next part needs – some practice.'

'Sure. Of course. I'm sure you're being much too modest though. You play brilliantly. Now – come. Sit here. On my lap. Watching you there made me feel so . . .'

'No. We'd better not. Arthur's due back – shortly.'

'He isn't. He can't be. Surgery's not due to end for another hour.'

. . . the pain was more than she could bear. She had forgotten its intensity. The sheer greed of the beast who writhed and licked its lips and anticipated the resumption of its feast. She remembered now why she had opted for numbness instead. Like a sleepwalker, she allowed Jonathan to guide her upstairs and lay passively while he poured his passion and his seed into her inert body. This time there was not even a moment . . .

'When shall we meet next? Can I come here again? There's something – terribly exciting – about having sex with you on Arthur's bed.'

'I – don't think so, Jonathan. I don't think we should meet at all any more. It hasn't been very – wise.'

'Why? Why not? Come along, Judith – you've been every bit as keen as I have. You know you have. What's happened suddenly? Surely it's a bit late to start moralizing now?'

'Jonathan, I've decided. I've had enough.'

. . . he didn't believe her. Finally, reluctantly, sulkily, he started to leave. 'I know all about addicts like you,' he said. 'I know you, Judith Goldman. It won't be long before you come begging for it.'

'No, Jonathan. Not me.'

He knew nothing about her. Nothing at all. After months of penetration into the deepest recesses of her body, Judith had made sure to show him nothing of her soul.

In the weeks that followed, Jonathan made a few half-hearted efforts to fill the gaps in his knowledge. 'Judith, I don't understand you. Can't we meet – just to talk.' But there were other women, a multitude of amenable gaps, legions of eagerly faithless wives. He soon gave up the chase for Judith Goldman. And she, in a self-induced sleep that was deeper than anything she had previously accomplished, erased all conscious memory of him and the blissful moments he'd induced.

It was a while before she discovered that Jonathan had left a calling card which even the profoundest sleep would fail to obliterate. She also learnt, around the same time, that her mother was ill. Dangerously ill and close to death.

'Dad – how is she today?' she would dutifully enquire each morning.

'Not good. Not good at all. I knew the last operation would be too much for her. Told Hymie Woolf to leave her alone. Let her be. But you know these doctors . . .'

'Is she worse though? Worse than yesterday? What does he say?'

'He wants to put her back into hospital. I said no. From now on she stays home – with me.'

'But Dad, she probably needs . . .'

'No. She prefers to be home. I'm keeping her here.'

Every evening, she and Arthur and Solomon would stand solemn-faced at Dora's bedside.

'Try and get her to eat, Pops,' Arthur would say. 'We need to build up her strength.'

'I do. I try. I'm sure she appreciates all the parcels you bring. Don't you, Dora?'

There would sometimes be a faint movement from the tiny figure with its gaunt face and hollow eyes and the hands with yellow claws that clutched at the counterpane. My mother, Judith would dreamily tell herself. That is – was – my mother. She wondered what would happen if she were to rest her head on the pillow, close to her mother's. What if she were to – hold her shrunken body and whisper in her ear, quickly, urgently, trying to catch hold of the last ounce of mothering before it all drained away? Would Dora twitch her response? Would she understand? Judith bent towards her, then stopped. She couldn't do it. She didn't dare.

'See! She moved,' said Solomon. 'She's aware of everything. Mark my words – she'll get better. That's what I keep saying to them. Just you wait. Don't be fooled by my wife. She'll surprise you all.'

But at last even Solomon had to acknowledge that his widowerhood was imminent. Early one Thursday morning he telephoned in a panic.

'Judith! Please come quickly. She's slipping. I'm sure she's slipping. She won't answer me at all.'

'Ring for an ambulance, Dad. Arthur's left for the surgery but I'll be with you as soon as I can.'

Judith had woken feeling even more tired than usual. Jonathan seemed to have left in his wake a cloud of fatigue. The body that he'd caressed and called magnificent had become a burden under which she staggered through her daily tasks. And for the past fortnight or so there had been nausea as well. Great waves of sickness that she tried to swallow back and suppress with weak tea and toast and denial. Surely not? Not her? They had sworn it was impossible. Quite unthinkable. No need to take precautions, she had loftily told her lover. I'm sterile. It's been proven. I am quite, quite barren.

But chance and nature had played a spiteful trick on science and morality. She knew. Despite all the logical reasons why this should not have happened, Judith knew with heavy certainty that she was pregnant.

'Get dressed!' she told herself sternly in response to her father's call. 'Drive carefully to Willesden and take yourself up to his flat and offer him your arms. Gently. Compassionately. Don't think about anything else. Don't think. Don't feel.'

'Judith.'

His tartan slippers. Faded, shabbily moulded to his bunions, but still there. So what? Surely she wasn't about to be moved by a pair of faithful old slippers? She glanced away – and saw the gap where her piano had once stood and then looked quickly back at him. Upward, past the sagging trousers, creased shirt and grey unshaven chin. Past the expectantly half-open mouth and up to his eyes. Those ever-bewildered eyes.

'Dad.'

Back to his slippers. Easier, after all, to focus on the slippers.

'You came too late. She's gone.'

'What?'

'I told you Judith. She – just – went.'

'No.'

Surely he was wrong? He had to be wrong. Mothers didn't simply – go. Not her mother. Surely she was coming back to stand plumply at her husband's side, seeing all and saying little? Waiting – waiting patiently for the time when Judith would finally reach out and melt into her soft arms? No – he didn't know what he was saying. She *couldn't* be gone.

'You're making a mistake, Dad. You must be. Did you call the ambulance? Why are they taking so long? They should have been here ages ago.'

'Judith listen to me. Believe me. Your mother is . . .'

'The ambulance? Where's the ambulance?'

'I – didn't phone. She said no. After I spoke with you I leaned over and said "Dora – Dora darling – hold on – I'm getting the ambulance," and her lips moved and she said "No – hospital – please Solly." So I sat with her. And watched . . .'

'The doctor. Did you call Dr Woolf?'

'Judith – please . . .'

She brushed past him towards the bedroom. She had to see. To find out for herself. 'Mum,' she whispered, peering through the dimness at the still form on the bed, willing it with all her might to flesh out and sit up and be. 'Mum,' she said, louder, putting a tentative hand on a shoulder that seemed to wither under her touch.

And she knew. She had never seen a corpse before, but death seemed as familiar as if she'd know it all her life.

'Mummy!'

It was the cry of an abandoned child. She touched her mother's inert arm and felt the presence of an illicit being inside her and saw her father standing, bowed with sorrow, at the door.

'Dad,' she said, wanting to touch him too. And she took a step towards him, through the sea of guilt and unsaid things and monsters that ate and ate. A single step. But she couldn't come closer. She was terrified that she would drown. The water would close over her and he, in the bubble of his sadness, wouldn't even notice.

'Judith – come – sit down. This is a shock for you.'

He was leading her out of the hot, airless death-room into the light of the lounge. She breathed deeply and steadied herself against the sideboard and heard the drone of distant traffic and footsteps on a faraway unlit pavement. A peal of laughter. The clatter of a milk-float. It was only another day, after all, and hadn't she slept through thousands like it? Didn't she have courage? Easily as much as her father, who had sagged into his armchair, sighing repeatedly. Look at him! She'd show him. She might have failed him in many ways, but at least she coped. She was brave.

Again she made a move towards him and this time the sea seemed to have frozen and she was able to glide across it unafraid.

'Dad – I'm so – sorry.'

She kissed him on the forehead and his sighs turned into racking sobs, but she hardly flinched. 'It's a shock – for both of us,' she said. Calmly. Compassionately.

And with the same calm and compassion she called the doctor and Arthur and made cups of tea and listened to her father mulling endlessly over his wife's last week, her last hours, the final moment.

'At least it was here – at home – the way she wanted,' he kept saying. Judith sat beside him and stroked his shoulder, his arm, his hand. Again and again. Calmly and compassionately.

'Try and sleep a while, Dad. You need to have a rest.'

'You're a good daughter, Judith,' he murmured, relaxing at last. 'No father could wish for better.' His eyelids drooped trustingly and she vowed that he would never find out how bad she really was. Even if it meant losing the being in her belly. She had lost a mother and she had no choice but to sacrifice her unborn child as well.

Dora's dead body received more attention from Gertrude Goldman than it had done during the whole of its sixty-eight years of life. The Hon Sec./Joint Treasurer of the Burial Society arrived promptly with her fellow volunteers to perform the last rites.

'Judith – Solomon – this is tragic. Tragic. What can I say apart from wishing you both a long life?'

It was the traditional greeting of consolation for the bereaved.

'Thank you,' said Judith offering her mother-in-law a determinedly composed cheek.

'Long life,' echoed Gertrude's colleagues with a practised air. They'd clearly had years of experience in processing departures. Judith, mumbling something suitable, remembered an old joke about pious Jews employed by an enterprising battery manufacturer to sanctify his products at the end of the assembly line. 'Long life,' they were paid to intone. 'Long life.' She wanted to laugh. How inappropriate.

'It's an honour to lay your mother out,' Gertrude was saying in her most sanctimonious voice. 'We consider it a great *privilege* to have an opportunity to carry out this – the most sincere act of benevolence. After all, from the dead one cannot expect any favours in return.'

No, thought Judith, picturing the pathetic body of Dora, small and still on her bed. She could do nobody any favours any more. Unless, of course, there was a place called heaven and her mother, by virtue of unquestioning obedience, had somehow made it through the gates and gained access to the ear of God. Hadn't Gertrude taken the hereafter into account?

There was no time to ask. The body had to be washed and dressed in a white linen shroud – a shapeless garment, unisex and universal. Since designer deaths were forbidden to observant Jews, even the richest and most famous ended up as poor and anonymous as Dora Epstein. 'May she come into her place in peace,' recited the surprisingly large group that had assembled around a hole in a North London burial ground to see her off. It included Arthur's colleagues, his mother's committee mates and former consumers of Epstein's meat. 'She looked – *lovely,'* Gertrude could be heard whispering to a friend. 'Hardly anything left of her, of course. But somehow we managed to make the most of it . . .'

A chill wind blew across the cemetery when they lowered the coffin into the ground. Judith and Solomon, the principal mourners, stood together. Judith shivered as the cold air found its way through the cardigan she had torn at the collar as a mark of bereavement. She glanced at her father. He was leaning forward with eyes shut and lips moving furiously – as though he were trying to say something of importance to his wife. There was a thud as the box reached the base of its pit. She took his arm. His lips moved even more urgently, then they were still. Tears slipped down his cheeks. Either he had finished whatever he'd been trying to say, or realized it was simply too late.

He was silent during most of the following week, when they sat in mourning on low stools in the small flat and received callers and recited prayers for the repose of Dora's soul. Judith didn't talk much either. She couldn't take her eyes off the memorial candle that burned on the sideboard and cast tremulous light on the two pictures flanking it. Wedding photographs. Solomon and Dora on the left of the candle, she and Arthur on the right. When Gertrude bustled by – dusting, cooking, organizing prayers – the flame seemed to cower and for a moment the pictures went dark.

Meanwhile, Arthur, who had employed a locum doctor so that he could join the mourners for the week, dispensed sedatives to the family and small talk to the guests.

'Are you all right, Jude?' he kept saying anxiously. She looked drugged. In a trance. And yet she hadn't taken any medication. She had refused each time he had offered.

'Yes, I will be, Arthur,' she was saying. He was sure she

was slurring her words. 'In a while – quite soon – I'll be fine.'

Her eyes stared fixedly ahead and her left hand rose to the place where she had torn her cardigan. Near her heart, Solomon had said. 'A child who has lost a parent should rip a garment in a place close to the heart.' She felt her pulse throbbing and thought about another tiny heart that was soon to be stopped. She imagined the wound, the blood, the letting of blood as, from very far away, from another country, another time, she heard someone saying 'Long life. I wish you long life'.

'Arthur . . .'

'What, Jude? Is something wrong? Can I get you anything?'

'You – asked me if I thought I – needed a tranquillizer earlier on. I think I'd like to change my mind.'

She didn't change her mind about the abortion. She never gave herself the chance. Secretly, unflinchingly, she set things in motion. The small-time thief had become a grand larcenist, but this time she took care not to leave the tiniest clue for she certainly didn't want to be caught.

'The – er – sample I brought in this morning. Is it . . . ?'

'Yes. It's positive. You're pregnant.'

'I am?'

Of course she was. This had been mere confirmation. A step to be taken before the – ultimate step. A surreptitious tube journey to an anonymous corner of London bearing a bottle to an ill-lit chemist shop with 'we do testing' in the window.

'Are you – sure? There isn't the slightest chance that . . . ?'

'Madam, the tests these days are highly accurate. But if you'd like to come back in a week or so, we can do a repeat. Certainly. With pleasure.'

'No. Thank you.'

She couldn't wait. Another seven days and the thing might feel like someone. Then she would lose her courage. Even she.

'Good afternoon. I'd like to speak to somebody about – ending – a pregnancy.' Once she had discovered that abortionists called their activity Family Planning and were listed in the Services section of the local directory (between Factoring and Fancy Dress Shops), it wasn't difficult to get estimates for the job.

'Certainly. If you'd like to hold on, I'll put you through to the right department.'

There was a long pause followed by 'Terminations,' announced in another bored voice. 'Can I help you?'

'Yes. Please. Is it possible to make – an appointment?'

Nothing to it. Arranging for a termination was the easiest thing in the world. She would choose a day when Arthur was busy and take herself off. It would be like going to the dentist to have a tooth out. Even simpler, in a way. Less blood. Hardly any blood at all, they assured her. During the first trimester of pregnancy, abortion was a most uncomplicated procedure. Under the right medical conditions, of course, as the bland-faced doctor pointed out.

'We'll give you a general anaesthetic and clean you out so that all the products of conception are removed. Everything. And you won't feel a thing. Well – perhaps a twinge or two afterwards. But you should be able to go home within a couple of hours. Any questions, Miss – er – Mrs . . .?'

'Epstein. Miss Epstein. No – I don't think so.'

'You're not eating anything, Jude,' Arthur observed on the eve of her appointment. They had told her not to. Nil by mouth, the nurse had said. Judith had nodded silently. Her lips were sealed.

'I – can't,' she said to her husband as she watched him cutting his chips into two and mashing the halves on his fork together with bite-sized bits of beefburger. The chips were the frozen crinkle-cut kind and the meat had been bought ready-mixed and moulded for the grill. But Arthur understood. After all, someone who had so recently lost a mother couldn't be expected to take much interest in preparing (or ingesting) complicated meals.

'I know it's hard for you,' he said sympathetically, squeezing a dollop of ketchup on to his plate. 'But I think you ought to start making a bit of an effort to do – normal things. Try and see some friends. Go shopping. It will probably be difficult at first. But if you were more occupied, it would make it easier for you to forget.'

'I'll try,' she said, turning in revulsion from the red sauce, rare meat and squashed chips and forcing herself not to think about the products of conception. She would make an effort. She'd have to. After she had got through tomorrow.

'All gone,' were the first words she heard, half-awake in the whiteness of the recovery room. They seemed to come from another world. 'Just as I told you – a good old mop-up and everything's back to normal. How do you feel?'

'Sore,' she managed to say. 'Terribly – sore.'

'A couple of pain-killers will fix that. In a day or two you'll be absolutely fine. We've left you in great shape down below, Miss – er – Epstein. Perfectly clean, just as I promised.'

Clean, she repeated in the taxi that jolted her aching body home. Perfectly clean. In great shape. Now, with a little bit of luck, she'd be home before Arthur and she would put herself to sleep. The longest sleep she had ever had. And when she awoke she would feel pristine. Virginal. Thoroughly clean. All the evidence scraped and scrubbed away. Everything gone. Everything?

'Wait – don't go,' she wanted to call out when she finally reached her bed and saw again (was she dreaming?) the departing back of the bland-faced doctor. 'Haven't you taken too much? I feel empty. Quite empty. Surely the unwanted products of conception didn't include – me?'

The hollow feeling persisted and at first she was unable to ignore it. She kept exploring its dimensions and touching its dark places. Recoiling then returning, like a tongue fiddling compulsively with a hole in a tooth. What if she hadn't been brave after all? Would her father have understood her attempt at – courage? And Arthur? Poor, sterile Arthur. Cowardly, lying Arthur. But had she ever really given him a chance . . . ?

She tried to fill the emptiness with food, vast quantities that she ate without tasting and never seemed to satisfy her. And duty. Tireless displays of filial consideration and marital concern. Small, thoughtful deeds. Sweeping gestures. Nothing helped.

After a while, though, she grew accustomed to living with a void. She learnt to avert her gaze from its terrifying blackness and she told herself repeatedly that it – whatever it had been – was all over and she'd been cleaned out and everything was in great shape. That things couldn't be better . . .

Until the afternoon that Arthur came home much earlier than usual and said, 'Judith – there's something I need to discuss with you. It's important. I can't keep it to myself any longer.'

'Yes – sure.'

He'd said 'Judith'. Not 'Jude'. 'Judith'. He knew. He knew it all. The void was gaping in front of her. The ground was crumbling. She'd fall. She wanted to fall. She wanted to die.

*

But he didn't know all. Not about the – baby. He had heard about Jonathan Bloom and after several weeks of indecision had finally gathered the courage to confront her.

'I – er – don't know how to say this and it's been on my mind for a while. But with your mother passing away – well, I couldn't. It didn't seem right . . .'

'Please, Arthur – say what you have to. There's no point hiding it. Not any longer.'

'Right. It's Jonathan. Is it true, Jude? Can it be true?'

He looked directly at her and she saw a film of tears over his eyes and shadows beneath them that told her of his sleeplessness and distress. She hadn't noticed before. In her own morbid slumber, she had been completely unaware. She had ignored his pain just as he had avoided seeing hers. She nodded, wanting to weep – for him.

'It *was* true. But it's over now, Arthur. Long over. I promise you.'

He believed her. Grew almost light-hearted with relief, the euphoria of an ordeal survived, danger averted. The thing was in the open and, yes, she had been unfaithful. But people made mistakes and hadn't she admitted that she'd been unwise? That Jonathan had meant nothing to her and never would?

'He's leaving. Going back to Leeds,' he told her, watching her face carefully to detect any flicker of regret. She reached across the table and tentatively took his hand.

'Arthur – it's OK. He doesn't matter. Honestly.'

She didn't add that nothing mattered except the life she had extinguished. She had owned up to the affair with Jonathan without feeling a thing, but couldn't bring herself to confess to its aftermath. It wasn't that she feared the punishment. Weren't adultery and murder both capital crimes according to Jewish teaching? And how many times could a person be hanged? Anyway, she told herself, hanging couldn't hurt someone already stone dead. So why didn't she tell him everything now? What did she have to lose? She hesitated, then looked straight at him. 'Arthur,' she began, 'Jonathan never mattered but . . .'

'Jude.' He cut her short. 'Now that it's all come out, you don't have to – um – upset yourself with guilt about it any longer. That would be pointless. D'you know, when I overheard the chaps in the squash club talking about it – you and him – I didn't believe them. Couldn't. Not us, I thought. That was naïve of me – wasn't it? To have – *trusted* . . .'

'Arthur, please don't. You said – about it being pointless . . .'

'You're right. Absolutely right. We have to put the whole business behind our backs.'

He repeated that resolve the following night over the *crème brûlée* (preceded by iced fruit soup and pineapple duck with saffron rice). She had cooked the meal as a kind of reparation. An avowal to continue carrying out the functions of efficient Mrs Goldman. A statement of intent.

'Let's make a – new beginning,' she agreed. 'We must try and forget.'

And for a while she succeeded. They managed. She switched on to auto-wife and fulfilled all her duties, and the days and months passed hazily. And meanwhile all the unsaid things, the unsavoury secrets, the unfulfilled longings that she had pushed aside into the dark airless void, were stagnating. Rotting with the putrefied remains of a Smile Monster and the products of conception. Until the odour grew so foul that she choked on it and tried in vain to cover it with air freshener and French perfume and the scent of simmering chicken soup. She tried household cleaners with antiseptic additives which the manufacturers claimed would wipe away doubt.

But still the bad smell seeped out until she could bear it no longer. Until that fine April Sunday when Arthur said – what *had* he said? Something about premenstrual tension and a dustbin that he'd emptied. Not much, considering. But it hadn't needed a lot to release the cloud of fumes and make breathing unbearable and suicide the only way out. An ending. A merciful release – into the factory-made fragrances of All Seasons.

And so? Why on earth did the despairing Mrs Goldman feel so cheerful this Wednesday morning, when she should have been dead? She ought to have been buried by now and beginning to decompose, despite all the enthusiastic ministrations of Gertrude and her team.

Instead of which, never mind a half-demented husband and a sick father and reluctant in-laws who were all on their way to a hotel that was clearly falling apart, she was humming to herself. Smiling irrepressibly at the memory of how she and Angela Cockroft had shared the last bottle of cooking sherry in the deserted hotel kitchen late the night before. The other guests had dispersed and the staff, it seemed, had disappeared.

'To us,' they said, and were overcome by wave after wave of helpless laughter. Judith had come upon the supper menu, conceived and abandoned by the runaway chef.

'It was to have been – escalopes of – sperm whale tonight.' The words were uttered with difficulty. 'Tossed in . . . how vile. Here – read it.'

'Oh.' Angela was speechless. She hugged her stomach, groaning. This was turning out to be the funniest evening of her life. Wait till the girls heard about it. 'Oh, I've lost – my – breath. Gosh. I don't think I can take much more . . .'

But she could. Of course she could. She didn't want it to end.

'D'you want to hear something *really* hilarious?' she asked Judith, who was still spluttering spasmodically as she remembered Steve Maplin crawling out of a cupboard with his flies undone. But Angela's description of what ambitious Eddie had been attempting in the way of sexual athletics before putting himself out of action – *that* took the cake.

'He didn't!' gasped Judith. 'What on earth made him want to do that? Honestly. The utter foolishness of men . . .'

Their laughter subsided. Judith sighed. 'Ah well, I suppose it's time to . . .'

'Poor Eddie,' said Angela. She was suddenly serious.

'Poor *Eddie*? I'd say he deserved all he . . .'

'It's hard for him to be a husband. The thing is, he's not really – cut out – for the responsibility, if you see what I mean.'

Judith nodded thoughtfully. Yes. She saw. She saw how the burden of virility could break a man's back. Virility. Fertility. Effectiveness. Strength. Poor, poor Arthur. How difficult it must have all been for him.

'That's marriage,' she said sadly.

'What? Tell me, Judith. Please.'

'About what?'

'Marriage. How it's supposed to work. Aren't you holding this – conference? I thought you were an expert?'

'No. Not at all. I don't really know – very much. It sounds ridiculous, but after almost twenty years I'm only beginning to find out.'

'Oh.'

Angela looked disappointed. Her lips began to quiver and she dropped her eyes down to the manicured red finger-nails clustered round the stem of her empty glass. She twirled it disconsolately. Judith reached across the table and touched her arm. Wasn't there *anything* she could tell her? Any advice she could offer her? Nothing at all? Not even a few handy household hints? Perhaps the recipe for shoulder of lamb? Or how to make succulent chicken breasts with rosemary and thyme? What would she have said to a daughter? What had her mother said to her?

Judith felt tears rising. Such a terrible sense of loss. Self-denial. The waste of her life, her music, her capacity for love. She remembered a day long ago, when Dora had been waiting for her. Those five nightmare weeks at Grove House had finally ended and Judith, having learnt her lesson in endurance, had at last been allowed to come home.

'Judy – darling. Here. Sit down. I've been cooking for you. All your favourite things.' Dora had tried to feed and comfort her. But Judith, furious and betrayed, had been stiff in her arms.

'I'm not hungry,' she had said coldly.

'Please, Judith – try to understand. We – he – didn't mean to make you unhappy. He couldn't help himself. Sometimes people try and find in their children something they haven't got themselves. I did my best. You know what Daddy's like when he's made up his mind . . .'

'It doesn't matter.' She had turned her back on the laden table. And then, finding herself facing the piano, had turned angrily away from it too. Judith had left the room, catching a last glimpse of Dora with her arms hanging limply at her sides. The sight had haunted her for years. It sometimes haunted her still.

'You're crying,' Angela was saying, looking concerned. 'I'm sorry. I didn't mean to upset you. It's just that you seemed so – tough.'

'No.' Judith laughed wryly. 'You'll probably find that no one is ever what they seem to be.'

Angela frowned, puzzled, while Judith rose to her feet.

'Let's see what we can find to eat in this God-forsaken place,' she said. 'I don't know a great deal about marriage but I'll make you the most delicious omelette you've ever tasted. How about that?'

Judith surpassed herself. It was the best omelette even she had tasted. She enjoyed every mouthful.

And now, still feeling amazingly content (all considering), she stood at the window and watched the unrelenting rain. Was that the sound of a vehicle approaching? Had the family arrived? Surely not. Not yet. She wasn't ready. On the other hand, she was probably as ready as she'd ever be.

Judith peered through the net curtain and saw a large van with Green Lease Limited Ornamental Plant Hire inscribed on either side. Two men in emerald overalls were busy loading it with several pairs of large ferns, four delicious monsters and a couple of yukkas. Chuck Wilmot, watching them with obvious dismay, was waving his arms, shaking his head and making other futile gestures of protest.

'You can't do this to me!' he was shouting.

'Sorry, Guv. Orders,' shrugged one of the men.

Backfiring with such ferocity that Judith feared for the welfare of the vegetation that it carried, the van made a rapid departure. Then it screeched and splashed to a halt in the wet narrow driveway, almost colliding with another vehicle making its way towards the hotel.

'We've come for the telecommunications equipment, Mr Wilmot, sir.'

Judith squinted through the hazy greyness and read 'Rent-A-Fax' on the side of the second van and wondered whether *everything* in the establishment had been acquired on the never-never. The bricks, the beds, the kitchen staff? The management team? The meeting room? Was the whole place about to be repossessed?

Arthur, meanwhile, listened dejectedly to the steady downpour, and kept telling himself it was time to get up and make a move towards regaining possession of his wife. Another move. Finally. He stretched his arms and legs, testing for remaining signs of muscular spasm from the stresses of the previous day, and was amazed to feel hardly a twinge. The resilience of the human body sometimes astounded him – even now, after all the years of exposure to its frailties. The night before, by the time he had finally reached his bed, Arthur had been sure he'd exceeded the limits of his endurance. He ached everywhere.

What a day. What an evening. When Solomon had got things out of his system and finally agreed to accept nourishment, Arthur had fully expected his mother to respond the way she always did to an urgent cry for soup. Immediately and enthusiastically. But at first it had seemed she was going to let him down.

'Arthur! Why are you phoning so late? Your father and I have just – got – home. Just walked through the door. Haven't we, Ralph? Sit down, dear, and I'll make us both some tea. Arthur, I thought you'd have been in bed long ago.' She had sounded breathless. Her voice had been unnaturally high. Arthur had felt uncomfortable. There had been something new and strange about this excited woman.

'Yes – I know it's later than I usually call. But Mom . . .'

'Honestly, Arthur. The price one has to pay to eat out these days. A small Italian place – nothing fancy – and – what did we have? I had melon to start with, and your father had soup. Then we had the tiniest portions of chicken – Pollo-something, they call it – with courgettes and sauté potatoes. And your father had cassata and we both finished off with a little Tia Maria – as a special treat – and it came to – Ralph, what was it again? The bill? How much did we . . .'

'Mom, listen –'

'Never mind, it *is* nice to be taken out now and again. One simply has to shut one's mind to . . .'

'Couldn't you manage to organize some soup for Solomon? He still needs building up – especially if we're still hoping to travel in the morning. I was – er – relying on you.'

'Really, Arthur, at this time of night . . .'

'Mom – please. Don't you usually have some in the freezer? I remember the time when Judith and I both had flu and . . .'

'Well, perhaps. I'll see what I can do.'

Thank goodness. Arthur had been worried for a while, which showed just how edgy he had become. He had always seen himself as a trusting sort of person, but suddenly he had become unsure of everyone. Even his mother. What was happening to him?

'She'll do it,' he had announced to Solomon, hiding his unease. 'I'll pop along to the house – there shouldn't be much traffic now – and we'll have something inside you in no time at all.'

Solomon had nodded. 'Good,' he had said absently. And later 'Thank you', equally absently, after Arthur had endured the double journey in the rain and his mother's martyred mutterings and transferred the miraculously steaming soup from its Thermos flask to a cracked china bowl. The old man had swallowed a few spoonfuls without much interest.

'Why don't you go home now, Arthur,' he had said at last.

'Well – if you're sure you can manage, Pops. Will you be all right?' Arthur hadn't been able to keep the eagerness out of his voice. His bed had beckoned enticingly. 'Of course, I'd only be a phone call away so if you needed anything . . .'

'Don't worry. I'm better. Come and fetch me in the morning.'

The delightful prospect of soaking in his sunken bath and snuggling beneath the duck down duvet had overcome Arthur's misgivings about leaving Solomon alone for the night. He had steered himself homeward, cocooned in his car, feeling tired but remarkably satisfied. Which showed how little he asked for. Only a bit of comfort and reliability. He had parked the BMW and given its fender a fond pat. Comfort and reliability. The features one paid for in a car. Surely they were the least one could ask for in a wife?

At first there had been more. Arthur had been sure of it. 'I know I'm a bit of a romantic,' he would say in the early years, modestly, as though he were reluctantly admitting to a quality that placed him on a higher plane than most other married mortals, 'but I do think we have something special going for us, Jude. Something more than most other couples. A bond. A particular bond.'

She would agree in a vague sort of way, and for a long while he refused to see the vagueness as a kind of absence. He so badly needed to believe that he had found the perfect partner. His helpmate. His other half.

'We're *right* for one another,' Arthur would insist. 'Aren't we an excellent match?'

She would nod, never meeting his eyes, and it took several years for him to understand that he had only married a small fraction of Judith Epstein. What Judith offered couldn't possibly be enough to be someone's other half. Not nearly enough.

But Arthur was prepared to make do, for he had long since stopped hoping for a winning hand. Wasn't it enough that he'd been dealt a few strong cards? For instance, hadn't Judith turned out to be an excellent home-maker – honest, reliable and intelligent? How much more did a person need in a wife? Practically speaking, hardly anything at all.

Sometimes, though, in the darkest pockets of the night or in the safety of his car on a lonely stretch of road, he would summon the image of a dark-haired girl in a Paisley shawl playing the piano with a passion and intensity that stopped his breath. He would remember how she would modestly acknowledge the applause. Then her eyes, searching the audience, would rest on someone who delighted her and she would break into a smile as radiant as the rising sun. Arthur had discovered that the someone had been her father. He longed, more than anything, for the sun to rise for him.

He gave up eventually. But when the memory of that longing came upon him unawares, he would find himself in tears. Silent, shameful tears that he could never confess to anyone, for who would ever understand?

Most of the time, however, he managed to appreciate her assets. He learnt to make the most of the comforts she provided and her sturdy reliability. In fact, he came to rely on those things with a dependency that sometimes frightened him. Arthur suspected they were the only aspects of Judith that he could, with any certainty, call his own.

Then, one Friday night, he had an intimation that even these things were not to be counted on.

It was during one of his mother's Sabbath suppers. Arthur had been finding these gatherings increasingly unpleasant, despite the abundance of maternal adoration and lashings of sisterly loyalty and vast helpings of food. His brother-in-law, Martin (the merchant banker), had taken to mocking him incessantly and, what was worse, he seemed to be in league with Arthur's wife.

A few weeks before, Martin had exchanged meaningful glances with Judith and elaborated on the sexual obligations of a Jewish husband. Arthur had squirmed uncomfortably. He had always been worried about not being up to par in this respect and, after Martin's snide allusions, had felt uneasy for days. Judith, whose behaviour seemed to have become somewhat erratic and secretive since that evening, had done little to reassure him.

'Shall we – er – repair to the bedroom to – um – carry out our conjugal duty?' he had suggested a few nights later. It had been a clumsy attempt at jocularity.

'Oh *Arthur,*' she had said with such scorn that he had been embarrassed to try again for ages. But, as he kept telling himself, these things weren't important. He managed to expel the conversation and the humiliation from his mind (he was good at that) and comforted himself with the knowledge that, whatever happened, there would be a hot meal awaiting him each evening. And the predictable presence of his wife.

'I must hand it to Judith,' he announced to the family at the next opportune Friday, the Friday of his intimation. 'Her suppers are excellent. She has never let me down.'

'Really? Is that so?'

Martin looked from him to Judith and back again with an eyebrow raised in droll enquiry. Arthur wanted to punch him. He clenched his fists.

'Yes. It is.'

'Let me warn you not to be too complacent though, Arthur dear fellow. I was just about to tell everyone what I'd discovered in the Talmud this week about the grounds women have for divorce . . .'

'Martin – honestly,' Gertrude interrupted. 'When I encourage the expression of religious thoughts on the Sabbath, the sort of information you provide is not what I intend. This, I'd like to remind you all, is a *family meal*.'

But Martin was unstoppable. He leaned forward eagerly and Fenella, Joanne and Judith were open-mouthed, eagerly swallowing his every word.

'Did you know', he began, 'that a man who's afflicted with boils is *obliged* to give his wife a divorce if she wants one. The same goes for a chap with bad breath caused by polyps in the nose. And the guy who collects dogs' excrement for a living. Not to mention the coppersmith and the tanner. Malodorous men, it appears, are not for marrying – say the sages.'

'Quite right too,' said Joanne. Fenella, wrinkling her nose distastefully, agreed. And Judith, clearly amused, wanted to know what the ruling would be if the wife had been aware of the man's failing before they were married. 'Wouldn't she have to stick to her vows then, Martin?'

'Not necessarily, Jude. Apparently – and the rabbis will support me – the rule is that even if the husband made it a condition with his wife to marry him in spite of one of those defects, she's allowed to say "I thought I could endure it, but now I see that I cannot".'

'Oh, I see,' Judith said – with what Arthur heard as heavy, loaded emphasis. She looked across at her husband. ' "I thought I could endure it, but now I see that I cannot",' she quoted. Meaningfully. And Arthur was angry at first. Furious. What the hell are you talking about? he wanted to demand. You think it needs endurance, being married to me? Most women would *kill* to have me as a husband. I'm a doctor. A doctor, you understand – not a dog-shit collector.

And then he was terrified. The idea of Judith having reached the limit of her endurance suggested a withdrawal. A gap. An empty space in which even things like comfort and reliability would no longer exist. A cold, uncertain darkness in which Arthur, deprived of any kind of sustenance, would shrivel and die. His worst nightmare.

Arthur knew then that he would have to cling for dear life to the part of Judith he thought he had. He would keep his eyes tightly shut and hold on as hard as he could. He had no choice.

And so, with his eyes closed and hands fiercely gripping the knife and fork she still provided with his excellent evening meals, he managed for a long while to avoid confronting the issue of Jonathan Bloom.

He made sure not to see either the open address book, or the cigarette lighter, or even the scrap of paper bearing Jonathan's name. And he told himself he was imagining things when, one July night, he tossed fitfully in a bed he was certain had been occupied by someone else. It smelled of sweat and aftershave.

'Nonsense,' he muttered to himself. 'What can I be thinking? Judith . . . ? No, Never. We trust one another implicitly. She wouldn't do something like that.'

He tried to use the same terms of denial when he walked in on a conversation in the squash club changing-room a few weeks later. He had returned unexpectedly to collect a towel.

'Why don't you try your chances with the Goldman woman?' someone was calling from one shower cubicle to another in a suggestive sort of way. 'I have it on good authority that she has a magnificent arse. Jonathan Bloom was saying the other day . . .'

Then they noticed Arthur. There was a sudden hush.

'What . . . ?' he began. 'What's – going on?'

'Nothing, Arthur – nothing at all.'

Morrie King cast a quick warning glance at Jerry Glickstein, who smirked and mumbled something about husbands generally being the last to know as he danced from foot to foot and rubbed himself down. Arthur pretended he hadn't heard and afterwards tried to convince himself that it had been gossip. Nasty, vicious, false rumour. Jealousy. Pure jealousy. None of the guys had nearly as good a marriage as his and Jude's. Very few couples had.

Nevertheless, he almost made up his mind to talk to her about it, to clear the air and confirm that the talk was untrue. Then Dora died and he didn't have the heart to confront a person who'd just been made motherless. How could he? Anyway, she needed him. He could see it. She stayed close to his side and clearly depended on his soothing words and his sedatives.

But finally he knew he couldn't put it off any longer. Somehow, he found the courage to ask her directly about her rumoured association with his partner, who had suddenly, mysteriously, announced his intention to return to Leeds. And afterwards Arthur was so hugely relieved that it was out in the open that he hardly considered the inescapable fact that, yes, she'd cheated on him. His Judith. Her body. Her – arse. He didn't even ask himself what had happened to that thing he'd so believed in – the quality called trust.

But at least the affair was over. Of that he was convinced. Arthur had carefully studied her face when he had spoken of Jonathan's departure and observed not the remotest sign of concern. Nothing. Robot-like, she had swept the floor and tossed the salad and served the steak. Arthur had watched her expressionless activity and it had struck him that he would have to be content with even less of his wife than he'd had before. A large portion of Judith seemed to have died.

'Arthur,' she had started to say, with a desperate intensity that terrified him, 'Jonathan never mattered but . . .'

He had stopped her. There had been something more she had wanted to tell him, something she had needed to share. Had it been about the part of her he had never had? The part he longed for and feared? He hadn't been able to hear it, to bear the pain of it, and quickly interrupted her and watched the dull mask close over her face and afterwards felt sick with the knowledge that he had shut his ears and pushed her away.

And so, when she later agreed to make a new beginning, to try and forget, he was glad – almost overcome with gladness – that once again he would have a segment of Judith, no matter how small. An easily digestible morsel, flavoured with enough comfort and reliability to allow him to float through the days on smooth lakes of home-made soup, dreaming of fields of strawberry mousse beneath drifting clouds of the lightest meringue.

Things were all right, Arthur insisted to himself as he basked under bright yellow egg-yolks cooked sunny-side-up and became intoxicated on the aroma of freshly baked bread. He swallowed antacids for his heartburn and kept things moving with laxatives and determinedly ignored the malady which no medication could cure. The unspoken, unheard things that festered inside them both like unattended sores.

Yet somehow he knew for weeks before it happened that the bubble would burst. There were ominous signs. Her long heavy silences. The way she cleaned and scrubbed and tidied, endlessly, obsessively. There wasn't a house in all of North West London as meticulously managed as that of Judith Goldman. The kitchen exuded lemon-scented scouring creams, the lavatories emitted lavender, the packaged aroma of orange-blossoms oozed from the bedrooms – and Arthur smelt trouble.

'Jude, why don't you relax? Take it easy. Give yourself a break,' he tried. 'How about the piano? It would be good for you to have another outlet. That's what I always tell my female patients.'

She glowered at him, as though he were suggesting something obscene.

'Leave the piano out of this. If you're so concerned about my over-exertions, why don't you try doing something round the house occasionally? How about picking up your dirty socks from the floor and putting them in the laundry basket, for a start . . .'

'OK, OK. I will. I'll make an effort.'

He did. Truly. It worried him to see her looking so strained and tired. Even his mother noticed his anxiety.

'You're looking pale, Arthur,' she said, studying him carefully. It was his father's birthday celebration and he had arrived on his own. Judith had announced that she couldn't accompany him.

'Can't you make an effort, Jude? My dad will be disappointed. He really likes you.'

'No. I'm sorry.' She hadn't looked up from the ironing. Her arm had swung back and forth, back and forth like a pendulum. 'Wish your father – the very best – from me.' The pendulum had suddenly seemed to lose some of its momentum. 'And tell him that I would have liked to have been with him – but I can't. I simply can't face them all. He might understand.'

Her arm had stopped moving. For a moment she had been quite still. Almost as though she were about to add something to her explanation. Then she had put the iron down with what he had thought to be an unnecessarily hostile thud and added another perfectly pressed shirt to the neatly squared pile.

'I see,' Ralph said later, understandingly, when Arthur tried to explain Judith's absence. Gertrude, however, failed entirely to see.

'Her *moodiness* must make things very difficult for you, Arthur,' she said. She knew all about her daughter-in-law's indiscretion, as she called it. Everybody knew. But although they talked about it amongst themselves, no one had ever mentioned it to Arthur.

'Mom – it's been a nightmare,' he wanted to cry. 'The pain she has inflicted on me seems to be more than I can bear.' But instead, blinking determinedly, he turned away from Gertrude and fixed his attention on the series of portraits hanging on the far wall.

There was thirteen-year-old Arthur, plump-faced in a prayer shawl on the day of his Bar-Mitzvah. It was the Saturday he was supposed to have become a man. And there was twenty-four-year-old Arthur, slightly leaner-faced in a graduation gown. That was the day he had become a doctor. And, finally, there was thirty-year-old Arthur on his wedding day, with his chest puffed out next to his new bride. A man, a doctor and a husband. What more could a person hope to become? Arthur, aged fifty, drew a deep breath.

'Things aren't so bad, Mom,' he said stoically. 'In actual fact, they're not bad at all.'

But the frightened little boy inside him knew they were very bad. That something momentous was about to occur. A climax. A confrontation. An ending. He dreaded it deep into the nights and most of each day. When it finally happened, it was almost a relief. A reprieve. Now he would do exactly as she demanded. Bring the family, talk things over, calm her down and then take her home. And then? Would things be perfect after that? Was it possible for people to live happily ever after?

Arthur so badly wanted to believe it, and still sometimes confessed to being 'a bit of a romantic'. These days he said it apologetically, for he had come to see it as a weakness rather than a virtue. Privately, he still thought that the best marriages were made in heaven, but if Judith wanted to talk things over, he would let her have her way. He would make absolutely sure that no one would ever be able to say of Arthur Goldman that he hadn't done everything possible to save a marriage, a wife or a life.

*

Chuck Wilmot was desperately trying to save his hotel. 'Morning guys,' he said with rather forced good cheer. Admittedly, he had given in to the heavy-handed withdrawal techniques of the minions of Rent-a-Fax Ltd. But, looking on the bright side, he had successfully resisted the pressures of the Kitchen Appliance Supply Company ('We lend a hand') and Sofa To Go ('Easy chairs, easy terms'). Chuck had made up his mind that, all in all, things could be worse.

Which was what he announced when he had recovered his composure sufficiently to call a meeting. It was to have been a crisis meeting at the uppermost level of management. Just the executive manager and his deputy. Wilmot and Maplin. The crack team. But Steve, answering his bedroom phone sleepily, had insisted that Sherryl Carter be included.

'She's got great ideas, Chuck. I'm sure she'll be a real . . .' He had broken off with a gasp followed shortly by a high-pitched female squeal and Chuck, disgusted, had replaced the receiver and resigned himself to a three-headed conference.

For a moment he had wanted to give up. To abdicate in favour of faith, hope and charity. But he'd caught himself quickly. Who knew where that line of thinking might end?

'The situation is grave – but not irredeemable,' he declared bravely in the Solstice Centre less than an hour later. Steve and Sherryl were locked together attentively. They had moved the furniture to cover the spaces formerly filled with electronic equipment and Sherryl had gathered rain-soaked blossoms and bunches of snowdrops to replace the repossessed rubber plants. After several moments of doubt (sudden change always disturbed him), Chuck had grudgingly conceded that the room looked 'Not too bad – considering'.

'Now guys,' he said, sitting down to establish full frontal contact with his depleted team. Sherryl's front proved somewhat distracting so he tried to concentrate on Steve's. 'What we have here is an organizational hitch. It's serious, but not necessarily fatal. Let us examine the possibilities.' His eyes wandered uncontrollably back to Sherryl's chest.

After a thoughtful moment, Steve cleared his throat. 'Milk them,' he said.

'What?'

'The Goldmans. The members of our meeting. Honestly, Chuck – Sherryl and I have looked at things from every conceivable angle and the only way out of our difficulties is to utilize the gathering. Squeeze them for all they're worth . . .'

'Sure,' Chuck said vacantly, picturing her nipples. Was he losing his grip? 'Miss – er . . .'

'Carter.'

'Miss Carter, would you please take a seat in a separate chair. It would be much more conducive to constructive thought. Steve. You were saying?'

'The Tanning Yard Effect, Chuck. The strategy they taught us at that Florida Convention. Remember?'

'But Steve . . .'

'You know. Keeping guests firmly anchored round a pool that's better for looking at than for swimming. Giving them a free sun-bed and lots of salty snacks – and watching the drinks profits soar. The simplest thing in the world.'

'Steve,' said Chuck wearily, tipping his head in the direction of the rain-streaked window, 'there's a slight problem.'

'The *concept*, Chuck. Surely you can see it. We don't have a pool. Not yet, anyway. What we do have is a meeting-room which, due to circumstances beyond our control, is better for looking at than for communicating in. So what do we do? Keep them here, feed them lots of Strauss (researchers say he's the guy for inducing intimate and expansive feelings) and watch them get hungrier and hungrier for – things. Fashion accessories. Illustrated socks. Personalized Belgian chocolates. Cuddly toys . . .'

'Steve, be sensible . . .'

'I am, Chuck. This is serious. Do you honestly think airports and stations survive on planes and trains? Or that the great cathedrals rely on God? What keeps the coffers of the Victoria and Albert Museum full? Tell me how a nation like ours can afford a House of Lords? Concessions, Chuck. Creating a demand for things that no one could possibly need – and supplying them. We can start with a food court.'

'A – *what?*'

'A food court. You know – burger bar, pizzeria, calorie-counted salad servery, palm-lined eating area . . .'

'I thought that's what you meant. Maplin . . .' He took a step towards his deputy and engaged him in some challenging eyeball-play. 'Are you aware that we don't have a chef? Or a kitchen hand? Or a single potted plant? Hasn't anyone informed you that we have only a few hours to pay for the furniture and to settle the gas and electricity bills and they're about to cut off the phones. And most of our couples have checked out. Two by two, as though they'd guessed the bloody ark had a leak in it. Be realistic, Steve. As I said – the situation's not beyond repair, but one has to look things straight in the eye and . . .'

'Mr Wilmot!' Back into his line of vision came Sherryl's breasts. They were heaving agitatedly. 'The *Sun,*' she was gasping. 'Mr Wilmot, the *Sun.*'

'There isn't any,' said Chuck irritably. Surely she wasn't back on the Tanning Yard tack? He'd had enough. He would have to reassert his authority.

'The *newspaper,* Mr Wilmot. The social affairs reporter. He's coming tomorrow. To cover the conference. And there's the man from the *Mirror.* And someone from the *Daily Mail* . . .'

'Oh my God. The press embargo. I knew there was something I forgot. Maplin, didn't I warn you about no publicity! The woman will be mad as hell. She might go and cancel the whole thing – and *then* where will we be? The meeting's the only thing we have going for us. Our single chance.'

'We thought it would be for the best. We still do. Listen, Chuck . . .'

'*No.* You listen to me. Both of you. The time has come to throw off all the – the hair-brained machinations. Instead, let's examine the issues. One at a time. Carefully. Methodically. Linda – er – Sherryl – will you please take notes.'

Steve glanced helplessly at Sherryl, who was fumbling in her handbag for her stenographer's notebook and a pen. Chuck had acquired a tight smile in the triumphant belief that he had regained control. Wasn't it wonderful how, in the end, decades of management training paid off?

'Right,' he said. 'Are you ready? Number one: Judith Goldman – mollification strategies. The extraction of a substantial advance from the – er – aforementioned, in order to placate the most pressing creditors. Two: the appeasement of other creditors by methods outlined in handbook entitled *Cash Crisis III (Fighting Back).* Three: reversal of illicit publicity moves. Restraint of press. Four: emergency catering arrangements. Five: physiotherapeutic assistance for last remaining male honeymooner. Six: psychotherapeutic support for last remaining members of staff . . . That's about it, guys – I think. Now. Shall we begin?'

By the time the second proposal had been carried by the crisis meeting (with two votes in favour and one abstention), Arthur and his passengers had hit the open road. Despite the rain and the traffic, they had achieved a flawless departure – after a minor delay when Gertrude had insisted on washing her and Ralph's undies from the day before.

'But, Mom,' Arthur protested, 'you were the one who said we should make an early start. I've had to rush like crazy to get here. Surely your knickers can wait until you get back?'

'Arthur!' Shocked. 'Surely you ought to know by now that it's a matter of principle with me never, ever to leave soiled laundry in the house when I go away. Can you imagine if, God forbid, something happened to us and . . .'

'All right, all right.'

He was pacified with a bowl of stewed prunes to eat while he waited. 'I hear you and Mom had a nice time at that Italian place last night,' he said to his father, who was sitting quietly opposite him, still apparently finding items of interest in the previous day's newspaper.

'Mmm?' Ralph emerged from behind the sports section with a bemused expression on his face.

Arthur started repeating his remark, in the condescending and long-suffering tone that he had always heard Gertrude using towards his father. 'I hear you and Mom . . .'

'She's quite a woman, your mother,' Ralph interrupted, speaking almost to himself. Then he looked at Arthur, as though about to communicate to his son a profound truth. 'She's really – quite amazing, Arthur. There aren't many like her, you know.'

And he disappeared into the folds of the paper while Arthur fed the final prune into his mouth. Its sweetness was suddenly cloying. He shuddered and tasted exclusion.

But when she returned and kissed him on the forehead, he felt better. 'There! All done. Thank you for being such a good and patient boy. Come along, Ralph.' It was her familiar, imperious voice. No, nothing had changed. He had imagined it. The tension of the past few days was clearly affecting his judgement.

There was another unnerving moment after they had arranged themselves in the car. 'Are you – comfortable – Ralph – dear?' his mother asked, and Arthur saw her turning round and studying her husband with concern. Real concern. Could it be – tenderness? He swallowed hard as he started the engine, which thankfully responded with its usual prompt purr. Arthur cleared his throat.

'We're on our way, folks,' he said resolutely. 'All Seasons. Without further delay.'

They reached Willesden in record time and Solomon was waiting at the entrance of Willow Court. A small upright figure sheltering from the rain in the doorway. His shabby leather suitcase was propped at his feet and his face, pale and gaunt, was a study in stoicism. A survivor, thought Arthur, with grudging admiration. Whatever the guy had said about not being a hero, he certainly knew something about endurance.

'Hi – Solomon,' he called through the window as he drove the car up to the kerb. 'Wait. Let me help. One second. We'll get you into the car . . .'

'Good morning Arthur. Gertrude. Er – Ralph. It's all right, Arthur. I can manage.'

Repressing a grimace, he lifted his luggage and wedged it into the boot. In silence, he took his seat alongside Ralph. Arthur was aware of Solomon's eyes fixed on his balding head and fidgeted uneasily.

'Sure you're OK, Pops?' he asked, sternly reminding himself of his medical status and assuming his most authoritative doctor-voice. 'I really ought to have examined you properly before giving you the all-clear to travel. You had us all worried yesterday, you know.'

'It wouldn't have mattered what you said, Arthur. I made up my mind. Let's go.'

The engine didn't ignite first time. 'Damn it!' said Arthur, unable to suppress the profanity. He was cross and unhappy and apprehensive and tired, and always felt worse in wet weather. His mother made a restrained gesture of disapproval as the ignition system reluctantly shuddered into action. It clearly wasn't keen on rain either.

'I do hope your motor car's not going to – create difficulties,' she remarked with the weary superiority of the practised passenger. For Gertrude, the moderate inconvenience of being a non-driver had always been amply compensated for by the critical opportunities it created.

'Of course not, Mom. Don't be ridiculous. If you knew anything about cars, you'd be aware that this is about the most reliable model on the market. Why d'you think I paid out all that money . . .'

'They took him away.'

Solomon's words, sudden and loud, cut into Arthur's protestations. There was a brief baffled pause.

'What, Pops? Who?'

'Seymour. Seymour Katz.'

'Oh?'

'My upstairs neighbour. The one who wasn't well. Last night they called an ambulance to take him – to a home, I think. An old people's home. His son came. I heard what happened – the whole thing. But they didn't give me a chance to say goodbye.'

Gertrude perked up eagerly. A parting never failed to arouse her interest. 'Solomon, believe me, these things are usually for the best. I've seen it many times. He'll be far better off where he is. They invariably are.'

'Oh.' Solomon had always been astonished by Gertrude's certainty. He wanted to ask her how she knew. Where had she acquired her all-embracing portfolio of opinions? He would have liked to have asked her if she ever had any doubts, but she didn't give him time.

'Here you are,' she said, unsealing the Tupperware box on her lap and releasing pungent sandwich smells into the car. 'Have something to eat. They've been in the freezer overnight, so they may be a little cold. But they'll do you good. I always believe that one sees things differently through a full stomach. Help yourself, Solomon. Arthur? Ralph?'

Solomon and Arthur, both deep in thought, declined. Ralph accepted cheerfully.

'Thanks, Gert. Excellent idea. Which route are we taking then, Arthur? Have you decided?'

'Through Oxford, I think,' said Arthur distractedly. He was attempting deep breathing to steady his heart-rate.

'At least I'll get some peace at night,' said Solomon. He was trying to talk himself out of an inexplicable sense of loss. He hadn't known he cared so much about Seymour Katz.

'What? When?' Gertrude asked sharply. She hated remarks that seemed irrelevant to a conversation.

'At night. Now that my neighbour has – gone. It was his bladder, you see . . .'

'Never mind. Try a sandwich, Solomon. It will do you good.'

The rain gushed down and the windscreen wipers squeaked. The warm breath of four bodies condensed on the glass. 'It's difficult to see,' frowned Arthur, stopping to wipe the window. 'D'you want to have a look at the map, Mom? We may as well plan our route.'

'Why don't I navigate for a change?'

Ralph's cheerful voice floated to the front. Arthur saw that his father's arm was resting on the back of Gertrude's seat. His hand touched her shoulder in an easy, affectionate way.

'That would be a help, Dad.' Arthur could hardly utter the words. His throat had tightened alarmingly. He coughed and blinked and reprimanded himself for being an idiot – and didn't see a warning light that flashed briefly on the dashboard. Nor did he notice a momentary lapse in the steady hum of the motor after he had slowed down for his assault on the Hangar Lane Gyratory System.

So caught up was Arthur in the turbulence of his emotions that he was blind to the distress of his car, which was exhibiting advanced symptoms of the imminent failure of one of its main engine life support systems. His trusted BMW was going to die.

The signs of mortality at ailing All Seasons were far less subtle than those of Arthur's car. Just as Chuck Wilmot was about to embark on the proposal dealing with emergency catering arrangements, the electricity was disconnected. The Solstice Centre, having little access to natural light, was plunged into semi-darkness and the sort of eerie sub-silence that reigns when technology fails.

'What the . . . ?' Chuck gasped. It felt as though someone had taken his breath away. 'Guys . . .' he said in a strangulated voice, wondering whether a person could suffocate (a merciful release?) when the air-conditioning failed. He suddenly wished some of his management training had been of a more practical nature. Why had he rejected *Understanding Your Wiring* in favour of *The Executive Mind*? Of what use was psychological insight when the lights went out?

'Don't panic,' said Chuck bravely. 'We must all keep – calm.'

Steve and Sherryl seemed calm enough. They were intertwined

in a position of mutual consolation and, although Chuck was a firm believer in the benefits of team spirit, he couldn't help feeling that the Maplin – Carter clinch was detrimental to productivity.

'Ahem. Chaps. Let's proceed with our meeting. It seems that we – er – have an additional item to add to our agenda. Sherryl – please make a note. Emergency lighting measures.'

Reluctantly, Chuck's team separated itself into two.

'We could get some candles . . .' suggested Sherryl eagerly.

'. . . or battery-operated torches and paraffin lanterns and oil lamps,' said Steve.

'Wait. Hold it.'

Chuck had always been opposed to the notion that an agenda could be flexible – even in an emergency. Especially in an emergency. When all around him seemed to have descended into darkness and disorder, he was convinced that it was essential to hold on to the safety of formal procedure. Wasn't that what civilization was all about?

'There are several proposals with which we must deal before we reach the question of lighting,' he said firmly. 'Sherryl – can I take it that you and Steve have composed a message to Mrs Goldman, alerting her to the necessity for a further down-payment? May I see it, please?'

'It's all under control, Mr Wilmot. The note's already been sent to her room. We're sure she'll pay up. Aren't we, Steve?'

He tweaked her nose and nodded. She winked and flashed him a conspiratorial smile.

At that very moment, Judith was pondering over Sherryl's note.

Dear Mrs Goldman (it said),

With reference to your forthcoming conference, there appears to be a short-fall in the sum originally charged to you as a deposit for the use of the Solstice Centre and its facilities. We would appreciate your co-operation in this matter. £500 would do fine.

Thanking you,
Ms Sherryl Carter (formerly Linda),
Administrative Executive.

P.S. News of your conference has been leaked to the press. Don't worry – we'll call them off *if you produce the goods*. It's up to you.

*

She had just reached the postscript when the lights went out. There was a click followed by silence. The grey and rain-soaked countryside suddenly looked brighter than the man-mixed spring tones of April, and Judith moved to the window to consider the postscript. She smiled as its meaning became clear.

The blackmailer being blackmailed, she thought. Just deserts. Retribution – if one could apply so grand a word to the sordidness of her situation in this seedy and disintegrating establishment.

And yet, crazily, she felt real in All Seasons. Wasn't it ironic that here, in a candy-floss construction that was founded on fantasy and greed and was dissolving before her eyes, she had found a sense of her own substantiality? She had sleep-walked through the supposed solidity of suburbia and been numbed by economic security and finally sought the ultimate oblivion. And here, in this hideously vulgar place where she had chosen to die, she was suddenly coming to consciousness.

Life was baffling, unpredictable and suddenly quite interesting, she decided, reaching for the phone. Barbie answered. 'Reception,' she trilled. At least *she* hadn't been repossessed. Not yet anyway.

'This is Judith Goldman speaking.'

'Yes?'

'I have a message for Sherryl Carter. Would it be possible for you to reach her? It's quite urgent.'

'I'm – not sure, Mrs Goldman. Miss – er – Carter is engaged in an important meeting with Mr Wilmot and Mr Maplin. They specially asked not to be disturbed.'

'Could you tell Miss Carter – as soon as you possibly can – that I received her note but will *not* produce the goods. She'll know what I mean.'

Judith smiled as she replaced the phone. Wasn't this fun? It had all become a game. A delightful game. Then she caught herself.

Who was she deluding with thoughts about the emergence of the real Judith Goldman in this crumbling hotel? In the end, she was seen as a wife. A fully paid up and respectable doctor's wife with an authenticated Gold Card. A sterling source of credit. That was all.

She sighed deeply. There had to be something more, she thought. Last night, when she had shared sherry and eggs with Angela Cockroft, she had believed there was something more. But would that something be discovered in a round table confrontation with the family? Through talk – and more talk?

She tried to picture Arthur, his parents, her father – but they were hazy shadows in her mind. Puppet figures in a shiny saloon car, being drawn towards her by strings made of duty, guilt, fear and recrimination. And love, they would add. 'We're doing this out of love.'

Judith tried to think what 'love' meant. Singers had crooned platitudes about it and poets had written odes to it and businesspeople had extracted all its juices. It had inspired movies and theme parks and vast leisure industries, where it was coupled with marriage and marketed and made into a product for family consumption. And a place like All Seasons, where it had been reduced to complimentary condoms in the bedrooms and Salad 69.

No – not love, she decided. Not that sort. Maybe affection or fondness or attachment. A kind of benevolence. Perhaps that's what it came to in the end.

Anyway, further philosophical contemplation seemed pointless when her practical situation was so dire. Judith squinted to see the time. Almost midday. She hadn't heard anything from Arthur, so she assumed they were on their way. In the rain. To a dark hotel and a wife who could no longer see much sense in her demand to talk. Since it was clearly too late to call the whole thing off, she decided to devote some thought to what she was going to say.

But first, she would find Chuck Wilmot and tell him that she utterly refused to submit to blackmail. Not another penny would she advance to the hotel.

At exactly 12.55, while Judith was insisting to Wilmot that no more money was to be had from the Goldman coffers, Arthur's car broke down. The rain had paused briefly to make space for a small snatch of sun.

'That's strange,' said Arthur.

'The sun's out,' exclaimed Ralph.

'Quiet! It's the car.' Arthur looked around disbelievingly. Surely not? This shouldn't be possible. 'She'll start again in a moment,' he said in a panic-stricken voice. 'She always does.'

Gertrude, Ralph and Solomon watched silently as Arthur fiddled with the automatic gear selector and moved his foot up and down on the unresponsive gas pedal. They heard his muttered dismay, but nobody said a word.

At 12.58, the rainfall resumed and Judith concluded her defiant speech. But Arthur's car, which had stopped short in the heart of a market town called Witney, showed no sign of life.

'I did think earlier on that there was something . . .' ventured Gertrude. But Arthur cut her short.

'Shush!' he said sharply. 'Be quiet, everyone. I need – to – think.'

A lorry behind them started to hoot.

'Shut up!' Arthur shouted, opening the door and stepping out into the wet road. 'Can't you see I have a problem?'

Cursing impatiently, the truck-driver reversed his vehicle violently and splashed mud over Arthur as it roared past him.

'Bloody hell!' Arthur sank into his seat and rested his exhausted head on the steering wheel. Had anyone ever been cursed with such consistent bad luck?

'Arthur! Your *language*. There's no need to . . .'

'No need? *No need?*' he demanded, turning indignantly to his mother – and then meekly accepted the Kleenex she held out to him. He wiped his mud-spattered face and sighed deeply.

'And so?' Solomon dared to ask after a while.

'So – what?' Arthur asked back belligerently. Didn't the old man understand anything about disappointment or humiliation? 'We're stuck, Pops. That's what. I'm going to have to call the AA.'

'Oh.' A worried pause. 'And Judith?'

'What about Judith?' The guy was the limit. Here they were, stranded in the rain in the back of beyond, and all he could think of was Judith. 'She's fine. Warm and safe in a luxury hotel and probably sitting down to her lunch. Don't you worry about Judith.'

'She's – waiting for us. We should let her know . . .'

'We will, we will.'

The rain drummed on the roof of the car and streamed down the windows. Arthur, suppressing a shiver, made a mental rundown of emergency resuscitation techniques and treatments for acute shock and the necessity of keeping a patient warm and dry and still. Someone hooted behind them. He didn't hear. He was puzzling over the case of a five-year-old automobile of German extraction whose presenting complaint was prostration by loss of both nervous and muscular power. Sudden and total collapse, with no medical history.

'The ignition system,' said Ralph. 'That's probably it. Wet distributor cap, damp plug leads. Something like that. I had plenty of trouble with cars in the rain in my travelling days. Let's take a look at her, Arthur.'

He had opened his door and was about to step out.

'No.'

Arthur stopped him. He hated the thought of his father fiddling with the innards of his car. And anyway, what could Ralph possibly know about the workings of such an intricate piece of machinery?

'We'd better not touch anything, Dad. It's all very delicate. Highly sophisticated. Automatic transmission and micro-electronic circuits . . .'

Someone was tapping on the window. Arthur wiped away the condensation and peered through the glass and was about to say something irritable when he realized it was a policeman. A large officer with a multitude of badges. Evidently a senior member of the Witney force.

'Terribly sorry about this . . .' Arthur began.

'Your vehicle is causing an obstruction,' the policeman pointed out with solemn deliberation. He looked at Arthur challengingly, as though waiting for him to contradict the accusation.

'Yes, but . . .'

'There's no denying it, sir,' he interrupted, pleased with the response. There was a fair chance of stirring up a case of insubordination here. It was always the same with the small rich ones in big foreign cars. Defensive as hell. 'No arguments now. You'll have to get it off the road.'

'I – can't. It's stuck. It – shouldn't be moved.'

'Course it should. Here. I'll give you a hand. Stick the thing into neutral and Bob's your . . .'

The officer positioned himself behind the car and began to push, and Arthur was sure he heard the engine groan. He grabbed hold of the steering wheel, turning it towards the kerb and trying not to think of the internal dislocation that was almost certainly being caused by this additional trauma to his stricken vehicle.

'There you are, sir. At least it's out of the way.'

Arthur couldn't respond. Stress had rendered him speechless. But Gertrude, beside him, was preening herself back to life.

'*Thank* you, officer,' she gushed.

'My pleasure, ma'am. Glad to have been able to help.'

'Tell me . . .' She leaned across Arthur and looked up winningly at the face of the law. Gertrude loved the law. The sight of a policeman made her feel safe and genteel and *especially* virtuous. Her conscience was always quite clear. 'Do you perhaps know of somewhere near by for us to go and – freshen up? We've been on the road a long time.'

'Certainly, certainly,' he smiled. The law reciprocated Gertrude's fondness. 'No shortage of places here in Witney, ma'am. Why don't you try the Horse and Saddle? There – see it? Just a couple of hundred yards up the road. Nice and clean. Good food. And there's a telephone handy, sir, if you should want to . . .'

'Thanks,' Arthur managed.

'We can phone Judith,' said Solomon, relieved.

'We will, Pops. Didn't I say we would? First I'll have to get in touch with the AA.'

The weary voice that answered the Automobile Association's emergency helpline reported a three-hour delay. At least.

'We're terribly busy,' it complained. 'The weather's been appalling. Cars stuck all over the place. Our patrol teams are going mad.'

'But it's urgent.'

'That's what they all say. I'm sorry, Dr Goldman. You're just going to have to wait your turn.'

Gertrude was surprisingly amiable when Arthur reported that help was not immediately at hand.

'Ah, well,' she said, daintily sipping the tea she had procured from the woman behind the bar at the Horse and Saddle. 'What can one do?'

She and Solomon were seated at a table in the dimly lit saloon lounge. Gertrude, having sniffed and expressed disgust at the smell of cigarettes and beer that hung in the air, had nevertheless pronounced the establishment 'jolly good'.

'We're in the country, of course,' she'd added to Solomon, wishing that he would relax for a moment and stop thinking about his daughter. 'In London I wouldn't *dream* of patronizing such a place. But I must admit that the — *ladies* – was spotless. And, as I always say, one can tell a lot from that. Forgive the expression, but toilets talk. They really do.'

She had paused, then lowered her voice confidentially.

'Actually, it was Ralph who taught me that little bit of wisdom.

An experienced traveller, my husband. Spent *years* on the roads. Extremely difficult for him – but it was his *work.* The children and I had to understand . . . didn't we, Arthur?' she asked her son, who had made his nervous return from the telephone with news of the lengthy delay.

'What?'

'Understand how *necessary* it was for your father to be away from home so much. Sit down, darling. Have a cup of tea. And then perhaps we ought to let Dad come in and warm himself. Wasn't it good of him to have volunteered to look after the luggage? The poor man must be miserable out there in the rain.'

But Ralph, sitting comfortably in the crippled car, was far from miserable. He was lost in a mist of memories that had risen from the rain-drenched countryside. Why was the past suddenly haunting him so?

In London, the streets of Willesden had brought back childhood smells of soup and soap, and the sounds of families squabbling and women sobbing and small boys taunting and old men praying. Real life? Had that been real life?

Or had it been here, where the earth smelt of rain and he had once driven alone through wet country lanes hating Gertrude and relishing his guilty secrets? He took a breath and remembered how, long ago, he'd inhaled cheap perfume in the sort of standard hotel rooms frequented by travelling reps. They had varied only in the names of their locations – and the female partners they had provided for Ralph.

How squalid that all seemed now. How – pathetic. And yet he'd felt good with these women. They had looked up to him. Seen him as somebody. Rich Ralph, they had called him. Generous, kind Mr Goldman. And each time he had returned home expanded, expansive, with gifts for the kids and travel tips for Gertrude, who never, ever travelled and was too stupid and too blinded by arrogance to have suspected a thing. She had never voiced any suspicion, at any rate.

At home, under his wife's self-righteous gaze, he would quickly shrink until he was small and empty and ineffectual – and couldn't wait to be off on his travels again. For years he had cherished a dream (could he really have been so naïve?) that perhaps in one of those hotel rooms, beneath one of the painted faces and somewhere under a padded bra he would find his other. His heart of gold. His love.

But the travelling days had come to an end and, of course, his perfect partner hadn't appeared and Ralph had decided that there was nothing more to hope for. The women had become spectres in his mind. Friendly ghosts, who comforted and amused him at times. Otherwise there were just the endless days and nights and months and years. And Gertrude.

And, until a couple of days ago, he would have sworn that everything was over. That, in the end, his life – married or otherwise – hadn't amounted to much. But now he was suddenly seeing Gertrude in a new light. He might have been imagining it, but she had touched him with tenderness. For a while, he had almost been happy. And now – now there was a strange ache in his chest. Could it be longing? Loss? Possibilities?

What nonsense. The chances were that it was the after-effect of last night's Italian meal. Ralph had eaten too much.

'Dad.' Arthur was at the window. 'Do you want to go inside? I'll stay in the car for a while.' The rain had stopped and the sun was shining. Ralph looked up at him, nodding, and shielded his eyes. He was blinded by the sudden glare.

'Any news about the car?' he asked his son. 'Arthur, don't you think the two of us should have a peep at the engine? I told you – I'm almost sure it's the ignition. Seen this sort of thing a million times in wet weather. You get water into the high tension system and . . .'

'They're coming Dad. The AA. It'll take a while – but one shouldn't take chances with a car like this. We'll have to wait.'

'And Judith? Did you manage to reach her?'

'I tried. Couldn't get through. The line's busy or something. I'll have another go in a . . . What's the matter, Dad? Why are you standing like that?'

Ralph, stepping out of the car, had leaned against the door with his left hand pressing against his chest. Suddenly conscious of his position, he dropped his arm.

'It's nothing,' he said. 'A bit of indigestion perhaps. That's all.' He squared his shoulders. 'The place is up that way, isn't it, Arthur?' he asked, pointing. 'The Horse and Saddle?'

'Yup,' said Arthur absently. He had been alarmed by the frailty he had suddenly sensed in his father. Ridiculous. Neurotic. He was starting to see imminent mortality everywhere. Ralph, for God's sake. Hardly the type to have a heart problem. He didn't have the build. Or the personality. Or the medical history.

'You'll see the place. Just a little way along the main road. And, Dad – can you try and get back here as soon as you've had something to eat? I must make another attempt to get in touch with Judith.'

Arthur could have saved himself the trouble. Telephone communication with All Seasons was impossible. All lines to the hotel had been 'regretfully disconnected owing to chronic non-payment of overdue quarterly accounts'.

'We're *most* sorry about the inconvenience, sir,' the Telecom clerk had told Chuck Wilmot with patent insincerity. Chuck had recognized the tonal cadences from exercises prescribed in Fitzwilliam's *Public Image – Private Lies*. The woman clearly still had some work to do, he had thought patronizingly. But that didn't help him to solve his telecommunication problems.

'Couldn't you allow us a little more time? There's been a temporary – er – hiatus in the cash-flow situation. A couple of days would make all the difference . . .'

'I'd love to. Truly, Mr Wilmot, this is extremely painful for me. But unfortunately I'm under tremendous pressure from above. You know how it is?'

'Yes.' He certainly knew. 'Tell them the – cheque – is on the way.'

So was the Second Coming. Chuck replaced the receiver with an undisguised groan of despair. The hell with public image.

'No luck?' asked Steve Maplin.

'No.'

'What are we going to do about cancelling the press?' enquired Sherryl.

'I don't know.'

'What about my husband – my family? Does this mean there's no way we can reach them – or they us?' asked Judith Goldman, who had interrupted their top-level discussions with a defiant refusal to augment her deposit and wild allegations about blackmail.

'Blackmail?' Chuck had repeated, aghast. An hallucination, surely? Hadn't he suspected from the start that the woman was seriously disturbed?

'Ask your – colleagues. They'll know exactly what I mean. In the mean time, I'd like you to get to the telephone *immediately* and call off the press. Now, Mr Wilmot. I'm waiting.'

'OK, OK.' He had retreated to the phone, wondering how many more hours of analysis it would take to uncover the root cause of his timidity in the face of an aggressive female. That had been when the Telecom person had called to warn of the impending disconnection.

But now the same Mrs Goldman, who had marched into the room with furious black eyes and a stinging tongue, was asking in a sad, lost little voice about her husband and family. Better. Much better. Chuck felt his self-confidence returning with her display of vulnerability.

'Mrs Goldman, I know exactly how you feel,' he said in honeyed tones. 'It must be terribly difficult for you to be cut off like this. Isolated from your family. No lights. No phones. But I do want to remind you that a solution lies in your – er – *lovely* hands. If you'd let us have access to your Gold Card – just *temporary* use, I'd like to stress – it would help us all enormously. Telecommunications, electricity, catering equipment, greenery – all would be restored. Mrs Goldman, you've no idea what a . . .'

'Forget it.'

She was turning her back on him. Walking out of the room. And he had thought he'd been doing so well . . .

'Mrs Goldman, please. Consider our position.'

'No. Not a penny more. I meant what I said.'

She slammed the door behind her. 'Oh well,' began Steve, resignedly. 'A good try, boss . . .'

'Shut up Maplin. Take a seat – both of you. There's unfinished business to conduct.'

He picked up his papers, unable – even he, iron-willed Wilmot – to still the tremor in his hands. His lips twitched uncontrollably. 'I'll get that card out of her,' Chuck muttered, almost to himself. He looked up. Steve and Sherryl were eyeing him curiously. 'Mark my words, both of you, I'll have Mrs Goldman's credit card if it's the last thing I do.'

Even in his demented state, Chuck knew that no Gold Card could possibly make a dent in the mountain of debt that was engulfing All Seasons. But £500 could buy him something more. A respite. A chance – his only chance – to hold on to his precious NALGEX membership and walk out with his head held high and an updated certificate to prove he was still a 'managing force to be reckoned with'.

No – nobody would ever say that Chuck Wilmot didn't count. Not even Judith Goldman, whom he suddenly despised with the virulent kind of loathing that those who are trapped and powerless and broke feel towards a free spirit with a well-lined purse.

Judith, unaware of Wilmot's malevolent thoughts, was rather pleased with her firm-principled stand. For a moment she had been tempted to hand over the goods. She had been panic-stricken by the idea of being held under siege in this dark, silent fortress and would have given everything she had to make contact with someone, to restore the lights.

But she had caught herself. She'd had an inkling of how much he despised her and how pathetically desperate he was. 'I won't give in,' she had resolved, marching through the door and down the corridor and past reception.

'Did you get hold of Mr Wilmot, Mrs Goldman?' called Barbie.

'Yes. Thank you.'

'I do hope his meeting will be over soon. I've been trying to reach the electricians to fix the lights but the phone's out of order and things are a little bit – difficult. Ah, Mr Cockroft. So nice to see you up and about again. What can we do for you?'

Edwin, limping painfully, had approached the desk. Angela was following in his wake, lugging two heavy suitcases. Judith looked at her enquiringly.

'We're leaving,' mouthed the recent Mrs Cockroft. Judith was sure she could detect a twinkle in her eye. 'I decided it was time to go – home.'

'Oh?'

'There's his back. And the food. He says it disagrees with him. Eddie likes simple meals. Home-cooked, preferably.'

'Ah. I see.'

Angela was wearing the white linen dress Judith had noticed when she had watched the couple sign in. But on Sunday a fresh corsage had been pinned to her chest. There had been bounce in her curls and innocent hope in her eyes. Now the flowers had vanished and her blonde hair hung limply round her face. And the hope had been replaced with an amused kind of cynicism.

'Thanks for last night,' she whispered to Judith. 'I'll remember it.'

Judith nodded. She would remember it too. 'Good luck,' she said. 'You'll be all right.'

'I think I – we – will.'

The Cockrofts made their way towards their red family saloon and prepared for their departure. Edwin took his place in the driver's seat and his wife settled down at his side. Judith watched as the car back-fired assertively, then skidded on the gravel and sped away in a cloud of dust.

'Silly idiot . . .' she muttered. Then she remembered what Angela had said about how hard it was for Eddie to be a husband. 'Poor man,' she said, watching the red dot disappear.

Ralph was feeling sorry too. Desperately sorry for himself. So sorry that his normally reliable appetite suddenly and completely deserted him.

He had made his way to the Horse and Saddle and settled himself at the saloon bar table and started tucking into the Ploughman's Platter Gertrude had ordered for him.

'I enjoyed mine so much that I thought you'd like one too,' she had said with a welcoming smile. Contentedly, Ralph had glanced at his surroundings, bringing an eager forkful of pickled onion towards his mouth. Then he'd stopped. His stomach had tightened. He had looked again at the person behind the bar and told himself he was imagining things. 'Course he was. How could he have thought for a minute that there was anything familiar about that busty blonde drawing beer? Silly old goat.

Ralph had sunk his knife into the chunk of processed Cheddar and started fiddling with his hermetically sealed pat of butter.

'Here, let me do that for you, Ralph dear. Modern packaging . . . honestly. It's enough to defeat the strongest of men. But at least this way one knows for certain where the butter's been. There! Eat up now. You look hungry.'

'Uh – thanks, Gert.'

No, it couldn't be. She would have looked older by now. Probably gone grey, lost her figure. This – person, the woman behind the bar, why – she wasn't a day older than say – forty? Which meant that fifteen years before she would have been around . . . twenty-five? Wasn't that about right then?

Squashing the square of butter deep into his French stick, Ralph had tried to expel a mental picture of a scarlet-lipped smile and a naughty wink. She'd always winked at him with her left eye, the eye above the dark beauty-spot on her cheek-bone. 'All real,' she had loved to boast. 'Boobs, legs, beauty-spot. No artificial additives. With Cheltenham Shirl, what you see is what you get . . .'

Cheltenham Shirl. But that had been centuries before, in another life. Surely it had nothing to do with the elderly husband who was allowing his Gert to butter his bread? Shirl wouldn't come back to spook him? Not now?

'Why don't I cut up the cheese for you? Then you can put it on your bread. I'd avoid the onion though, Ralph. The most appalling cases of heartburn have been brought on by pickled onion. Arthur was telling us only just now . . .'

He'd taken one more careful look at the woman. To confirm it was a case of mistaken identity. After the way he'd been indulging in nostalgia all day, it would hardly be surprising for his imagination to be slightly overactive.

'What's up, Ralph? You're not eating. We don't want to spend all day in this place, pleasant though it might be. Do we, Solomon? Come along, Ralph dear. This isn't like you at all.'

'No. I'll eat. In a minute. I'm – not terribly hungry, Gert.'

He forced his gaze back to the bar and watched her, deeply engaged in animated conversation with a customer. Almost facing him. He heard full-throated laughter. Then he saw the wink and the beauty spot and he knew. No denying it any longer. It was Shirley Griffiths. The one and only Cheltenham Shirl. Ralph's heart started pounding and his mouth went dry. He wanted to sink beneath the table. To run. Hide. Disappear.

Gertrude had placed a solicitous hand on his arm. Ralph felt its weight and its warmth and wished that he were still sipping *stracciatelli* soup with his wife at the Trattoria San Marco in Golders Green. He had felt cared for and the future had seemed safe and for a time he had almost dared to think it might be – pleasant.

'Gert . . .' he hesitated, desperately seeking inspiration. 'Your sandwiches.' Of course! Amazing what the mind could do under stress. 'They seem to have quite spoilt my appetite . . .'

'Oh? Was there something the matter with them, then?'

'No, no.' Now he'd done it. 'On the contrary, Gert. They filled me up. And they were – um – so much better than anything a place like this could possibly produce, that it seems a pity to waste them.'

'Absolutely. That's what I've been saying all . . .'

'So, instead of forcing myself to eat now, why don't I go out to

Arthur and keep him company and later, when I'm hungry . . . you'll excuse me, won't you Solomon?'

'Of course,' Solomon said, puzzled by everything. This place was unlike any other he had ever eaten in. He couldn't understand Ralph's odd behaviour or Gertrude's unfamiliar warmth. His departure from Willow Court seemed to have taken place centuries ago. And Judith? How many decades stretched ahead before he would finally see her?

'Well – uh – cheers.' Ralph was rising from his seat, glancing furtively in the direction of the bar. 'I'll be off to the car then. We'll send for the two of you as soon as the AA people have done their thing.'

He took stealthy steps towards the door, eyes down-cast, back hunched, wishing he'd brought along his old checked trilby. Why had he been deterred by Gertrude's scorn? 'Surely you're not going to wear *that,*' she had said, rolling her eyes to the ceiling. 'Arthur's taking us to a very posh hotel, Ralph. A hat like that would be quite inappropriate.' It would certainly have been useful now.

'She'll never recognize me, anyway,' he thought. Step by cautious step, he decreased the distance between himself and the door. 'Not after all the years.' He was doing well. Head down. No noise. Only a few paces more . . .

'Ralph! Ralph Goldman!' he heard in an excited falsetto. 'Gosh. I'd never have believed it. What a surprise!'

Quickly he glanced back at Gertrude. She didn't appear to have noticed anything.

'Shhh!'

Ralph turned to the bar, frowning fiercely. His eyes met Shirley's, which seemed to be staring at – through – beyond him to that once-upon-a-time when he was another person. Rich Ralph. Her cuddly sugar-daddy. 'We're made for one another, you and me,' she had often whispered, tickling his ear with her tongue. 'Leave the bitch and set up home with your Shirl. The times we'll have together . . .'

He remembered how he'd been tempted. Sorely tempted. Of all the women who had fed Ralph's illicit dreams of rescue and redemption, there had been no one who'd matched Shirley Griffiths's persuasive powers. Or her sexual skills. Or her hypnotic way with those cobalt blue eyes – which now, still almost as blue, had shifted their gaze from the face of her erstwhile sugar-daddy to his still-prattling wife in the saloon bar.

'So that's *her*?' she asked, winking.

Ralph nodded. Shirley's beauty spot seemed to have grown. Darkened into a black hole. The end of matter. Perhaps soon, he thought dazedly, he would disappear into billions of anonymous waves and particles. Please God. But, just in case that didn't happen, he would take surreptitious side-steps towards the exit.

There. At last. Gratefully, he gave the brass knob a shove. There was hardly enough strength in his arm to push the swing door open.

'Nice to see you again,' he mumbled over his shoulder as he stepped out into the street. His last glimpse of Shirley had taken in an extravagent head of bleached hair and a black dress that clung to pale crêpe paper skin. Her curves appeared more voluptuous than ever and her narrowed cobalt eyes seemed to be fixed on him appraisingly. Ralph gulped greedy mouthfuls of fresh spring air as he stepped hurriedly over the puddles on Witney High Street. He was hugely relieved. He thought he had escaped.

But he hadn't.

The Automobile Association's harassed patrolman eventually arrived on the scene of the breakdown and decided, after much deep contemplation and examination of parts, that the BMW's prognosis was 'not good'.

'I'd hate to be unduly pessimistic', he said darkly, 'but I've always felt that it's better to face the truth. Brutal perhaps – but kinder in the long run.'

'It's not – fatal?' Arthur couldn't hold back the question. *The* question. How many times had it tremulously been asked of him?

'Well, sir, the thing is . . .' And, with a look of disdain at Arthur, the layman, who couldn't possibly understand the esoteric complexity of his field, he proceeded to reel off a string of technical terms and diagnostic assessments.

'What's to be done?' asked Arthur helplessly, feeling diminished by the weight of knowledge of the Automobile Association and the might of the mechanical establishment. He particularly resented the fact that his father had joined the repair-man at the engine-side and seemed to understand his jargon. 'What course of treatment – er – action do you suggest?'

'I'd have her transported to a garage, for a start.'

For a start? Arthur glanced up and down the unfamiliar High Street with its stone buildings and foreign-looking people and wet patches that sparkled teasingly in the afternoon sun. Was this really happening to him? On Wednesdays he held his weekly Blood Pressure Clinic. He ought to have been gravely in attendance, warning his loyal group of hypertensives about diet and abnormal diastoles and the dangers of stress. Yet here he was, stranded in an old Cotswold town with a car beyond repair and a wife beyond reach. He had learnt from the telephone operator that the lines to All Seasons had been disconnected until further notice.

'I don't know what to do,' he sighed.

'Let's go home,' suggested Ralph eagerly.

'We can't, Dad. Having got this far, we may as well try and reach Judith. Can't be too many miles from here – *and* she's got the Volvo. If only I could get through to that damn hotel . . .'

By the time Arthur had finally given up on the restoration of telephone communication with All Seasons and a low-loader had come and gone with the BMW, the shadows had lengthened over Witney and the single car hire shop was shut. And Gertrude had decided she was 'staying put'.

'I'm *exhausted*,' she declared. 'I absolutely refuse to travel another inch. Not without a good night's sleep.'

That was how the party came to avail itself of the 'Superior Accommodation with Olde English Breakfast' advertised on a prominently displayed brass plaque in the saloon lounge of the Horse and Saddle.

'It's a known quantity,' urged Gertrude. 'At least we're sure that – things – are clean.'

'But Gert,' Ralph tried, 'there must be several other *proper* hotels in the town. I know for a fact that there's a good place called the Crown just a few blocks away. Stayed in it once myself. Wouldn't you like me to . . .'

'No. Don't argue, Ralph. Please. I'm happy here and refuse to move another inch.' She gave him a fond peck on the cheek and he, filled with wistful longing for the kind of marital harmony he had glimpsed the night before, protested weakly but soon surrendered. Minutes later, he found himself helping Arthur to carry the luggage upstairs.

They had been allocated three of the Horse and Saddle's eight bedrooms. Mr and Mrs Goldman were to spend the night in what the management liked to describe as the Bridal Suite. Dr Goldman and Mr Epstein each had a single room. Only one other bedroom was occupied – by the Home and Affairs reporter on the *Milton*

Keynes Evening Echo. He had been sent by his editor to cover a conference on marriage, but seemed to have lost his way.

'And so, Gert. Here we are,' Ralph said, not unhappily, after he had shut their bedroom door and sat down on the (rather small) double bed with a grunt of relief. His wife was completing her sanitary inspection of the facilities.

'Spotless,' was her verdict. 'Not a speck of dirt anywhere. Excellent accommodation. Ralph, darling – aren't you pleased you listened to me about staying here?'

He agreed. Pointless not to. It would be fine, he convinced himself. A peaceful night, tucked up tightly with his wife in a nice country inn. It would be idiotic to spoil things with silly fears about Shirley Griffiths – who seemed to have disappeared. She had probably knocked off by now. Gone home. The odds were that Shirley had forgotten entirely about old Ralph Goldman walking into the bar that morning. It was probably the last thing on her mind.

But Shirley had not forgotten. Celebrating with solitary glee, she had already knocked back four cans of Guinness in the staff quarters of the Horse and Saddle and made several toasts to a more prosperous future. Shirley was convinced that her ship had come in. Laden with goodies, like Father Christmas's sledge. Yup – that's who had arrived. A little early, but who was counting? The one and only, good old Santa Claus.

'Shirls, my poppet,' she said jubilantly, 'if you play your cards properly, all your troubles will soon be over.'

She hadn't recognized him at first. So much had happened since the days with Ralph Goldman (not to mention all the others) that she had sort of wiped him from her mind. And anyway this morning she'd been so caught up in her worries that the Queen Mum might have walked into the pub and she'd not have batted an eyelid.

Money problems, basically. Didn't things usually come down to that? If only she hadn't signed her name to that ridiculous Spanish pub scheme. But it had sounded like a gold-mine – especially after Dick and the guys had fed her a few pints. A winner, they'd said. A dead cert.

But she'd been taken for a ride. Again. Lost the flat, the car, the microwave, the telly. About the only thing she'd been able to hold on to was her Burberry trench coat. They'd have to kill her before they took that! And of course she still had her looks – what was left of them, anyway. She'd been on the point of despair (and Shirley Griffiths wasn't one to give up without a fight) when Ralph Goldman had appeared. Wonder of wonders.

She had seen the way he'd looked at her – craning his little neck, eyes like saucers, hardly eating a thing. And naturally, she'd known at once what was on his mind. 'Naughty, naughty,' she'd thought, winking at a customer and remembering how Ralph had once loved the way she had winked at him. She had sucked in her stomach and stuck out her boobs and felt sexy – and imagined him lusting after her.

That was when she'd cottoned on to the opportunity he presented. And then, her luck being what it was, she'd thought for an awful few hours that he'd left. Just like that. 'Nice to see you again,' he had said – as though he'd meant it. She'd been convinced he had meant it. But then he had walked right out and she had thought her chance had gone.

A little later, though, she'd heard the wife – *Christ* what a battleaxe – talking about staying over and Shirley had known why. Ralph had come back – for her.

'My quarry,' she thought with relish, licking a bubble of foam from her lip as she planned her strategy. Then she suddenly felt bad. Hadn't she always thought of herself as a decent sort? And she'd liked Ralph. Honestly. Of course, he'd have been more of a *man* if he hadn't been under the old lady's thumb like that. But still – she'd grown quite fond of him. Fonder still of his wallet. But she gave as good as she got. Always. It was a point of principle with her.

But now principle time was over. Fate had brought Ralph Goldman back to her, looking as solvent and randy as ever. He probably wouldn't mind helping out an old friend. And if, by chance, he did object – well then, Shirley would have to apply a little pressure. Just a touch.

God, it would be *something* to have a few quid in her hot little hands again . . .

Gertrude, Ralph, Arthur and Solomon had agreed to meet at seven for supper in the Horse and Saddle's saloon lounge. They had washed and changed and Gertrude, for one, was feeling remarkably pleased with things – under the circumstances.

'I think I'll have a small sherry,' she announced mischievously. 'How about you, Ralph? Go on. Have a drink. We're on holiday.'

'Are we?' asked Ralph, who seemed to have lost sight of what this journey was all about.

To his dismay, Shirley Griffiths had far from disappeared. He had spotted her immediately they had entered the bar. There she had stood, with a glass and cloth in her hand, sporting her tight black dress and a surreptitious (and most suggestive) wink. Ralph had almost choked. But, ignoring Shirley pointedly, he had gripped Gertrude's elbow and marched with great determination to the lounge.

'All right – I'll have a whisky then,' he said. His voice had lost all his morning cheer and his chest ached again. 'And you, Solomon? Why don't you have something too?'

Solomon shrugged. He didn't mind one way or another. Four days had passed since they'd had the call from Judith, and he had travelled from Cricklewood to Witney (with a side-trip to an outpost of death) and was worn out. Once, long before, he'd had the vigour to be on speaking terms with God and to complain about his Meals-on-Wheels and to have something important to say to his daughter. Now he felt ancient. A little wiser, maybe, and not quite as – proud. But who knew? Did anyone ever really learn anything? 'Perhaps I'll have a whisky too,' he said. 'Why not?'

'Why not? And Arthur? How about you?'

'A gin and tonic, I suppose. I think I could – do – with a drink.'

Arthur didn't say that lightly. As he frequently liked to remind people, alcohol was a potent drug and was not always treated with the respect it deserved. In this case, though, he reckoned that a medicinal dose was in order. For the pain. A deep, raw, searing sort of pain. The kind that – if it were described to him by one of his patients – would lead him to suspect an internal trauma. A massive haemorrhage.

But Arthur was aware (as far as one could ever be with such a convoluted mechanism as the human body) that his physical organs were in reasonable shape. Something else was hurt and bleeding. Something to do with a wife who had betrayed and eluded him and parents who were behaving – differently. And a car, supposedly one of the most reliable money could buy, that had let him down.

'Sit down, Dad. I'll get the drinks,' he offered. Even in his acute distress, Arthur's conditioning to appear helpful and polite came to the fore.

'Aren't you *good,*' enthused his mother, offering instant reinforcement. Arthur's pain eased as he went to the bar.

The four sat in silence, swallowing their drinks. The men were immersed in their thoughts. Gertrude's eyes darted from one corner of the room to the other and her ears were trained for interesting scraps of conversation. She was having a wonderful time.

'What's the matter with you all?' she asked at last, eager to share her unfamiliar *joie de vivre* with an audience. 'So gloomy! One would have thought there'd been a death . . .'

There was no response. Solomon shifted uncomfortably in his seat.

'Lack of food,' Gertrude announced decisively, after considering for a few moments. 'That's what it is. Hunger. I'm absolutely sure that a good, hot meal will improve everyone's mood. Ralph . . .'

'Mmm?' He turned to her reluctantly, dreading what was coming.

'. . . I'd like you to go the bar and find out what we can possibly have for supper.'

Judith had decided to search the hotel kitchen to see what it offered in the way of ingredients for a hot meal. It was the least she could do to welcome the family. When and if they finally arrived. Thoughtfully, she inspected the meagre array of tins and packets that she had extracted from the grimy cupboards. A few tins of tuna, some button mushrooms, instant white sauce and a bag of salt and vinegar crisps. Hardly an inspiring collection.

The most she could manage would be Tuna and Mushroom Casserole, one of her most reliable short-cut meals. She turned on the oven (amazingly, the gas was still connected) and drained the cans, crushed the crisps, mixed the sauce and baked the mixture until it was golden brown.

Gertrude would probably despise the dish, with its heavy reliance on convenience foods. She was loudly contemptuous of 'heat and eat hostesses' and the 'fish finger school of mothering'. Arthur would be torn between his loyalty to his mother and his appetite. But easy-going Ralph wouldn't object to the food. He never did.

And Solomon? What would her father think? Judith considered

carefully and realized with amazement that for the first time ever she didn't care what her father thought. It simply didn't matter. His views on bravery or music or marriage or even Tuna and Mushroom Casserole weren't of the slightest importance. She was interested, certainly. But suddenly she couldn't imagine why his opinions had mattered so much.

'We all have to do what we – have to do,' she sighed, extracting the casserole from the oven and smiling at the enigmatic, Gertrude-like epithet that had sprung to her lips. Were she and her mother-in-law so very different, after all?

Gertrude, meanwhile, was finding it hard to be philosophical about the length of time it was taking for her husband to make the necessary enquiries about supper at the Horse and Saddle.

'Where on earth do you think he's got to?' she asked Arthur testily, having drained the last drop of her sherry. 'Do you know he's been gone for at least ten minutes?'

'Shall I . . . ?' began Arthur.

But, just then, Ralph reappeared. He looked grey. In shock. Like someone who'd been kicked in the guts. Or worse.

'Where were you? What happened?' demanded Gertrude.

'Nothing happened. Nothing at all,' he answered quickly, managing to recover some composure as he sank into his chair. 'I was feeling a bit – off-colour. Had to go to the loo. The – um – menu will be along in a minute. Supper begins at eight.'

As he spoke, Shirley Griffiths entered the saloon bar and placed a typed card on the table.

'Evening, all,' she said cheerfully. 'Let me know if there's anything special you'd like to order.'

And she was off, hips swaying provocatively, cool as a cucumber. Ralph wasn't a violent sort by nature, but if (theoretically) he'd had access to a weapon, he'd have had no hesitation in killing old Shirl. Making quite sure she was painfully and thoroughly dead.

'Ah – so you remember me then, Ralphie?' she had whispered meaningfully when he'd approached the bar. He had nodded briskly, willing her with all his might to go away.

'I – er – wanted to enquire about supper. What sort of meals do you serve?' He had kept his tone as distant and businesslike as possible.

'Ralph,' she'd breathed, 'it's me, Shirl. Cheltenham Shirl. The George. Room 414. How could you ever forget it? God, the things we got up to. The games. That night you got me tipsy and we dressed up in . . .' Her voice was rising alarmingly.

'Sshhh!'

'What?'

'Be quiet. You don't have to . . .'

'Oh. *Her*. You mean you've been keeping it a secret all those years? Our little secret?'

'Well, Shirley – it's not the sort of thing . . .'

'I – er – don't know about that, Ralph. I quite like being *open* about these matters – and in fact, I've always been – well – *proud* of our – liaison. Such a decent type of fellow, you were. Still are, I presume. And a sense of humour too. When I think of some of the . . .'

'Shirley. Please. Keep your voice down.'

'Serious then, are you? You really mean it then – about keeping her in the dark about who I am? Even now?'

'Of course. It's all over and done with, anyway. There'd be no point in . . .'

'There might. For me, certainly, there just might be some point. In fact – it suddenly occurs to me – why don't I go over to her now and have a little chat to her meself? We could have a real old giggle together – having certain things in common, if you know what I mean . . .'

'Shirley!'

'On the other hand, Ralph. Come – let's slip outside for a moment. It'll be easier to talk. Where was I? Oh – yes. I was going to make a – well, a suggestion. And with you being a generous, understanding sort of man (not like some, I can tell you), I've got a feeling it'll all go smooth as a baby's bum. The thing is, I'm having a touch of – financial embarrassment at the moment. Nothing serious. But if you could see your way straight towards – relieving me – then *maybe* I might lose interest in that pow-wow with the wife.'

'Shirley! What are you saying? This is . . .'

'. . . Bribery? 'Course it is. We're grown-ups, Ralphie. It's the way of the world.'

'I'd simply deny it. You've got no proof.'

'Come, come. Proof? No *proof?* How about that cute little

birthmark I remember so well on your left buttock? Not to mention the scar on your thigh – you know the one from when your Mum bought you a Swiss Army knife for your birthday when you turned – eight, was it? Hmm? Hmm? Golly, I can see them still, plain as a picture. There are no flies on Shirley, Ralph sweetie. Never have been.'

'Listen, Shirley . . .'

'And so?'

And so – reluctantly, he had agreed to subsidize her shortfall. To pay for his past to the tune of £500 in the form of a cheque, which he had promised (what else was he to have done?) to deliver to her personally. They had arranged to meet late that night, after he had made sure, absolutely sure, that Gertrude had fallen soundly asleep.

'Now, Ralphie, don't you let me down, mind,' Shirley had warned him, patting him playfully on the cheek. The cobalt lights in her eyes hadn't been playful at all.

'I'll be waiting up – and if I haven't heard from you by – um – let's say 1 a.m., I might just get a teeny bit impatient and come knocking at the door with some news for the old lady.'

Who wouldn't have felt off-colour after an interlude like that? Ralph had been telling the truth when he had finally forced himself back to the saloon lounge and faced Gertrude and the others. He had indeed sought refuge in the loo. That had been where he'd retreated, making futile attempts to convince himself that the encounter with Shirley would, in the end, turn out to be a mere hiccup. A minor, soon-to-be-forgotten inconvenience. He returned to the table uncomfortably unconvinced.

A while later, after they had thoroughly perused the menu, Gertrude, Arthur and Solomon were engaged in earnest debate about whether or not to risk the Horse and Saddle's Wednesday Supper Special. It was 'Fish 'n' chips in a Basket'.

'Sounds safe enough,' said Arthur.

'The frying oil,' warned Gertrude. 'How sure can we be that it isn't contaminated?'

'Germs,' hesitated Solomon. 'After yesterday, I'm a little nervous . . .'

'Ralph – what do you think?' Gertrude wanted to know. Ralph started. He wasn't used to having his opinion asked. But he couldn't have joined in, even if he'd wanted to. He was dumb with dread.

Judith, too, was feeling uneasy. She had suddenly become aware of the time and the distinct probability that the family would not be joining her for supper after all. She had found and lit a couple of candles, which partially illuminated the darkening kitchen and wondered what she should do next.

The Tuna and Mushroom Casserole, meanwhile, had succumbed to the accelerated ageing process to which quick meals were particularly prone. Its golden crust had become soft and grey. Judith probed the limp surface disconsolately and tried to cheer herself up with the fact that at least Gertrude wasn't there to make smug observations about slipping standards and the dangers of taking short cuts.

'Ah – Mrs Goldman. *Here* you are.'

Chuck Wilmot had slipped into the kitchen holding an electric torch. A bright beam settled on the casserole, spotlighting its deterioration.

'Nice work,' lied Chuck with great zeal. 'Beautiful! I could have sworn the minute I set eyes on you that you'd be an expert in the – er – culinary arts. Never been wrong about that kind of thing. Shall I tell you something, Mrs Goldman? I've always believed that accomplishments in the kitchen are highly underrated. If one thinks about . . .'

'What do you want, Mr Wilmot?'

'Er – nothing. Nothing in the least.'

He switched off the torch and the candles flickered ineffectively in the large dark room. Chuck's body was a shadow and his face looked bleached. He was taking slow steps towards Judith.

'Why don't you leave me alone then?' She was suddenly frightened. For the first time since arriving at All Seasons, she had a tug of real longing to be home.

'Mrs Goldman,' he was saying, 'we need to talk, you and me. No – don't move away from me. There's nothing to fear. Honestly, Mrs Goldman, we're *friends.* We could be, anyway. You're a very attractive woman.'

'Mr Wilmot – what do you want? If it's . . .'

'For us to understand one another. To talk. Explain things. That's all. To assure you, for a start, that I had nothing to do with the – er – threatening tone that you perceived in the note from my colleagues.'

'Where are they? Where's everyone?'

'Ah. Well. Mr Maplin and Miss Carter have been – er – summoned by headquarters. For a meeting. As for the rest . . .'

'How come nothing's being done about the lights, the phones? Will you please tell me what has happened to all the people?'

'Mrs Goldman, don't you worry your – delightful – head about such matters. Leave these things to me. You're a guest. *My* guest. It's enough that you should have been good enough to have prepared this *magnificent* repast. Come with me. Let's find somewhere more comfortable and we can have a nice cosy drink together, the two of us, and get to know each other properly . . .'

He placed his arm round her shoulder with a subtlety that, over scores of seductions, had been perfected till it had achieved the optimum balance between masterly assurance and divine sensitivity. Judith found herself being guided to the sitting-room, which could no longer be called Summer with any degree of authenticity. It was dark and chilly and almost bare.

'Here. Take a seat. Next to me. Mmm – you feel wonderful. Delicious. In fact, I could . . .'

'Mr Wilmot.'

Judith stood up sharply. Surely she hadn't almost fallen for his technical dexterity – again? This time his smell had brought her to consciousness. A puzzlingly familiar combination of sandalwood and soap and sweat that she couldn't quite place. Then suddenly, with a sick churning of her stomach, she had remembered the aroma of Jonathan Bloom. She struggled to control her voice.

'Mr Wilmot, I'm not really in the mood for – exchanging confidences – right now. It's late and I'm tired and worried about what could have happened to the people I've been expecting. So, if you'll excuse me . . .'

'Wait. One second, Mrs Goldman. You know what they say about a trouble shared?'

But she was unyielding. She strode resolutely to the kitchen where she appropriated Chuck's torch. He was about to object.

'Help yourself to some Tuna and Mushroom Casserole,' he heard her calling. 'I'm sure it tastes better than it looks.'

It couldn't taste worse, he thought spitefully. The hatred he'd felt for her earlier that day returned in a poisonous wave. She had denied him a temporary loan. Refused him a chance to hold on to his NALGEX card, his dearest possession, his identity badge.

And now she had spurned him sexually. She had rejected Chuck Wilmot, body and soul.

She would pay for this, he vowed with manic intensity. Judith Goldman had better watch out.

Ralph was on high alert. He was terrified that the mixture of alcohol and fatty food (they'd taken a chance on the fried fish) would defeat his resolve to stay awake. What a prospect. Wouldn't it be a nightmare if, while he lay snoring, the door burst open and in stormed Shirley?

'Right. Game's up. Ralph – what have you got to say for yourself?'

He could hear it. Knew exactly how it would feel – waking to the shame of being stripped in front of his wife and seen to be a pathetic old lecher with a past. He would lose any chance of late-life serenity. Oh *God*. Ralph pressed his fist against his chest.

'Dad?'

Arthur had noticed. If only that – *boy* – would stop looking at him. Ralph had always been uncomfortably aware of Arthur's suspicious watchfulness. He turned abruptly to his wife.

'I think it's bed-time,' he said, placing a tentative hand over Gertrude's. She covered it with her other hand and he forgot his irritation with Arthur.

'You look tired, Gert. Why don't we go upstairs, us two? The others can follow when they're ready.'

'What an excellent idea, Ralph.' She produced a gratified smile. Gertrude had made allowances for the poor cooking and general unsophistication of country folk and consumed the greasy battered plaice and soggy chips with immense enjoyment. She had even spoilt herself with a dollop of tomato ketchup once she'd got properly in the mood.

Solomon and Arthur didn't linger for long in the lounge after Ralph and Gertrude had retired.

'Shall we – uh . . .?' suggested Arthur, nodding in the general direction of the stairs.

Solomon agreed wearily and started rising from the table. He hadn't enjoyed the meal at all. As a recent veteran of gastric germ warfare, he had been reluctant to venture into another fray and nibbled cautiously at his food. There had been a brief period of geniality, for Gertrude's unusual sprightliness had been infectious. But that had long since subsided. And now all Solomon wanted was solitude and a soft, warm bed – and for the hours to pass swiftly so that he could reach the end of his journey.

'Good night, Arthur. Sleep well,' he said politely when they had mounted the uneven staircase and reached the short corridor along which all the bedrooms were ranged. There was another flight of stairs at the end of the passage, but that was closed to the public with a large sign saying 'Staff Only'.

'Night, Pops,' said Arthur absently, fiddling with his key.

Solomon had stopped trying to correct the familiarity. It was pointless, he decided, as he entered his small room and began slowly to undress. Some things were impossible to change.

'G'night, Gert,' Ralph was saying next door, in the most soporific tone possible. He was relieved beyond measure that his wife had agreed to tranquillize herself for the night.

'Take a sleeping pill, Gert. You really should. It's important that you have a good rest,' he had said, trying not to sound too imploring. 'It's been a difficult day – and, after all, this *is* a strange bed . . .'

'Good night, Ralph dear,' she now responded drowsily and so fondly that Ralph, who had assumed a dormant position at her side, was filled with so much regret that he wanted to weep. He would have prayed if he'd known how. Instead, he squeezed his wife's arm and lay as still as possible.

Judith was struggling with insomnia. Neither sheep counting nor relaxation exercises had succeeded in making her the slightest bit sleepy. For hours she tossed fitfully in her four-poster bed. At last she sat up and decided that a walk might take the edge off her restlessness.

The room was stuffy. It smelt of decaying daffodils and the scent of Aromatic Herbal Bath Oil. This had been the last of the pack of Four Sensual Experiences that she had found in the bathroom cabinet (with the Management's Compliments). Judith had decided that a long, hot herbal soaking had been preferable to a sensual experience with the Manager himself. Cheaper, too, considering his designs on her Gold Card.

Chuck Wilmot's financial desperation occurred to her again later, when she had given up on sleep. She suddenly worried about the location of her handbag. Where had she put it?

With the aid of the torch (it took her some time to remember where she'd placed *that*), she finally came upon the bag and rummaged through its contents until she found her purse. Intact. Naturally. How silly of her to have suspected anything else. Surely in a place like this one didn't have to worry . . .

On impulse, nevertheless, Judith extracted the Gold Card from the purse and tucked it into the pocket of the hotel bath-robe, which she had put on against the late night chill. Holding the robe tightly round herself, she stepped out of April into the dark and draughty silence of the passageway. All Seasons, she imagined with a shiver, was probably haunted by the spirits of generations of lost honeymooners. Sad, battered brides. Disillusioned grooms.

'Hello-o,' she called. Surely there was someone about? Anyone? No one? A sheep bleated in a distant field, but from inside there was not a sound. Tentatively, Judith followed the torch-path she lit towards the sitting-room.

There had been no response to Judith's timid call but someone was there. Very much there. Chuck Wilmot was waiting with the master key, biding his time to pounce.

He had planned to ambush her in bed. To fling open the door and demand her money or her . . . he hadn't quite worked out all the details. But Chuck had no doubt that when the time came, he would know what to do. Logic and reason would prevail. Once again, he would be able to rely on the cool, studied sort of reasoning that he had learnt in scores of Step-by-Step Thinking seminars and a protracted postal course on The Pragmatic Approach.

After all, who knew better than Chuck Wilmot about the dangers of hearts ruling heads or pulling carts before horses or leaping without looking? Or about systems and corporate pyramids and Getting Along with Your Team? No one. No one at all. In fact, there was nobody, *nobody* in management more highly-trained than the superbly-skilled senior executive of All Seasons. Never mind management. There was no match for Wilmot in the country – or Europe – or the whole wide world.

So why the hell was such an organizational genius in so much of a fucking mess?

It wasn't fair, Chuck thought angrily, as he clenched his fingers round the master key and wondered whom to blame. His mother had been killed by an out-of-control bus in Clapham High Street when he was eight and he'd never knowingly had a father, and the uncle who'd looked after him (a reformed petty thief, pimp and Salvation Army recruiter) had long been incarcerated in a home for the most advanced cases of senility. So there was no one to denounce – apart from the fates. The cruel fates and the even more heartless Judith Goldman.

And since the fates weren't around to take their punishment, he would have to mete it out to the Goldman woman. She would pay and pay and pay.

He was carefully calculating exactly how much he could demand – taking into consideration the credit-limits to which even the best authenticated Gold Cards were subject – when, without warning, his quarry emerged from her room.

Chuck, caught unawares, pressed himself against the wall and held his breath. What did she think she was doing, wandering through the corridors like an over-sized Lady of the Lamp? He listened to the soft padding of her footsteps and allowed himself to breathe again when the sound had disappeared. What now? The possibility of her not being safely tucked up in bed hadn't occurred to him.

On the other hand, thought Chuck (who prided himself on an immense capacity to turn the unexpected to his advantage), there was no need for the presence of Judith Goldman herself when it was her money he really wanted. Her absence would make things easier. No conflict. No sweat. A direct line to the lady's bag. Perhaps the tide had turned and the fates had swopped sides. Weren't they opportunists – the lot of them? He was chuckling admiringly as he sidled towards the door. They'd picked their winner, had the fates. They had clearly decided that Chuck Wilmot was their man.

Cautiously, noiselessly, euphorically, he turned the key. Her handbag – quickly now. Before she came back. He shone the torch round the room and, miracle of miracles, there it was, propped against the bed – in full blatant view. Take me, it may as well have been saying. Tear me open. Ravish me . . .

With hands suddenly clammy and unsteady, he fumbled with the clasp. There. Ah, bliss. How he'd always *longed* to penetrate the secrets of a woman's bag! All those mysterious bits of paper. Used tissues. Lipsalve. A bottle of tablets – contraceptive pills, most likely. And – what was this? A personal vibrator?

Chuck lifted out an oblong object which, after a hurried examination in the torchlight, he decided looked disappointingly like the remote control device for a television. A strange inclusion. But there wasn't time to ponder on its presence. Here it was. The purse. *Her* purse. It was finally in his grasp.

Breathing heavily, he opened it. Seven pounds and eighty-four pence. Nothing. Peanuts. But the card. That was the important thing. The Gold Card. Where had she secreted it? Where? Where? Where?

At last he gave up.

And the euphoria that had covered him like a magic dream-cloak slipped to the ground. He shuddered as he saw the utter hopelessness of his plight. The letters NALGEX danced meaninglessly and faded before his eyes as Chuck saw with awful clarity that there were no initials that would hide his failure and no Gold Card in the world that could save him from his bankruptcy. He dropped the purse back into the bag and heard it bump against the bottle he had noticed earlier. Mechanically, he inserted his hand and lifted it out.

'Amitriptyline 50 mg,' he read on the label. 'Take one at night. Warning: This may cause drowsiness. If affected, do not drive or use heavy machinery. Avoid alcoholic drinks.'

Amitriptyline. A tricyclic antidepressant. Even in his delirium, Chuck recognized it as one of medicine's favourite answers to misery. The drug especially recommended by the authors of *The Unhappy Executive*. To be used sparingly, they advised – only after the most alluring tax-free perks had failed to lift corporate spirits. Prescribe one for cheer, two for pleasure, three for . . .

Chuck examined the bottle. There were at least a hundred there. A hundred for ecstasy. Extinction. The end. He knew, as surely as he had read every training manual in the land, that a hundred amitriptyline would be fatal.

Like a well-programmed automaton, he pocketed the pills and shut the handbag and returned it to its place. Then he left the room soundlessly and stepped into the passage – where he stopped sharp, listening. What was that? Not music – *real* music – here at All Seasons? Chuck believed he was hallucinating. Or was he already dead?

At first Judith did not believe that the piano she had come upon could be in working order. She had recognized its shape in a corner behind one of the chintz-covered sofas and drawn her fingers curiously along its smooth, white-lacquered surface. Tentatively, she had lifted the lid, expecting to be blasted by an electronically arranged Bridal March or some syncopated Strauss.

Nothing happened. Judith sat down before a keyboard that gleamed in the moonlight like a perfect set of teeth. Cautiously, she pressed middle C. Then E. Then G. Such clear, true notes. Softly, she tried a scale, a run, an arpeggio, a chord, and then began to play.

K 331. The Sonata in A. First movement. A simple, graceful theme followed by six variations. Wasn't it amazing the way she remembered them, all of them, off by heart?

'So you should,' her father was saying. 'It was the first sonata you ever played. You played and we cried. A little girl and you made us all . . .'

'Hush!' she said fiercely. 'The music. I'm listening to the music.' This time she wanted to hear it properly, to explore every note.

'You play brilliantly. Really. But – come. Sit here. On my lap. Watching you there made me feel so . . .'

'Do be quiet!'

Her father's mutterings ceased. Jonathan Bloom's hollow words died away. And the sad, oboe-like strains of the A minor variation swelled to fill the space created by their silence. Judith listened to the music in wonder, for it suddenly seemed that she had never really heard it before. She leaned forward as she played, intent on each note that her fingers produced. The theme. The thread. She had always known the sonata was beautiful but it had never sounded quite like this.

She paused for a moment to draw breath before the final variation. Then she abandoned herself to its triumphant *forte* passages, and it was a celebration. A feast. A victory. When at last she reached the final chords, it occurred to her that for the first time ever she had made music to please no one other than herself.

When Judith finally returned to her bed at All Seasons, her father-in-law at the Horse and Saddle was leaving his. He had a cash cheque for £500 tucked into his top left pyjama pocket. Ralph moved stealthily, careful not to rouse the snoring sleeper at his side.

She turned over, grumbling, and he froze. Afraid to breathe, he waited until her regular deep grunts were re-established. Then, inching onward with supreme delicacy, he manoeuvred himself off the bed and trod on a squeaky floorboard as he tiptoed across the room. He stopped, but this time she didn't stir. At last he reached the door and turned the knob and opened it slowly and crept outside.

The door clicked shut and Ralph, with pounding heart, leaned against it, listening. No sound. He pressed his ear so tightly against the wood that at first he could hear nothing but the rush of his own blood – then, finally, Gertrude. Grunt. Wheeze. Grunt. Wheeze. Thank the Lord.

'Ralphie!'

A throaty stage whisper. He swung round. There she was, in full view, at the foot of the staircase marked 'Staff Only', dressed (for God's sake – what did she think he was?) in a black satin slip with – nothing underneath. Her breasts heaved pendulously. Shirley looked old.

'Shirley . . .'

His mouth was dry and his voice sounded hoarse. Ralph beckoned her towards him. 'Here. The money. Here's – what we arranged. Come. Before – my wife – wakes up.'

There was no response, apart from a broad, inviting smile. Shirley wobbled slightly as she held her suggestive pose against the bannister.

'Shirley . . .' He felt sweat rising in every pore. 'Please.'

But instead of coming to collect her payment, she was turning the other way. She was mounting the stairs with her right arm behind her back and her forefinger wagging for him to follow. Seeing no option, he obeyed as quietly as he could. It was as though he were hypnotized. He fixed his eyes on her finger with its long red nail and tried to suppress the gasps with which his breath was being expelled. The flight of stairs seemed higher than Everest. He wasn't going to make it. His jaw, arm, chest hurt. Christ – he felt sick.

'Here we are.'

She had extended an arm to help him up. The smell of lavender was choking him.

'Shirley . . .' he tried again.

'Come – let's go into my room, Ralphie,' she was cooing. 'Then we can do our – little transaction. Just like old times.'

And she led him up another single step into a small attic bedroom. He was in pain. Extreme pain.

'Nice?' she asked, taking hold of his hand and pressing it against her breast. 'Eh, Ralphie?'

'Shirley,' he managed at last. 'This isn't what we . . .'

'A bonus,' she said, slipping down his pyjama bottom. 'An extra. For old friends. It's always been a matter of principle with your Shirls never to take nothing for nothing. Besides, you may still like it and we could – well, work something out. An arrangement . . .'

Her words were coming from further and further away. The pain had settled in his chest now. It was crushing. Unbearable. The world was going dark.

'Ralphie, you're sweating,' echoed from a vast, vast distance. 'Here – lie down. I'll help you on to the bed.'

That was the last thing he heard.

THURSDAY

At exactly four minutes past midnight, all the occupants of the Horse and Saddle except one were woken by the terrified noises made by Shirley Griffiths. But these were mere whispers compared with the storm of lamentation produced by Gertrude when she saw the state of her husband.

She'd been dreaming – and, unlike Gertrude's run-of-the-mill dreams which were rather uneventful and mostly in monochrome, this one had been a full-blown technicolour production of the most lurid kind. Her digestion, badly battered by the onslaught of fried fish and chips, had retaliated with high-budget horror.

There had been a body. Unsurprisingly. Gertrude frequently dreamt of laying out bodies. This one, however, had been different. Alive, in a macabre sort of way. She had felt emanations when she had touched it. Her flesh had crawled.

'I – don't think I can continue . . .' she had confessed shamefacedly to her Burial Society colleagues. She had been embarrassed. Never before had Gertrude Goldman balked at a corpse.

'You must,' a familiar voice had insisted. It had belonged to someone who'd been watching over her shoulder. A person who had sounded peculiarly like Arthur. Arthur? Her son? What had he been doing there?

'You have no choice,' he had said into her ear in a relentless monotone. Yes – it had been Arthur all right. 'This body has to be prepared for burial.'

'I can't. Please – let me leave. I cannot. I – simply can*not*.'

She'd been panic-stricken and tried to walk away, but her feet had been rooted to the ground. Then he'd taken hold of her shoulders. Her head. He had forced her to face the – thing – half-dressed in its shroud.

'Look. Look who it is. Can't you see, Mom? Open your eyes.'

'No. Please, Arthur. I need some air. Can't we leave? Get away? Me and you . . .?'

'We will. Later. When I've had the car fixed. First things first.'

And he had torn off the sheet covering the dead person's face and revealed the waxen features of her husband. In terror, she had forced herself awake.

'Ralph!' she had cried aloud, instinctively feeling for his presence at her side. Why was he sleeping so far away? The bed was cold. The bed was empty. 'Ralph . . .?' she repeated, properly awake. The dream. Had it ended? Of course it had.

Gertrude managed to turn an involuntary shudder into an impatient shrug, telling herself that her husband was probably in the toilet again. Honestly, the man devoted a disproportionate amount of his time to his ablutions. Day and night! Came from not having enough *productive* activities with which to occupy himself. She'd go and find him. Tell him he ought to come back to bed. She crossed the room and opened the *en suite* bathroom door (having observed that Ralph was doing – whatever he was doing – remarkably quietly).

Then, as Shirley's first sharp scream shattered the silence, it dawned on Gertrude that Ralph wasn't there.

'Ralph – where are you?'

Her throat was tight. She shuddered – uncontrollably now – with a premonition of doom.

'Ralph!' she called out, opening the door to the darkness of the corridor. 'Ralph . . .' imploringly. 'Won't you come back to the room?'

'He – can't.'

Gertrude jerked her head towards the staircase with the 'Staff Only' sign and half-way up, hugging her shoulders and shivering pitifully, was a blonde woman in a revealing black petticoat with a mascara-streaked face. The screamer. No longer screaming, but sobbing. Hugging herself and sobbing convulsively.

'Come . . . please . . . help,' she was gasping, indicating upstairs.

Gertrude followed, dread making her as stiff and silent as a mandarin guard. Up the stairs – left, right, left, right – and into the small attic room, where she saw Ralph on the bed, still as . . .

'No, oh no. Oh my God – NO. I knew it. The dream . . .'

And she stared from her inert husband to the – disgusting old tart snivelling at the door. Then suddenly she snapped. Years and years of suspicion and hate and pain exploded in an eruption of the shrillest, most anguished sounds that the 320-year-old passages of the Horse and Saddle had ever heard.

'Arthur,' she cried, as her son, rubbing his eyes, came towards her in bewilderment. 'Arthur – your father. Look. No – don't look. I'm so – ashamed. I – hope he's – wish I were – dead.'

But Gertrude remained painfully, noisily alive. And so, much more quietly, did her husband.

It had taken several seconds for Arthur to comprehend that this wasn't a nightmare. It was real. Horrifyingly real. His mother, his indomitably strong mother, had fallen apart. All her certainty and self-respect were pouring away in the torrent of those uncontrollable tears.

'What do I *do*?' she kept begging of her son. The disgrace of it all. The mortification. 'What do we do . . .?'

'We must get him to a hospital,' said Arthur, amazed that his voice sounded so normal. He looked around and saw expressions of shock. The blonde woman rocking herself and sobbing quietly in a corner. The publican, worried and disapproving, shaking his head. Solomon, blinking bemusedly at the door.

And his father. His grey-faced father, taking shallow breaths, lying unconscious on a strange bed.

'Can someone – get an ambulance? Urgently. His pulse . . .'

His pulse. He had never taken his father's pulse before. Funny that tonight, after all the years, he should be feeling his father's heartbeat for the first time. And it was so faint. Almost non-existent.

'Arthur, what has happened? What's the matter with him?'

She was pulling on his sleeve imploringly.

'How could he have done this – to me?'

'Myocardial infarct,' Arthur was muttering, bending over the perpetrator, the patient, the father. Touching him. His skin was damp and cold. 'A pulmonary embolism . . . ruptured aortic aneurysm . . . impossible to tell.'

A shot of atropine. That's what he probably needed. His blood pressure must be dangerously low. Atropine. Deadly nightshade to bring his father back to life.

'Dad!'

His pulse had weakened and his breathing was even shallower.

'Can you hear me, Dad?'

Arthur didn't want him to die. Not now. Not after he'd touched him. Gertrude's wails were unrelenting. If only his mother would calm down and support him and if only he hadn't left his medical bag in the car. And if only the car hadn't let him down and if only Judith hadn't gone and started the whole damn thing in the first place. If *only* things had worked out differently, he would now still be safely at home, tucked into his king-sized bed. If only . . .

But Arthur knew, as surely as he stroked his father's clammy forehead, that there was no real safety in a king-sized bed. That nothing was safe.

'He isn't going to . . .?' Gertrude was still tugging at his sleeve. She didn't dare to complete the question. *The* question. Hadn't he asked it himself only hours before? Of his car? Or had it been of his marriage, his wife, his life. Now he wanted to protect Gertrude from the answer. Wasn't that ironic? He, little Arthur, protecting Gertrude Goldman from mortality?

'I can't tell anything yet, Mom,' he said. 'We'll know more when we've got him to the hospital.'

The ambulance arrived. ''Scuse, 'scuse. Mind out the way, folks,' the attendants said briskly. They clapped an oxygen mask over Ralph's face and eased him on to a stretcher and prepared to descend the stairs. Arthur watched numbly.

'Maybe you should go with him to the hospital?'

Solomon had put a hand on Arthur's shoulder. He was squeezing it gently. Arthur nodded.

'I'll tell them to wait for you. Quickly – go and get dressed.'

'I'd better come too.' Gertrude had decided to forego hysteria in favour of any dignity she could salvage out of the situation. Surely there must be some nobility in bearing with fortitude the role of wronged wife? 'After all . . .'

'Judith,' Arthur suddenly remembered. He turned to his father-in-law. 'What are we going to do about – Judith?'

'I'll fetch her,' said Solomon quickly. 'I'll get a taxi to the hotel – then we can meet you at the hospital.'

'Are you sure you can . . .'

'Don't worry, Arthur. I can manage. Do you think I haven't taken a taxi before?'

*

Solomon asked the question with scorn. A taxi? He? Of course he'd taken taxis. But there was one taxi ride in particular that came to him as he offered to fetch his daughter. How many years ago had it been. Twenty? Twenty-five? No, at least thirty years before. He shivered, remembering the way she had shivered that evening. It had been in the fancy country house where she had been chosen to make music.

Oh, the pride when he had heard the news. 'You've heard about my daughter, naturally?' There hadn't been a customer at Epstein's butchery who had been spared the tale of her achievement. How would he have explained it to people if he had brought her back home?

So he had left her there, shivering. He had returned home by taxi alone. And no one, not even the driver, had seen the tears that had soaked the front of his best suit. He had disappointed her. He had told her about courage and survival but, deep down, Solomon knew that it had been pride that had persuaded him to leave without Judith. His pride had meant more than his daughter's misery. Bravery? Heroism? What right had he ever had to preach?

Now he was being given another chance. 'Thank you, Lord,' he muttered, a little uncomfortably. It felt like ages since he had spoken to his Maker and he was suddenly unsure of his mode of address. 'This time – I'll bring her back with me. And I won't say a word about courage, nothing about heroism. Not a word. That will be between you and me. And, Lord, while we're talking again, will you give Dora a message for me? Tell her . . .'

But he didn't have time to complete his communication. Arthur, who had rushed to get dressed, had returned to the room. He was standing at the door.

'Solomon,' he said.

'Hurry, Arthur,' Gertrude was calling from downstairs. 'Come. I can hear the ambulance. It's about to leave . . .'

'Solomon, I'd like to fetch Judith.'

'You?'

For a moment the two men stood silently, looking at one another. Her father and her husband. Then Solomon spoke.

'Perhaps you're right, Arthur. I – think this time *you* should go.'

Arthur watched as Solomon helped Gertrude up three steps into the back of the waiting ambulance. The doors were slammed shut and the vehicle roared down the deserted moonlit street.

'D'you think – Solomon – will talk?' Gertrude had whispered to him urgently, when he had told her of the change in plan. She had objected at first, then nodded a subdued agreement. She would wait at the hospital with Solomon until Arthur arrived with his wife.

'What?' Arthur had asked wearily. The night had seemed endless. 'Talk about what?'

'You know. Tell people at the hospital. About . . .'

Oh yes. He had known. The woman. The disgrace. His mother, Arthur had realized, would bear anything as long as she could hold her head high.

'No, Mom. He won't breathe a word,' he said with complete assurance.

He had known that too. Solomon had other things on his mind. Things he wanted to tell Judith. The things that Arthur had been so reluctant to hear. Judith, too, had once wanted to tell him something. 'Arthur, there's something else . . .' But he had shut his ears. He hadn't wanted to be upset. Just give me comfort and reliability, he had cried. That's all. Surely that's not a great deal for a son, a man, a doctor or a husband to want? Now he understood that they meant constancy and that was everything. And nothing. A dream as impossible as eternal youth and immortality, and a season that lasts forever.

Judith awoke to a perfect spring day. Blue sky, green fields, clusters of bright yellow daffodils. The sort of day starry-eyed brides dream about as the perfect setting for their nuptials.

But Judith hadn't dreamt at all the night before. The music she had made had been her lullaby, soothing her to a deep and restful sleep. Now she had packed and was waiting to leave.

The hotel was silent and deserted. Judith remembered how, not long before, it had seemed to be flourishing. Everything had been in orderly matching pairs. The armchairs, the guests and the staff had all had partners and even the fire safety precautions had been in rhyming couplets. There'd been nothing single at All Seasons until the day she had arrived here to die.

But the hotel had perished and she alone had survived. She wondered what had happened to the family, but decided there was time to find out. Plenty of time.

She was picking up her suitcase when she heard the sound of a car. A taxi? Could it be . . .?

Judith turned to the door. She was ready to face anyone. The honeymoon, as they said, was over.